I0452015

Spires of Aurora

NATHANIAL COVELL

Blue Lantern Press
Spires of Aurora
Nathanial Covell

Copy Editor: Christopher Nelson
Cover Design: Diogo Lando

Published in the United States by Blue Lantern Press
ISBN: 0996090908
ISBN-13: 978-0-9960909-0-2

Version 1.1 (Muzen)

For Mike.

SPIRES OF AURORA

CONTENTS

PROLOGUE

Kingdom of Kitan – Ten Years Ago

Night falls upon the world of Aurora, but its very air ignites. Ubiquitous lightning sets shadow against shadow, the algae glow in the seas, and swarms of life illuminate the winds. Trees, fields, and mountains pulse like the star-filled skies in blue and green bioluminescence. Lightning strikes are visible in all directions, more on the high ground, less in the valleys. In the distance, a mountain is struck dozens of times in an instant, accompanied by the low cacophony of thunder. Roads and buildings are studded with tall lightning spires: protection from the mercurial eddies of ions.

Smoke rises from a small wooden building, old but aglow with the sounds and light of life. Atop the creaking boards, a few local inhabitants, men of varying social classes in wont of camaraderie, are drinking around a large fireplace. They speak with the zest all afford the present.

"I simply refuse to believe this. Those with faith do not sway so easily." The speaker wears fine, but worn, clothing.

His friend retorts, "I saw the dead and the burnt-out buildings. Perhaps if you took your nose out of your books and traveled …"

Frustrated, a third adds, "The rumors are the same no matter who you ask. The monks have laid waste to several villages."

"It defies all for which they stand. They would sooner burn the libraries they fill than destroy a town or kill a single person. Anyway, I will have it straight tomorrow. I'm headed north." The scholar brushes the creases from his clothing, affecting nonchalance.

His friend is incredulous. "That is where the most recent incidents have occurred. Haven't you been listening?"

"Rumors, nothing more. More like ungrounded lightning spires led to a few strikes and a fire. Carelessness, that's all."

The largest patron, with a deep voice, speaks up. "I thought they disappeared years ago. Are you sure it's monks that are being seen or just those fissin' sparkies?"

"It's been three years since the monks were excommunicated from the lowlands and there was never a shred of proof connecting them to their supposed crimes." The scholar is emboldened by an injustice unrighted.

"I don't care what you say. I don't like 'em. Never have. Secretive, sneaky. Always hiding their faces. And some of the things I heard they do—" the large man continues.

"All explained and repeatable science by their own admittance. They were even committing their scientific findings to literature for anyone to read. Extraordinary times were upon us and then they were gone. Now we have only this age of darkness."

"I've heard of the weapons, too," adds another man.

The scholar, shutting his eyes a moment summoning tolerance, recites, "Yes, their teachings, but wrongly applied. Crude abominations of—"

The scholar's friend turns suddenly, leaning back, and the others turn toward the doorway. A dark, cloaked figure stands inside, a wide trapezoidal hat obscuring his face. Just over a flange rising from the circumference of the monk's straw hat are several small holes through which the monk's eyes gaze. They appear to burn red in the firelight.

"Ah, you startled us … didn't hear you come in."

"A monk!"

"I told you!" hisses another.

"You're just in time to show your goodwill to these unsophisticated galoots." The monk does not speak. "Have a seat, please. Your faith is always welcome."

More silence.

The large patron stands, grabbing the offered chair. With a heave, he shatters the chair into fragments, but retains the leg. "Sorry, he's mistaken; no seats left, ya fissing mute. Now why don't ya go jam a lightning bolt up your arse and ride it home." He punctuates his comments with the jagged chair leg.

A few patrons smile and raise eyebrows. The pleading man's faith in the monk is shaken by the silence, as he looks back and forth nervously. In his large friend's huge arm, the chair has become a potent threat. Now he raises it menacingly, growing impatient and encouraged by the others. "Get flashed!"

Finally the monk speaks. "You see how inaction only emboldens the violent?" The monk weaves his hand through the air and creates a small, floating ball of light, and blows. It slowly floats toward the large man. "Whereas exacting pain delivers a permanent, indelible understanding." The man does not retreat as the ball approaches. The other patrons stare on in wonder of the beautiful, floating blue orb.

"Actually, that's a misquote," adds the scholar. "The proper phrasing—"

When in arm's reach of the man, the ball pops, firing tiny lightning currents in all directions toward the ground, most scalding him. He howls, literally shocked. "That's it!" Two of his companions stand and draw their swords. But no sooner are their swords drawn than the monk makes a pulling motion toward himself and they are jerked from the patrons' hands. Simultaneously, the monk produces a finger-size knife and flicks it toward the three men.

As the knife and swords pass in the air, thousands of tiny blue electrons are seen drawn to the metal weapons, forming a distinctly concentrated electrical path between the monk and the men.

The large man perceives that something has struck him and looks down to see a small knife protruding from the chair leg he's holding. Its small size and his mild relief combine as he looks back at his companions and shows them the chair leg. They begin laughing, but the scholar's face is a mask of dread.

Moving his arms, the monk's random movements now begin to affect the immediate area: nails, cutlery, pots and pans jiggle and skitter arrhythmically toward the monk. With one arm high and one low and a final motion, he pushes the air down the path of the thrown blade. An invisible wave, like wind, stands the patrons' hair on end and metallic objects scatter. Suddenly, light erupts between the monk and the men, a flash of lightning that blinds and burns indiscriminately. Those not yet fallen are swept from their feet by the accompanying thunderclap. Tables, chairs and people are smashed against the tavern walls, while the glass windows explode into the night.

The monk emerges from the tavern as a squall of lightning assaults the night. The skies over the town explode in light, sound and fire. Antiquated spires, meant to protect, melt under a fusillade from the sky, stone explodes, wood burns, livestock sizzle and panicking villagers die in the strikes for lack of cover. The monk walks amongst the chaos and lightning, unaffected.

ONE

Kingdom of Yvan – Present Day

Two young men in light wooden-plated armor trudge up a steep, rocky road, under the protection of lightning spires, following switchbacks, their breathing elevated but controlled. Jirai is the first to reach the plateau. He bends his knees out of habit and gets closer to the nearest spire. Standing straight, he absorbs the green of the valley and gray of the mountains, whose glass peaks, melted from the constant lightning, glitter in the last light of day. His broad, lopsided smile widens as he watches Shotoku struggle to make the rise. Arching his eyebrows, Jirai looks at him without turning his head.

Feigning impatience and shifting his weight, "Oh, by thunder, I feel like I'm smoldering with my grandma."

Shotoku looks up at his friend, who is thin, but wound tight like coiled steel. Jirai reminds him of a mongoose: fast, lethal, then at once mischievous and easygoing—a quicksilver wit that always seems to strike too close to truth and a temper that can sprawl like black powder against his enemies. His black, shoulder-length hair is tied in back with a knot. "Why? Why do you always drag me off to such obscure locales? Don't they brew beer in the valley? And why did we leave the horses below?"

Jirai feigns gravity: "I'm ashamed. Ashamed. There is just no gratitude. *Dragged* you? Never have I seen it in life. Gratitude: useless fissing word. Just look at that view." They take in the beauty and danger of Aurora: Hamlets and towns dot the valleys and mountain ridges, all with long spires stretching high above to protect them. At a distance, dark clouds and striations mark rainstorms above lush growth. Luminescent plants pulse, easier to see in the waning light.

"At a whopping 20 years of age—gods, that *is* beautiful—*you* haven't experienced something? Well, soon you can console yourself in the arms of some of the local swill."

"Swill? You wanna good arse grounding? Here hold this spire … a bolt'll be along soon …"

"Be my guest." Shotoku pushes Jirai toward the spire. Jirai stumbles much harder than Shotoku's push warrants and trips, narrowly missing the lightning rod and falling to the ground. He looks up as if shocked.

"You coulda killed me!"

"Oh, zounds, that was the worst fake you've done." Shotoku rolls his eyes.

Jirai continues his protestations, "*I did not fake it*."

Sounds of merriment begin to waft to their ears from the village which is now in view and Shotoku looks into the distance, optimism returning. "What a jackass. Let's go." He offers his friend his hand. Shotoku's clear eyes reflect amusement as he wiggles his fingers, waiting on Jirai's hand. His shortly cropped hair accentuates a clean jaw and chin, still only lightly stubbled at 20 years of age. He is not overly tall, but well built, with a natural athletic prowess. He has an inclination to spend his time in introspection, which leads to an affinity for philosophy.

Jirai hesitates to take his hand, peering at his friend as if betrayed. This is Jirai, his best friend, but one who will concoct an incident and play it out forever. A genuine trickster.

Shotoku's eyelids grow heavy forced to witness this conduct. "Okay, I'm sorry," he utters perfunctorily.

Jirai hesitates again, then rises with sudden alacrity. As he walks, he dusts fluorescent flower pollen from his pants with a plaintive expression. Shotoku follows, bewildered and laughing, as usual, at his friend's peculiar behavior. He looks back down the slope. "Are you guys coming?"

Two more young warriors achieve the plateau. Chillson and Char-ton look like brothers, but their philosophies differ greatly. Originally both from the kingdom of Corville, they have fair hair and blue eyes. But while Char-ton is studious, Chillson likes to grapple with the material world. "I wonder if they have a library here," Char-ton muses.

Chillson rolls his eyes. "Seriously? You're going to look for books and whatnot?" He wears a loose, white shirt with buttons tucked into brown trousers. His body is lean, but muscled from a life of vigor. His clothes are well kempt, his boots new. He runs ahead, skipping a bit and twisting his long curly hair, enjoying the Bright Guard's detour to this mountain village. "Look at this town. So full of … possibilities!" Char-ton considers, but does not demur. "Girls … girls we've never met—" Chillson proffers.

Char-ton laughs, Chillson's enthusiasm contagious. Like most from Corville, he is attentive to his appearance. His tailored, buttoned shirt tucks into tweed trousers and, though his boots are a bit worn, they are of expensive construct: pure Mujong leather. He carries a satchel, usually containing a few ancient tomes. He looks back as he hears the last two of the six members of the Bright Guard make the plateau.

"Are you harassing or helping me? I can never tell, whelp." Starov's chin bobs as he laughs, like a cackling skull. Devukai appears to help him, but slips and only keeps from falling by grabbing on to Starov.

Somewhat hurt, Devukai says, "Whoa, close one there. What? Helping, of course. I'm carrying your stuff." He takes the bag off of his shoulder and holds it up.

"I know, lad, but you damn near dragged me down the mountain three times." Starov yells to the others, "Would you tell this young'un to let me be? He's already part of the Guard. Enough kissin' of me arse."

Chillson smiles next to Char-ton as he yells back, "Dev, you helping Starov up a mountain is like helping a mountain goat. He couldn't fall if he wanted to. Go ahead, push him."

Devukai pushes Starov, whose body rebuffs his efforts. Devukai pushes harder and, without turning,

Starov swats at him with one hand. Chillson runs to help the youngest member of the team and Starov points a stout finger at his blond head. "Now don't you do it. I put on me bleeding nice travel clothes for this little bit of fun and I won't have you muddy them." He straightens his colorful patchwork vest and his green trousers supported by suspenders. His cloth boots look too soft for long distances, but his unique sense of fashion demands them.

"Is that really what they wear in Yvan? Are they all color-blind there?" teases Chillson.

"That's it. Time for a lesson from your elders." Starov moves quickly at Chillson, who runs for the village. The others pursue eager to join the quaint village's festivities.

+++++

Townsfolk dance throughout the large wooden tavern while all the smells and warmth of festive times swirl in the air and into the night. Shotoku and Jirai sit at their own table, soaking up the jubilant spirit.

"These are the times we live in. These, right here." He grabs the air, laughing. Jirai looks on his intoxicated friend, raising an eyebrow and leaning back in his chair. "We have got this thing licked. Unification. And my dad did it."

Jirai waves at a few ladies across the room and they giggle. He looks at Shotoku as he hoists his mug. "And this is what we pacified the outer kingdoms for: making nice with the locals, good beer and …" his eyes drifting back to the ladies, "companionship."

"I wish my brother could have seen this." Shotoku grows sullen and Jirai leans toward him quickly.

"No, no, no, don't go dark on me. And don't get in a poor-me pissing match, either. I lost my parents; you don't see me sulking."

"I know. But he saved you."

"That's right, and now I'm your brother. See, dreams do come true." Jirai spreads his arms, grinning. Shotoku resists, but a smile creases his face as he shakes his head and looks away.

"A trade of dubious value."

"There's my little soldier!" Jirai turns his head and motions for the ladies to come to their table. He feigns begging and proffers a chair as if it were a rare delicacy. Shotoku eyes the ladies and speaks without looking at his friend.

"You're quite the seducer. Why don't you just point at your jewels?"

Sneaking an unappreciative glance at Shotoku: "I am a master of subtlety. Now quiet! Here they come."

Shotoku searches the crowded room for the others and sees them at a table nearby. Chillson is speaking to the youthful barmaid who has just delivered their drinks. His curly blonde hair, not often seen in these highlands, causes her to tarry a bit longer than normal. He speaks to her animatedly, his hand lightly on her forearm, as he tells some story. Devukai and Starov listen and watch, grinning. She laughs at Chillson's exuberance and shakes her head walking away. He turns back to the other men, impressed with himself and laughs loudly.

Devukai's smile is bright under a mop of shaggy, dun hair. Just recently promoted to the Bright Guard, he is enjoying growing his hair out. The Sterling regular army is not allowed that luxury; all soldiers have shortly trimmed hair. Certain privileges come from joining an irregular unit—a unit whose missions are often more clandestine and focused on gathering information. His ability to endure physical and mental hardship has won him a spot with the Bright Guard while he's also inherited the strategic acumen of his father, Sterling's General Douzen.

Starov's chin bobs as he chuckles at Chillson's antics and he draws deeply from his pint. Even while relaxing, he surveils the room, ever watchful. Having survived the unification of the kingdoms under the one king, Saiak, his past is notched by poignant and violent memories. He knows that war is won not just by battles but by determination. He is stout and short of stature, but of immense constitution. A bald pate accentuates his resilience. In spite of a hard life, however, his good-nature prevails wherein so many people it does not. Shotoku regards his council as indispensable.

Shotoku returns his attention to Jirai. "Okay, this time don't start with a bunch of lies. I can't keep up with that all night."

"I know. You're awful at it." Its Shotoku's turn to lean back in his chair staring at his friend. Jirai speaks without breaking eye contact with the tentatively approaching maidens, reassuring them. "Everyone lies, Shock."

"Well, we can try. The world is what we make of it, after all. My father has sacrificed to realize his vision."

"Your father burns books. You know, that sounds a little suspicious to me."

"The monks wrote those books. Are you taking their side? After the destruction they dealt?"

"I just don't know how you can believe so strongly in what's offered up to you. Don't you question for a second what's been happening around us? Something's foul …"

Shotoku squints, attempting to discern the level of his friend's conviction in this remark. Jirai only sneaks a peek at his friend, but his eyes are defiant. "What would you know? You're a liar and a thief," Shotoku teases. "My father runs a kingdom; what do you or I know about it?"

Jirai pinches his fingers at Shotoku and makes a penetrating gesture upwards: lightning up your arse. "Ladies, ladies, ladies, what took you so long? Your beauty did rise like an ocean's sweet swell and fall as you glided 'cross the room."

"Buy us a drink, lads? Some Talan wine?" the young lady asks.

Jirai is impressed. "Ah, a woman who likes the good stuff. So be it."

No sooner do the ladies sit, however, than a hand grips Jirai's shoulder. The ladies look up, fear in their eyes.

"Oh, Rison, go home. We're just chatting," says the girl nearest Jirai.

"Not with you they're not. Time for you to go, sparker."

"Don't mind him—" Suddenly Jirai stands, chest to chest with the man. Panic overwhelms the young lady. "No! He's my brother."

"Are you too stupid to know your enemy before you start some static, boy-o?" challenges the older, much larger man. Seeing the silver crest on Jirai's chest makes

Rison pause for only a moment. "Sterling's Bright Guard. So what?" The men's eyes lock and all can divine the future. Shotoku forces his way between them as the man tries to pull his dagger from its scabbard.

"No, no, you don't need that." Shotoku's hand is slightly extended, floating over the man's hand without making contact. Rison pulls with all of his strength, but cannot budge the weapon. He looks at Shotoku's hand and then his face, witnessing an event he cannot comprehend. "Hey, hey! Rison, right? Not even gonna be an issue, okay? I guarantee it." Jirai and Rison try to maintain eye contact, but Shotoku pulls Rison aside. When Shotoku glances back at Jirai, ire in his eyes and his concentration broken, Rison manages to loose his dagger. Moving quickly, Shotoku pivots and strikes the dagger with an invisible, magnetic burst, knocking the blade from his hand and sending it across the room. As the blade closes on an innocent bystander he is forced to motion magnetically again, causing the blade to change direction mid-flight. It careens upward, lodging firmly in the wooden ceiling. Baffled, Rison allows himself to be guided by this youth as Shotoku puts a hand on his shoulder. "Slippery blade, huh? You're a big guy. Whaddya do?"

"But … What the …?"

"What do you do?" A few tables away, the rest of the Bright Guard finally notice the altercation, but Shotoku indicates "stay put" with a quick shake of his head.

"I'm a lumberjack, okay?" Rison finally focuses on Shotoku, who nods and smiles.

"That makes sense up here. It's a good living?"

"Of course. Hard work."

"And you can't raise the axes high, can you? Or you'll get flashed."

Rison's expertise is piqued by Shotoku's interest. "Right. We use a special technique. Horizontal strokes at a particular angle. Scientific stuff. You have to be a guild member to know."

"Impressive. Well, master lumberjack, we are only here to share in the festivities and wonderment of your honorable village. I swear to you that the virtue of not only your sister, but all the ladies of your village, is safe with us." Shotoku and Rison lock eyes in a much different way. His eyes reflect not resolution alone, but also a taint of profound sadness for all the wrongs and pain the living must endure. Rison knows he can trust Shotoku, even without his oath.

"Have a nice time."

"You, as well, my friend." Shotoku rejoins Jirai as Rison walks away, tall frame reaching the dagger and having to apply some force to wrest it from the ceiling.

The young ladies are clearly impressed. "Wow. You are good with people. I've never seen Rison back down."

Shotoku eyes his friend disapprovingly. "I should have let him beat you like a rented mule. You're such a fire starter."

"This one keeps me out of trouble. To Shock!"

The ladies giggle and they all clink glasses.

+++++

High above the village, lightning flashes upon the mountain peaks and a dark figure's cloak blows in the wind. From beneath his amigasa, Maji grins, surveying the light and sounds of the jubilant hamlet. He cracks his knuckles and adjusts his numerous silver rings, many studded with magnetic lodestones. He wears notched metal scalemail over a double-woven dark red gi, the loose-fitting jacket and pants traditionally worn by warriors in Aurora. The pants tuck into knee-high armored boots that end in two split toes.

Another monk, face hidden under an amigasa, approaches behind Maji. "It is time."

Maji exhales, "I've waited far too long for this. The time of the Kuroshi has come. I shall enjoy making them all suffer." The monk hands him a bow. He takes it, knocks an arrow and points it at the sky. The arrow flies high, a long, thin filament of metal in its wake. When lightning hits it, the long metal wire burns and strobes bright red in the night sky.

All along the mountain ranges, the inazuma, black, gnarled humanoid creatures, pour down the slopes toward the inhabitants below. They climb over one another, clattering like crabs, eyes glowing red from the lightning on which they subsist. Some tuck and roll, their hard exoskeleton increasing the speed of their descent. Some run, eerie, modulated roars escaping craggy mouths. The breath from the inazuma's wailing flows through rudimentary vocal chords, their congenital electrical capacitance coercing the waves into digital emanations. The results are limited harmonic tones that seem to strain and increase in volume violently under the variation of frequency.

Screams rise in the cool night air as the invading inazuma find their first prey.

+++++

The alley doorway of the tavern opens, spilling warmth and light into the darkness outside. Shotoku and Jirai, a girl in each arm, stumble outside laughing and narrowly avoid barrels of libations. A guard sits on the barrels, enjoying some beer himself.

"Oh this air feels nice. Stuffy in there. Come on boys ... up to Glass Lake with you." Rison's sister pushes Jirai from behind, playfully.

"Oh, I do love to be pawed at, darling. Do it again." Jirai smiles and looks back, but straightens. "What in the world? Shock!"

Shotoku turns from smelling his girl's hair and follows Jirai's gaze. Shotoku's girl looks up at him, dreamily, as he is forced to close one eye in order to see straight. Lightning seems to be striking the rock face that lies behind the village. The lightning grows rapidly closer until it begins exploding buildings and eating up the alleyway. "That is not natural," he utters, sobering. These are the rarely seen inazuma: creatures of the high mountains who subsist on lightning and blood.

The guard takes heed of the spectacle, uncomprehendingly, but drawing his sword. In a flash, the inazuma set into him from above, tearing his flesh. His sword skitters across the cobblestone to Shotoku's feet.

The rest of the Guard enter the alley. "What the devil—" says Starov.

Jirai looks at the approaching horde and, feeling there's no other recourse, implores his friend, "Use your power, Shock. We've *no* chance."

"*I'd kill us all*. I won't kill someone else's brother so we can live. Run," yells Shotoku as he picks up the sword and intones his vow again, like a mantra, "I will die before I use lightning again, I swear."

They all sprint down the alleys and out of the village pulling the young ladies with them as six inazuma leap at Shotoku. Lightning arches between them and into Shotoku, but his talents allow him to channel it unscathed. He whirls and cuts and slices, through their chitinous exoskeleton, sundering limb from body. Their talon-like fingers seek him out, but he parries and thrusts, beheading one while stabbing another attacking from behind. Then he stands in the light of the door, the bodies of six inazuma at his feet, his sword shining with the brown tint of their caustic blood.

More inazuma crash down the street and he pursues his friends. As he runs, he risks a glance behind and sees the black humanoid creatures with red eyes scaling walls and leaping incredible distances, all the while being struck by lightning from the sky, unaffected.

He reaches the edge of the village, when one leaps high enough to catch him. Shotoku bares his teeth and launches himself at the creature. Electricity jumps from the inazuma, sizzling Shotoku's clothes, but he channels it without resisting as they fall hard to the ground. He loses his sword in the fall, but his dagger is already out, as he strikes but cannot pierce the creature's solid exoskeleton.

"Use it, Shock! Use your powers, damn you," Jirai urges from somewhere.

His plea only strengthens Shotoku's defiance and, groaning in effort, he sneaks his foot up to its chest and pushes it away. It looks at Shotoku, emitting an oddly digital roar. At that second, the inazuma's head pops off of its shoulders, mechanized roar hollowing and electricity arching from its neck. As the creature falls, Rison's form rises, axe in hand.

"Go! Save the girls!" Rison turns to face the wave of oncoming inazuma. Shotoku hesitates, but Rison looks back and emits a yell that is both a command and a plea. "Goooooo!"

Shotoku runs, looking back at Rison who whirls and strikes, stopping their advance. A moment or two and the glint from his axe dims, engulfed by red eyes and blackness.

"Over here! Shock!" At first, Shotoku can only see a cliff where he believes his friend's voice to be, but then he sees Jirai's hand waving some fluorescent moss. He runs and Jirai yanks him down into a small cave just before the edge of the severe grade they'd recently climbed. Bioluminescent moss coats the cave walls, adding surreal qualities to already scared faces.

"I used to hide here," whispers Rison's sister.

"Shhh!" They all listen in the darkness. The Guard have their daggers out and Shotoku frowns.

"They are tough. Zuma?" Jirai just nods, grimly. Shotoku's eyes move quickly as he fights down panic. They stop breathing as a clicking sound approaches and stops short of the cave. Two red eyes emerge from the top of the cave entrance. "Grab that fisser!"

Determined, Jirai grabs the inazuma's head and jerks hard. Static discharging from the contact, he falls to the floor cursing. The creature drops and clatters on the rock face. Jirai recovers quickly and, trained soldiers, they set upon the inazuma, searching for chinks in its carapace. It writhes, but the lights in its eyes soon dim. Their foe finally dispatched, they breathe hard, worry on their faces. Rison's sister, teary-eyed, asks, "Do you think my brother is okay?" Shotoku just looks away solemnly, unable to answer.

Jirai shudders at having been shocked so many times and looks at the young ladies. "Has this happened before?" he asks; both women shake their heads. "Then we can hope this is a fluke."

"What else could it be?" says Shotoku.

Jirai looks at him, impatient. "A beginning."

"To what?"

"Flashers. Look," moans Rison's sister. They all creep toward the cave entrance. In the darkness, along the mountain range, the towns they admired earlier, as far as the eye can see, are engulfed in fire and lightning.

TWO

Kingdom of Sterling

Shotoku, soiled from his flight back to Sterling, runs, a satchel over his shoulder, staggering up the stairs toward Sterling's war room. "Father! Father! Invasion!" He rounds the corner and Saiak, the king of Sterling, catches him at the entrance, fairly crashing into him. He holds his son at arm's length and Shotoku dares to believe he sees worry in his father's eyes.

"We know. Are you injured?" Behind him at the table are his generals: Douzen and Kurukov. Douzen frowns at the scene, but Kurukov smirks. The generals wear the uniform of Sterling, dark blue gi's under woven, wood-plated breastplates. Douzen has graying black short hair over thick eyebrows. He conducts all the training of soldiers and is fast and deadly; strict, but fair, he is held in high regard by all who know him.

The gray hair on top of Kurukov's head is as thick as his beard. More of a strategist these days, he has gained some extra weight. Secretly, he enjoys his days behind a desk, instead of in the field, sipping wine and planning. Logistics agrees with him and the fact that there are more maidens in the castle than in the barracks. Even with the extra flesh, however, Kurukov is respected as a cunning swordsman.

"Zuma. They were everywhere. I've never even seen a live one and then ... boom. All those villages. All destroyed. The mountain range was like a wave of fire. Lightning cascading on the villages as if from one of our lightning catapults." Hearing this, Douzen sits up and looks at Saiak questioningly. Shotoku continues, "... and mouths. I thought they didn't have mouths."

"They don't," Douzen states, deadpan.

Shotoku takes the satchel off of his shoulder and dumps out the contents. An inazuma head clanks upon the floor, red eyes dim and mouth agape.

Douzen moves to examine the head. "Red eyes? These northern creatures are not like their cousins in the south. And the skin is gnarled and grotesque—"

"—not smooth, like you taught me," Shotoku says. Douzen gives him a knowing smile, witnessing his instructions bearing fruit.

"It's okay, we will avenge the fallen. This is what we fought for. Unification of the kingdoms has granted us the collaborative might to resist such an incursion. Kurukov and Douzen, please leave us." The two generals rise slowly and exit, although Douzen does so with no small measure of frustration at being unable to hear more new intelligence.

"They seemed almost organized. How is that possible?"

"No. They have occasionally frenzied. It can look like an army, but it's no more than a mob."

Shotoku considers this a moment, eventually acquiescing. "Father, it's time to implement my plan."

Saiak turns his back to his son and walks to peer out of a large glass window through which sunlight pours. "They have denied our appeals. They will suffer in the end by one fate … or another."

"We must invade. We need Mujong for such a defense. I'm telling you the zuma are too many. All those villages, as far as I could see: destroyed. We steal the king's precious princess and force them to ally with us. Such a powerful kingdom. Mujong's army would turn the odds in our favor." Shotoku, incensed by his brush with death, becomes bold. His father stares at him, assessing.

"No, and that's final. I cannot risk you, not now, with the zuma so close to Sterling. Instead, you will practice with the Spark again. No more childhood games."

The young man feels his father watching him closely, gravity mounting. "I swore never to use it. It can't be controlled."

"You heard me," Saiak voice grows harsh, then softens. "One brave man inspires a thousand, son. Make me proud." Saiak turns and Shotoku reluctantly backs out of the room and strides down the gray stone hallways.

+++++

Shotoku walks out of the dark halls and into the

sunlight. Seeing the green of the valley, the white of the clouds and the blue of the sky, he stops at the battlements. Hanging against each spire, glass orbs clink gently against one another in the warm breeze. When severely stricken, the non-conductive glass breaks, alerting the builders to the possibility of severe damage. Far below, he sees children playing and hears their laughter. Jirai joins him.

"What are we doing, brother? What begins this day?"

"My father says we're staying here and I'm taking up the Spark again."

Jirai sighs and rolls his eyes. "And what *are* we doing?"

"We're going into Mujong hard and fast, that's what."

"Yes," says Jirai, smiling broadly and slapping Shotoku on the back. "That's why I love you." They begin to walk together, conspiratorially.

"Will we fail? How many will die? And what do the zuma want?" Shotoku's eyes search the horizon as they move.

"Yeah, failing would be painful. Hey, we'll die together, though, right? And Mujong probably has the nicest dungeons in all of Aurora, if we're caught," Jirai says.

"Well, if we get chased I'll just shoot you in the leg; they'll catch you and all your dreams will come true."

Jirai smirks and looks down at the children. "'Who's more ready than us?' is the right question."

Shotoku sees the truth of the words and gives Jirai a determined look. "Damn right."

+++++

Kingdom of Mujong

The massive, regal stone Castle of Mujong, carved from a mountain with fields of long grass on three sides, glitters in the sunlight. Grand, ornate lightning rods extend toward the clouds from the bleached walls and magnificent towers of the castle. Not just for protection, the spires are revered, and a kingdom's disposition toward the welfare of its people is often ascertained by their grandeur or lack thereof. These spires, wider than a man at the base, rise from the ground through the castle walls. Once in plain view, they twist and split in random, often beautiful ways, but also to safely rob the castle's aura of Aurora's constantly encroaching electrical eddies. Colored glass decorations hang from the lower branches of the spires.

Kenshi, the king of Mujong, his son, Junchi, and daughter, Makiko, sit in the prim garden's gazebo practicing calligraphy. Makiko smiles as she helps her younger brother grind and mix the black and fluorescent charcoal with water as they prepare to draw. The king focuses on the character that represents "truth." Makiko shows her brother how, with controlled but firm motions, he can reduce the charcoal rock. He tries, but, feigning exhaustion from the task while trying to entertain his sister, he spills his ink. Giggling, yet chastising, she frowns and helps him clean up.

"I'm not as good with a brush as I am with my black steel swords." The boy reaches over and grabs the sheathed swords and makes a crazy face. His sister continues to dab up the liquid.

"Oh, yes. You are menacing. Oh my, that is your fiercest face yet." Encouraged, the boy sticks his tongue out and crosses his eyes. Makiko affects vexation. "Now what's that? Oh yes, your face does that when you try to do math." Her eyes widen playfully and lips form a small circle. Junchi's face droops and he tightens his lips. Then he's zealous again.

Yelling quietly, he says, "You know I hate math!"

+++++

Two trail-worn, hooded figures ride fast down the spire-protected road approaching the Mujong castle. Mud flies from the hooves of the horses as they burst through the courtyard and through the internal portcullis, reining in their steeds before the gazebo. The two figures dismount deftly and stride toward the king, taking a knee and removing their hoods. Long blond hair tied behind his head and matted with sweat, the Mujong Captain of the Guard's thin, handsome face emerges. Finn's austere gaze quickly visits Makiko, then rests upon the king. Just behind, his companion, Sono, wears a tired, worried look, blond hair disheveled and haphazardly tucked behind his ears.

"It has begun. The zuma pour from the mountains in the north, destroying all in their path."

"And the Iridians?" Kenshi replies.

"They have refused."

The king puts down his brush, face dire.

Sono speaks, hesitantly, "Sire, we saw them, a sea of red eyes in staggering numbers, flooding, crawling atop one another … consuming the dead."

Kenshi nods, "Yes, they are not so refined as their blue-eyed brethren in the south. How many?"

Finn exhales, "As you suspected, we cannot defeat them alone."

"Tens of thousands, sire," says Sono. The king rises at this, perturbed, and turning away. "Sire, we must ally with Sterling. It is our only chance."

At this, the king whirls to face the young sergeant, his face that of a warriors. "No!" Makiko starts at the ferocity of his answer while Junchi's eyes dart nervously, uncomprehending. Sono lowers his head, while Finn meets the king's eyes, experienced enough to handle conflict with equanimity. "Never would I ally with Saiak. His tactics are the manifestation of a tormented soul. How soon you all forget the slaughter at Lunabi! Something is foul in that kingdom. I do not understand his people. They seem to have supplanted his will for their own."

"It is easier to follow than lead," Finn says, condemningly.

"And drivel rather than think." Makiko looks at Junchi. "And we haven't had any of the North's delicious jams since Saiak's embargoes. Perhaps they will finally receive justice under the foot of this new horde."

The little boy nods and looks serious. "Jam justice."

Makiko's eyebrows arch whimsically as she frowns at her brother. She stands, her back to the others, pensive.

"Regardless, princess, it is time for your training to begin in earnest. Every man, woman and child will suffer under this invasion."

Offended, she looks back at the young captain. "You trained me how to fence yourself. Suddenly that is not good enough?"

"I trained you to duel, my lady. Now we will train you for war."

She turns away again, eyes scanning the kingdom around her. She sees villagers laughing and children playing beneath the protective spires … safe. Tears form. "Someone must seek an understanding between all good peoples of these lands. Someone must forge new bonds, find a compromise. Someone of courage—. Beneath what veneer does this intrepid soul hide?"

THREE

Kingdom of Mujong

The Castle of Mujong lies in the darkness. The cool grass and trees are peppered with glowing insects. In a copse of trees across the field, Shotoku's blue eyes search for signs of activity on the battlements. He pauses, contemplating the violent task before him. What are these forces that drown our hopes? That make man and beast descend to willful harm? How does one break the cycle? If I knew the names of these sordid causes … if I knew the names, I vow no force could convince me to give them quarter. It would be my destruction or their own.

A tiny blue light blinks three times, disturbing his reverie. Shotoku answers with two quick blinks of his own red light and four dark figures emerge from the bending trees, prostrate as they make their way across the field toward the castle.

When the team is halfway to the castle, a deer, startled by a predator, bolts from the trees far behind them. It makes it twenty feet into the field before being stricken by a lightning bolt and falling to the ground smoldering.

Shotoku raises a fist above the undulating grasses and the team hesitates, watching for a reaction from the castle. Seeing none, Shotoku rotates his wrist, indicating to proceed.

The team achieves the invisible protective cover of the castle wall's large lightning spires. Luminescent, organic pods growing from the walls cast the exterior of the walls in a dim greenish light. Still prostrate in the dark, ensconcing grass, Shotoku again signals discreetly. Jirai, expecting the order, fires a single arrow into the nearest pod. It pierces the pod and its cool, fluorescent liquid oozes to the earth below, effectively shrouding the area in darkness.

With great speed, the team moves to the wall, the first standing and creating 90-degree angles with his arms and legs. The next member climbs the first, assuming the same angular stance but standing upon the shoulders of the first, and so on, until the final member's hands tightly grip the top of the wall. He peeks furtively over the battlements and sees a single guard snoozing in a chair near the closest tower. With two red blinks to the team beneath him, he signals the all-clear. The bottom member scales the others and so on until they all drop lightly into the cover of an impeccably groomed oriental garden.

The garden is dark, green and expansive. The team makes its way quickly and confidently through the garden and immediate open-air passages. The buildings are constructed of beige stone blocks, high vaulted ceilings and beautiful archways. The team makes numerous turns without indecision, sprinting in impossible silence across the polished stone floors with their cloth-bottomed shoes.

As they approach the courtyard in front of the main keep, with higher, more formidable walls, they fan in separate directions, taking cover. Two guards stand on either side of the large, open wooden doors marking the entrance. This area is well lit, but the team dissolves into the shadows.

+++++

The young Mujong guard is tired, but striving to remain attentive. His eyes scan the courtyard's pathways, grass and trees, but land on nothing. The glow pods are fresh and bright and he averts his eyes from staring at them directly.

There's a sound to his left and he turns his head quickly. It is the older guard, standing on the other side of the large, open entryway. He has been waking himself every few minutes with his own snoring. Annoyed, the young guard returns his head and notices something out of the corner of his eye. He squints in an attempt to focus on the shadows to his right, but they are too far and obscured by foliage. He is ambitious, however, and refuses to risk any error.

Attracting the other's attention, the young guard urgently indicates the shadows on his right and raises his crossbow, indicating that he should do the same. The older guard does not raise his crossbow, but wearily makes his way over to the younger one.

"Yeah? Light playin' with yer eyes again?"

The younger points to his ear. "Not unless it's making sounds too."

The older guard turns as if to go. "Well, I'll go wake up the captain, then." The young man grabs him.

"Ha, ha. I'm serious this time, I—" A distinct sound comes from the shadows near the wall. They look at each other and make their way with crossbows raised. The young guard smiles confidently, his opportunity for recognition at hand. Surprisingly, they still cannot make out an intruder. The young guard steels himself, imagining the coming action.

"Alright, enough of this hiding stuff. We know you're there." Bamboo chimes can be heard in the distance. When the old guard opens his mouth to speak again, a blur emerges from the darkness. Wooden sticks knock their crossbows astray as a black figure rises before them. The hard strikes are devastating, as if they come from everywhere at once. The young guard's training drives his feet to flank his opponent, but with the older guard already falling, the dark figure instantly counters and drops the young guard, as well.

Shotoku stands in dim silhouette, listening and looking at the young soldier without satisfaction. With two quick blue flashes, he signals the team and pulls the guards out of sight. The men emerge from shadows surprisingly close to the entryway, and all enter the keep.

+++++

Princess Makiko lies in her bed staring into the darkness. Her wooden bed is low to the floor, large and soft. Her thick duvet is covered by a dark green and gold fabric with a pattern depicting mythic lightning dragons and festival lanterns. Her headboard is simple with inlaid leather. Pillows lie to either side of the princess, showing the glow pandas of Mujong munching on lightning bamboo. A fist-sized pair of metal balls, or dama, rest on her ornately carved mahogany desk, the legs of which turn into claws at the floor. Scrolls hang from her walls bearing calligraphy. She reads one aloud, "The wise falcon hides its talon," and sighs. Nighttime, far from a respite, always makes her mind wander. Mujong will soon be drawn into something dreadful. She can feel it. Her country is prosperous, lucky compared to most in recent years. Those Sterling bastards. They choke us slowly and stifle trade with other kingdoms. The desperation is easily seen in the few messengers that make it from the outside. Most trade routes leaving her virtually landlocked kingdom traverse Sterling lands, which had grown increasingly dangerous. Finally, they were closed by Sterling for the good of all. There are rumors that Sterling itself has been attacking the trade caravans. When news does not flow, rumor never fails to take up the cause. That leaves only the sea to her south, and Mujong ships are not technologically advanced enough to withstand the huge waves of open ocean. Not that that would do any good, she curses. Lightning would decimate any ship fool enough to sail out alone on a huge flat surface. "Damn you, Sterling."

Her muscles ache and she massages her sword arm gently. Cuts and bruises pepper her body. Her training with Finn and his men was has been rough, but she is getting fit and fast. She would not wait for a terrible fate to befall her country. She would be ready, come what may. Finn and his men give her no quarter, either. They are strong, quick and smart: the best Mujong and perhaps Aurora have to offer.

Surprisingly, her father did not forbidden her training. "To rule, you must know what it is to send your subjects into harm's way. But more important is that you learn to keep them from harm to begin with." He looked older as he spoke. "You and you alone will bear the magnitude of your decisions. Diplomacy could save mankind from so much misery. Far too quickly do men go to war."

His words have not faded from her memory.

Makiko sits up in bed as she hears footsteps in the hallway. They cease before her door, which begins to open, slowly. Tiny feet are visible in the light beneath the door and she smirks.

"Hello?"

Her little brother sticks his head around the door, smiling. She lets her head fall back onto the pillow.

"Junchi." She opens the sheets. "Hop in." The boy runs and springs into the bed. "No, no, Junchi, take off your swords," she chastises. Expecting this, Junchi removes the sheathed swords from his robe and places them beside the bed. Makiko throws the sheets over them both and Junchi settles in happily.

A moment later, Makiko hears more muted footsteps from the hallway. Again, they seem to stop outside her doorway. She raises her head from the pillow to look at the door. Junchi, also hearing the noise, grabs his long sword and affects anger by furrowing his brow. He glances at Makiko to see if she notices his impressive state of readiness.

The door opens quickly and Shotoku enters, nearly

closing the door behind him. Though his nose and mouth are covered, his eyes register surprise at the presence of the boy.

Junchi lunges from the bed, sword swinging wildly as he is overwhelmed by bravado.

"Junchi! No!"

Shotoku backs up slowly, repelling the boy's uncoordinated attacks with his wooden batons. The sword is sharp and notches the dense wooden sticks. The boy yells ineffectually as he attacks, eyes closed, swinging repeatedly with all his strength. Shotoku looks at Makiko, uncertain. She is still in the bed, frozen with fear for the boy, but her hand seems to move toward something. He has many opportunities to raise a baton over his head and strike the boy, but does not. Cannot. He almost smiles beneath his mask, admiring the boy's crazy enthusiasm. Then only misery washes over his soul as the scene invokes a memory of long ago.

+++++

Shotoku remembers himself and his brother, young, wearing gi's and pointing wooden sticks at each other in the middle of a golden field. His brother, unrelentingly silly at times and, at others, capable of an amazing degree of focus, a fanatical focus that made him a challenge to control. His hair, impossibly tawny and wild like a lion cub's fur, could obscure his presence easily in the golden wheat. Four tall spires form a square around them, giving harbor from the lightning. His father, young and broad, but lithe. Handsome with jet black hair and eyes over prominent cheekbones, his strength manifesting a disposition born of discipline and resolve. He offers them guidance. But his brother keeps goofing off, hitting Shotoku's sword instead of listening to his father. Shotoku attempts to hold his stick in place before him as father grabs his wayward son with one hand, attempting to calm him.

"Zarushi! Now, when you attack, you can kiai—let out a loud scream." Zarushi pounces on this chance to misbehave by yodeling and making crazy expressions while running after Shotoku, who runs, unable to resist laughing. This only stokes his zeal. "Zaru! Stop it! It's to help you breathe and disrupt your enemies—" Their father tries to foil Zarushi's enthusiasm, but he continues to attack Shotoku like a madman, yelling all the while. Shotoku falls to his knees, weakly holding up his stick and laughing. Zarushi focuses more on face-making than attacking.

Unable to stop the boys' play, their father tackles them both and they tumble, simultaneously scared and delighted. They end up on top of him, laughing. He recalls his father's eyes, the happiness then, and its vacancy since. The remembrance sucks the breath from his lungs, but the faces on the boys beam as Zarushi feigns victory, responding to the lauds of an imaginary crowd. Removed, Shotoku views the scene and then the moment is gone. His father looks past his boys to the skies, eyes telescoping, once again distant as dark clouds gather: a murky future roiling all of the brilliance that might have been.

+++++

Devukai enters the room, distracting the boy. Shotoku quickly scoops him up from behind, pinning his arms and causing him to drop his sword.

"What's going on? Let's get the shrew and go,"

whispers Devukai. As Shotoku kneels to bind the boy, Devukai approaches the princess. Remembering, Shotoku's eyes go wide and he turns.

"Wait! She's got something," Shotoku warns him too late. In that instant, her feigned look of fear transforms to pure resolve as she brings the boy's short sword up from beneath the sheets. The blade is fast and she screams for effect, but Devukai is highly trained. His head returns to her in time to deflect the blade from his heart and into his shoulder. He grinds his teeth, but bears the pain in silence. He rends the short sword from her in order to reciprocate, but Shotoku is already at the bed. He punches her across the jaw crisply an d she falls back unconscious. Shotoku shoulders the princess and turns for the door.

"Bind the boy and let's go."

FOUR

Kingdom of Mujong

The team rides through the day and gallops down the dimly lit forest pathways at dusk. When exiting the cover of the trees, they affix slender lightning rods to their mounts and raise them to the sky. Then, leading their horses from the maximum length of the reins, they span the open ground, running to the nearest cover. Lightning is ever visible near and far. The mountains loom closer, strobing, illuminated by the abundant strikes that accompany the high ground. As night falls again, the team enters a narrow pass leading up and disappearing into the rugged mountain range.

At an area of relative sandy smoothness and surrounded by mountains, they rein in their horses and dismount. The steeds breathe hard and sweat in the warm night air. The men are quiet and quickly create a fire from dry wood and feed their horses. Long, razor-sharp shards of fulgurite, sand-embedded glass created from lightning strikes, cling to the rock surfaces and litter the ground. Moving the shards, they make themselves comfortable around the fire, squeezing water from their water skins. They chew on dried, cured meat and allow their muscles to slacken.

Shotoku dismounts and pulls the princess off of her horse. Though he sets her on her feet, her aching, cramped legs crumble beneath her. Her hands bound, her fall upon the fulgurite shards promises severe injury, when Shotoku catches her deftly. He suspends her a moment, checking his balance before leaning her gently against the rock face. He is not altogether unconscious of her softness, a fact which angers him.

"Wouldn't want to bruise your highness on her lowness."

She eyes the ubiquitous glass shards, but sighs, acquiescing. "That doesn't stop me from wanting to stab you … like I did your other Brilliant Guardian."

Shotoku draws his knife, leans down and cuts the rope binding her hands. Her face is dirty and the sweat makes her hair sticky. Shotoku hands her a skin of water and she accepts it, drinking quickly. Her wrists are raw. When he extends a piece of the cured beef to her, she hesitates and then accepts.

"I think my Bright Guard will survive your opinion of them."

"Do you honestly believe you'll make us an ally by abducting me? If you knew my father, you would have refused this task."

"It's a sound strategy and has worked in the past."

"I would kill myself before I allowed such coercion

of my people."

"I understand. But you should know that we do not plan to harm you. And we have a mutual enemy, do we not?"

"I have heard of the inazuma's invasion in the north, and I concede that the lowlands need to be defended. But history has proven your father untrustworthy. Abducting me? This is how he forms alliances?"

"He is not a politician. He is a warrior. Where others waver, he resolves. Your kingdom is fortunate to lie to the south and has the luxury of deliberation. But the zuma will be in our lands in days. Already, the refugees of conquered realms overwhelm Sterling's resources, and Mujong sits to the south and ponders a solution. A kingdom bloated with riches."

Shotoku sits down across from her, back against a different rock wall. Their faces are half-visible in the firelight. Makiko chews on the meat and rubs her jaw.

"Did you say you wouldn't hurt me? Too late for that."

"You did stab one of my men. If it makes you feel any better, I could swear no harm will come to you. I'm not sure you'd believe me, though. And, yes, abduction is what happens when diplomacy fails. Your father had a chance to ally with us many times."

"Believe what you want. Your kingdom is good at that."

Shotoku smiles against his will. "I heard you had a mouth, too. That much is true. We'll soon be back in Sterling. You'd be wise to figure out who you can trust."

She chews, looking at Shotoku distrustfully. "And I suppose that's you, right? And you'll believe me at my word, in turn, no doubt?"

Now Shotoku looks distrustful. "A person's word may be cheap in Mujong, but not in Sterling. You can do worse than have mine."

Her face drains of emotion and her eyes narrow, "Right. Your kingdom is the standard for virtue."

He reconsiders his position not without irritation, "Is it not Mujong that has cut off shipments of provisions, wood for winter?" Shotoku's eyes steel in the firelight. "Last winter hundreds died from cold and starvation."

Makiko responds, puzzled, "That's because Saiak cut off all trade with Mujong last year. What we usually export rots at our borders. And because of your embargos, our exports can't even reach the kingdoms in the north, and so they starve as well. Your father has spread a desolation like the worst of plagues."

Shotoku stands, unwilling to hear her words. "Okay, honey," Shotoku closes his eyes and shakes his head as if to clear it. "Did you really think you would be able to sell this little fantasy to me? To those who have witnessed the results of your policies?" Shotoku leans toward her quickly, his face alight with the campfire and with resolve. Makiko does not flinch but locks her eyes to his with equal fervor. "I assure you that Saiak will set right by force what you would seek to obscure. And, princess, no matter who is the coming victor, the fate of Mujong for its defiance will be terrible."

Realizing and encouraged, Makiko leans back and then forward again. "I finally understand. Saiak has deceived you all."

"Why would he starve his own people?"

"Fear … desperation … I don't know, but these

elements can cause people to rally around a kingdom's flag."

"But to what end?" Shotoku waits and the question looms heavy between the young ambassadors. Makiko, satisfied by the conversation, leans back, eyes confident, and an almost indiscernible smile on her face.

Frustrated, Shotoku turns and joins his team by the campfire.

+++++

"Tie her up again would you? Nice and tight. And give her a blanket." Shotoku sits down on a boulder by the fire.

Char-ton gets up. "Sure."

"How you doing, Dev?" Devukai is rubbing his shoulder, but, at his captain's words, sits up affecting nonchalance. "General Douzen is going to kill me."

"Great. It's not bad. Don't worry, my dad will say, 'It's good for you,' or something equally gruff."

Shotoku smiles, "That's true. I've heard it many times. You know, regardless of who your father is, you did well today."

Devukai nods, watching Shotoku, and adding, "I know if you say it, it's true."

Shotoku stops, eyes smiling as he invokes the general's image. "Your father has a big mouth. And a fast blade." They all laugh, having felt it many times. Shotoku sits down at the fire, stretching out, and unconsciously glancing back at Makiko.

Jirai picks up on Shotoku's mood and grins. "How's the princess?" he asks, innocently.

"Deluded."

"That's royalty for you," Jirai jibes, resignedly, yet

expectant.

"Indeed. So now I'm gonna get a hard time from you, too?" he retorts, admiring the constant glow of aurora borealis in the night sky.

"Ha," Jirai guffaws as they all smirk. "There's the juice."

A gust of wind suddenly brings the sound of high-voltage discharges. Devukai looks into the distance and points at a long wall of light in the distant mountains. "Is that sound coming from that? And what *is* that? It's a solid wall of lightning!"

Char-ton returns from tying up Makiko. "That is the Crown of Aurora."

"That's the Crown? What's inside it?"

"Heaven. Hell. No one has lived to tell," quips Jirai.

"No one can survive it," Shotoku says, head turned to take in the spectacle. "It is a solid wall of lightning. The magnetism is erratic. They say not even the fabled warrior monks can endure its might. That if you pass close enough, you can see blue, red and green jewels sparkle in the sky."

"The heat and noise, too, are said to be intolerable," Char-ton adds.

Devukai looks back and forth. "Even the warrior monks don't go there ... the Iridians? Even though they eat lightning and sleep in the storm clouds?"

Shotoku grins, "Those are just stories, Dev." His eyes sneak another peek at Makiko.

"She's pretty," comments Char-ton. "Didn't get a good look at her 'til now."

Shotoku quickly leans back and closes his eyes. "Is she?" The others lean back, following Shotoku's lead.

"Worse than that: she's a challenge," jibes Jirai.

"I suggest you rest. We've got a good distance to the border tomorrow." Shotoku sighs absently, relaxing. "How do I get myself in these situations?"

"Being the king's son doesn't help," Jirai says.

"King?" Jirai and Char-ton share a conspiratorial glance: they enjoy implying that Shotoku is soft like a courtier. Shotoku sits up and quickly arcs lightning between his fingers, a crisp snap resulting. "If I were a prince, shouldn't I be lying on pillows … instead of glass and rocks?" He gestures, feigning frustration. "And having my … body washed by a virgin?"

Devukai laughs, "A virgin? Why do fantasies always have to contain virgins?"

Jirai frowns, explaining, "Dev. It always has to be a virgin. It takes the fantasy to another level. Throw one in for me, Shock."

Shotoku closes his eyes and feigns concentration, placing his fingers on his temples. "Okay, there! Devukai's on the bed with you now!"

"Bastard!" says Jirai, laughing.

"Hey!" yelps Devukai, offended.

"That's the only place virgins exist, Dev, in fantasies. Except you, of course."

Devukai nods at Makiko. "What about her?"

They all turn to look and she looks back, quizzically. There is a tangible pause. "No, let's not kill her, yet. She kinda smells good," Shotoku says, speaking loudly. He looks over his shoulder again to face her and feigns surprise: "Oh … hi, princess. Relax and go to sleep."

He lies back down and closes his eyes. Like waves on a beach, distant thunder rolls over the mountains, a tactile cadence they have known since childhood. "We're not out of danger yet, boys. Let's remember that. Ji, you found a good observation point?"

Jirai nods and motions, "Up that way. Perfect spot."

"Good. You have first watch. Wake me when it's mine."

+++++

Jirai wakes Shotoku a few hours before daylight. He stands, adjusting his clothes and gear. Fireflies dance in the darkness. He walks over to the princess, who is still slumbering in the gravel, head on the blanket Char-ton gave her. Shotoku's face belies regret. He knows taking hostages is wrong, but he is bound by circumstance. War and desperation have long quieted those with delicate sensibilities. Now is the time for action. Yet, somehow he cannot convince himself that wrongdoing is justified by the situation.

He heads up the mountain toward the observation point they chose earlier. It grants visibility for several miles in the direction of Mujong. Shotoku can see several of the copses of trees through which they have come in order to find the discreet mountain pass, the only one to afford protection from the charged skies. Anyone following them will be forced to use the same path and would need several hours to reach their position. Shotoku looks out over the dark lands. Lightning strikes are visible near and far. He can feel the thunder resonate through his body and over the mountain ranges. Looking behind and up the mountains, the lightning is even thicker. The changing shadows blink and dodge nervously over the terrain.

Shotoku reaches a hand out to feel the energy in the

air. Cupping his hand, he motions as if to scoop it up and make a snowball. Faster now, he moves his hands back and forth low behind the rocks so as not to be visible from afar. Deftly, he turns his hands palms inward, as if holding a ball, and squeezes against an invisible force. An arc appears between his hands, but he remains calm. The bolt dances between his calloused palms. His face betrays no pain and his hands no burns. He moves them farther apart, slowly, until they reached shoulder width. Now he struggles to maintain the bolt, its arc increasing, searching for a better conductor. Then it breaks, the bolts falling directly from his hands to earth. He ceases his effort, the light gone, and he exhales.

Unfinished, Shotoku holds a hand out over some of the metallic rock and slowly lowers it. He strains, but the rock does not budge until he is nearly upon it. Finally, dust and a few small stones jump the short distance to his hand. He looks at the pieces, firmly affixed, defying gravity. His disappointment is obvious.

"No better than in the castle, and here I am in magnetic mountain paradise."

He looks again, making sure no one is approaching the mountain pass. His eyes take a moment to focus, and the ever strobing lightning doesn't help, but he can see the pass is clear. Quickly and smiling in effort, Shotoku folds his arms and begins circling each forearm around the other. Aware of how he must look even in these mountains, he cannot help smiling in embarrassment as he increases the speed of his arms, circling faster and faster. Beginning to lose his balance, he stops suddenly, drawing his hands outward again with palms facing each other vertically. A blue ball of flame lightning ignites between them. It is bright and beautiful and he yelps with triumph. He slouches lower behind the rock face and slowly removes his top hand from the vertical position and the ball of energy remains. His eyes dance as he stares at the orb of blue lightning above his right hand. Though he moves that hand away now, the ball remains floating. "This is how they did it. The ancient monks." Consciously extending the magnetic fields from his hands, he moves the ball now without burning them. He begins to wonder how to dispose of it. Releasing his influence, the ball floats slowly down the path he ascended, moving this way and that, hovering above the rock surface, sliding with the unseen magnetic eddies. Encountering a strong pull, the ball is sucked against the rock face, which begins to heat up. Slowly, the ball sinks into the rock, penetrating the solid surface while simultaneously diminishing in diameter. Finally, the ball seems to struggle, its light dimming more and more until it winks out of existence.

"That has never happened in the castle. It held its shape!" He examines the smoldering, orange-hot circle in the rock face as it rapidly cools. His mind races at the possibilities. Turning to lean back against the rock, Shotoku remembers that he is supposed to be surveying the area. He leans forward again quickly to focus on the mountain pass. Lightning flashes and Shotoku furrows his brow. Between the copses, black shadows jump from place to place in the mercurial play of dark and light. His face relaxes a bit, but he remains attentive. In a far clearing, shadows move in a straight line, low and quick: Mujong pursuers. Shotoku's face slackens with dread and resolve. With a whirl, he hops from his perch and slides down away from the approaching soldiers. Jumping, sliding, running, he descends the treacherous, rocky path.

It is just before reaching the camp that Shotoku hears a high-pitched sizzling. It is barely audible. He looks in the direction of the camp, but the sound seems to convey panic. And then he hears another sound: the growl of a predator. He climbs a low set of rocks and sees a large, four-legged, one-horned beast, black with glowing, lava-red veins. Its stance is wide and its head is facing away from him. Cornered in the rocks is a small black humanoid figure, its hands extended in defense. Two glowing blue eyes blink rapidly, set into an almond-shaped black head. Between its two long fingers on each hand, bolts of energy crackle in a frenetic manner that could only be discerned as a call for aid. The infant moves, its back against the rock, uncertain and trembling.

Shotoku scales the remaining rock quickly and draws his sword. The beast hears him and turns in his direction, roaring and furious. With a paw at the dirt, it charges. Shotoku waits confidently until the last moment and makes a practiced pivot out of the beast's path, bringing his sword down with tremendous force on its thick neck. There is the sound of metal on rock, but the beast's hide is unscathed. Its horn comes fast looking to fillet him, but Shotoku rolls across the dirt and away. He runs to the infant, who is still creating the noise with its hands. It ceases the electrical display and reaches up for Shotoku as he approaches. Shotoku hesitates, but sheaths his sword and picks up the creature rapidly, its blue eyes blinking at him. He notices it has no discernible mouth or nose. Its skin is rough except on its face and it is considerably heavier than a human child.

He runs up a low slope of rock circling the beast, which anchors its front legs and points its horn at Shotoku. "What the—" blurts Shotoku, trying to increase his speed away from its ominous pose. Lightning leaps from its horn to the wall, chasing him. It crackles loudly, followed by thunder that nearly knocks Shotoku and the infant to the ground. The beast eyes them both and moves to ascend the wall. Shotoku leaps down the wall back toward the encampment, stumbling under the weight of the child and almost dropping it.

+++++

Dawn is breaking and most of the camp is awake when Shotoku bursts into view and past Makiko, who lies on the ground, hands still bound. The men are startled and move for their weapons.

"Forget your bow! Here!" Shotoku hands Jirai the infant.

Before he can protest, Jirai takes the infant and eyes the beast, "Whoa!?"

Shotoku draws his sword and turns to face the beast, which rounds the corner into the camp at a reckless speed. It stops short of the far rock face, pauses and assesses the newcomers. Incensed by the intruders, the two-ton beast charges at them all.

Devukai, shocked and still in pain, moves the slowest, but Char-ton yanks him out of the way just in time. The beast stomps over the provisions and campfire, whirling, searching for its original prey. Instead, it sees Makiko on the ground helpless only a slight distance away. The beast anchors its feet again and lowers its horn. Anticipating, Shotoku leaps in front of Makiko just as the lightning erupts from its horn. The lightning courses through him, but Shotoku angles his sword and effectively grounds the bolt. The others look on, stupefied.

Frustrated, the beast exhales and all four thick feet dig into the earth, ready for rapid acceleration. Makiko tries to stand and fails, yelling "The neck! Under the chin! It has to be under! You have to—" she motions as if shoveling. Hearing her, Shotoku considers, grips his sword with two hands and walks toward the beast. It sets all of its terrific weight in motion, charging. Almost too late, Shotoku spins and drops to his knees with his back to the beast. With all his strength he thrusts his sword blade back and up. The sword catches the beast just under the chin, careens off one hard scale and then sinks into the soft flesh of the throat. Its head jerks reflex-fast up and away from the pain, but its inertia is too great. The blade slides in to the hilt. It tries to emit a torn, visceral bellow, but all that's heard is a great sigh. In the loose gravel, Shotoku is propelled, still gripping the sword, sliding on his knees in front of the beast, raising his center of gravity so as not to be trampled. Terrified, Makiko sees the rapidly approaching mass, but only manages slinking a few feet away. The beast's head finally slackens and drapes over Shotoku's shoulder and head. He tries to support it, but buckles under the weight, still sliding, head in the dirt. For a moment he lies there taking stock of his injuries. All stand speechless.

A muffled voice is heard from beneath the beast, "Get it off, get it off!" Everyone scrambles to help.

"Help him! Get it off! Quickly," Devukai says, trying to budge the beast with one arm.

"Hurry up! Does this thing look light?" Shotoku complains again. With great effort, they raise the beast enough to pry Shotoku out from under the weight. Char-ton kneels to examine him. Jirai chuckles, setting down the infant and laying a hand on the beast.

"Are you hurt?" asks Char-ton. Still on the ground, Shotoku dusts himself off.

"No, my health is actually enhanced."

Char-ton smiles, "Not hurt. And no improvement in your humor," as he backs off.

"Makiko hurt my feelings last night. Does that count?" quips Shotoku. Devukai hands him some water. Shotoku gives him an appreciative glance.

Char-ton looks to Makiko. "That was unbelievable. This thing is like a rock. How did you know where to stab it?"

She shrugs, "Every Mujongese knows where to strike a rava." She looks Shotoku up and down, appraisingly. "Though few can actually do it."

"Well, gee, you're welcome." The others gather around the beast, examining it. Makiko speaks only to Shotoku.

"You should thank *me*—though I served myself, not my captors," she says dismissively. Shotoku regards her curiously. "But you are brave," she admits—then, seeing his surprise, adds, "a trait abundant in fools."

"There's the juice," Shotoku smiles, exhaling and continuing to remove dust. He stands and moves to examine the beast with the others.

"But precious and rare in the wise," she whispers to

herself, eyes following in his wake.

"Is that what I think it is?" asks Char-ton, looking at the infant on the ground. The group turns their attention away from the beast.

"It's an inazuma child," states Makiko, puzzled. "You've never seen one?"

"No," replies Devukai, dubiously. "You have?"

Jirai kneels and looks at Char-ton. "It's not moving. It was, but stopped." Char-ton offers a blanket and Jirai moves the child. Its tiny legs and arms limply spread across the cloth.

"I can't see a mouth or nose. Shotoku, turn its head," Char-ton says, examining the inazuma. As Shotoku reaches for its head, he feels an invisible pull on his hands. His hands draw closer to the infant and it takes all of his strength to keep from making contact. His hair begins to rise and he feels a tingling sensation all around his body.

Panic seizes his eyes. "Strike! Get down!" Everyone dives for cover, but no lightning occurs. Instead, two bolts leap from his hands to the infant. He strains to resist, but the draw is too great. The infant moves with the dance of electricity all over its body as Shotoku's face contorts.

"Get him away!" yells Char-ton.

Devukai moves toward Shotoku to help. "Shotoku, ah, fiss!"

When they try to approach, lightning jumps from him to strike Char-ton and Devukai. They recoil, thrown to the ground. At last, Shotoku manages to break the bond and falls back to the earth, breathing hard. Eyes adjusting, he looks up to see a full adult inazuma standing before him. He rolls back, a little off balance, but manages to retake his feet and draw his sword. No sooner does he stand than he is hit by another bolt from the towering adult's raised arms. In that moment, inexplicably, he does not feel attacked. The strength of the bolt is weak and he can sense a conduit before him. Relaxing, Shotoku extends his arms and wills the flow into the conduit. The impact on his body is felt immediately, as the bolt he is receiving is directed back to the inazuma. A secondary bolt leaps forth from its chest and connects with his drawn sword. It glows a brilliant translucent orange and then, just as quickly, the bolt ceases and the blade cools. With this action, the inazuma ceases the flow of energy and lowers its arms. Shotoku's blade, now polished and jet-black, is engraved with strange red, glowing symbols.

In the light of dawn, Shotoku can see now that three adult inazuma stand before him. The rest of his unit closes ranks with him, swords drawn, but he waves them back and lowers his own sword.

"It's okay. He didn't hurt me." The infant scuttles over to the adult on the left and nimbly climbs its legs and torso to set its chin on the top of the adult's head. Its body blends with the adult's, and where there were two eyes there now seem to be four. The lower set of eyes pulse several times. The infant's eyes flash and Shotoku cautiously sheathes his sword. The infant disengages from its carrier. Suddenly, it leaps and deftly curls into a ball, rolling around Shotoku once and stopping. Its eyes strobing again, it begins to ascend Shotoku's leg, climbing around to his back, onto his shoulders. It places its chin on his head, just as it did with the full-grown inazuma. Awkwardly, Shotoku tries to relax. A cool, steady current tingles through his body. Then the infant jumps down, curls and rolls back to its former carrier. With this, the inazuma turn and scale the rock face with incredible agility and disappear over its peaks.

"Was that communication?" asks Char-ton.

"I think it was an attempt," says Shotoku, nodding.

Char-ton adds, "Wait, how did you—I mean, without dying? That lightning was all over you."

"It would seem that Shock has a few talents he has not yet brought to light," muses Jirai, looking at Shotoku expectantly. Guilt and disappointment cross Shotoku's face and, stealing a look at Jirai, he turns his back to them. Motioning with his hand indiscriminately, he orders "Let's get this camp cleaned up! Come on!" The others look at each other, bewildered, but begin packing up.

Jirai approaches Shotoku and speaks softly, "Hey, don't be like this. You just did a good thing with your power. I think you saved that … kid." Shotoku stares at his hands and then into the distance.

"I've been fooling with it more and more. In secret. Like I've just forgotten my promise."

"Maybe it's time. Maybe you should use the Spark again."

Shotoku turns his head to face Jirai, visibly angry. Jirai looks away and inhales, knowing what's coming. "Yeah, it was a long time ago, right? You kill your brother and just move on? I keep my promises, Ji. And you in particular should be happy for that." His agitation mounts, "You know: I'm sick of all you telling me to forget my oath. The day I do, I won't be who I am anymore. Don't you understand that? All of my promises will be worthless."

Quickly, Jirai turns his head to face Shotoku again. "Don't keep any for me and I won't for you. Just forgive yourself. It's what Zaru would have wanted."

Their voices having risen, Shotoku notices the others have stopped to listen. His eyes fall upon the princess and his mind recalls the mission. "The Mujong are onto us. We need to move out quickly."

FIVE

Kingdom of Mujong

The team lies prone on the rocks looking down at the Mujong encampment, dismayed. A large, forbidding river meanders across the land. A bridge lies at a distance, and guard houses can be seen on either side of the river. Two catapults lie on opposite sides of the river as well. On the near side, several dozen soldiers are making camp just beside a road that leads to the bridge. Portable spires are set in place, which, combined with those on the road, will protect the encampment from strikes. Closer to the mountains, there is thick forest. An expansive field separates the forest below and the river.

"Damn. They can't have been here long. They're still setting up tents," says Shotoku, grimacing.

Devukai points at a group off to the side. "There's the usual contingent of guards in gray. We would have been up against only four soldiers and now there are dozens."

"I count forty-three that I can see. Probably a full company," adds Jirai.

"Can't be connected to those following us. They must have sent reinforcements directly to all of the border crossings."

"How much time do we have?" asks Char-ton.

"Eight hours before they're on us, I'd guess."

"Sterling before us, yet so far away," Char-ton continues.

"We'll just have to wait 'til dark, then, and ride through at speed," shrugs Devukai.

Shotoku turns from the encampment. "Through fifty men? You know they'll barricade the bridge and the river is too swift. We'll need time to dismantle the barricade. And even if we make it, they can loose those catapults. We need time," Shotoku looks to the skies.

"Shotoku. They've just sent out groups of two away from the camp. Looks like in each direction. Are they searching for us?"

Shotoku takes his previous position on the rocks and looks. "Not sure. Definitely searching for something."

The soldiers disappear into the surrounding woods. Others continue setting up spires throughout the camp, which is loosely stretched along the road making maximum use of the spires already there. Some begin barricading the bridge, while others stand around cooking fires. A few tents are tall enough to stand in. Everyone, even the border guards now, is working to establish camp. The dark red Mujong standard flaps in the wind from one of the spires.

The soldiers wear solid, dark blue clothes with covering silver breastplates, helmets, and gauntlets while the border guards wear the same but with white diagonal stripes on their clothes. One man walks about directing the others. They move hastily with his commands. He then strides over to one of the larger tents and enters.

"There's the captain. He runs a disciplined unit. Fiss. We know his tent. We're going to need some kind of distraction."

The sound of a horn echoes from the valley below.

"Two of the troops are pushing something out of the woods," Devukai whispers, excited.

One of the groups of soldiers emerges from the woods and angles toward the sound, but is careful to follow the tree line. Others in the camp stop what they're doing and look in the direction of the two troops.

"What is it? Apparently, it's what they were searching for." Shotoku defers to Devukai's enthusiasm and looks at him in expectation.

Jirai smiles and turns away from the encampment. "It's wine. Talan, by the look of it."

"How can you possibly tell from here?" says Devukai, incredulously looking from Jirai back to the soldiers.

Jirai points, impatient, "The wood is cedar—see the reddish color? It's the only wine to use cedar."

"How much did they find?" adds Char-ton with renewed interest.

Shotoku turns and looks at Makiko. She returns a demeaning look. Returning his eyes to the troops, he squints with effort. All of the patrols converge at the barrel and disappear into the forest. More barrels begin to stack up at the tree line.

"A lot. Wow." Char-ton licks his lips and Jirai smiles, entertained by his zeal.

The captain exits his tent and signals for his mount. He and his two lieutenants mount their horses after erecting the portable spires attached to their horses' saddles. They ride across the meadow between the encampment and the location of the barrels, the chains which ground and protect the horses and their riders dragging behind. They arrive at the barrels and, after a moment's inspection, the captain signals back to the camp. A wagon with two horses begins to make for their location.

"These boys are at the edge of their kingdom, two days' ride from civilization, the probability of us turning up decreases with each minute, and they just found a huge stash of liquor and flash knows what else." Shotoku turns his back to the scene again and grins hopefully, looking to Jirai. Jirai returns a knowing smile. "I believe we have our distraction."

+++++

The team moves silently about their horses, unpacks and assembles a makeshift camp. A small, smokeless fire burns. They place gourds at their belts and in easily accessible satchels.

Shotoku walks over to Makiko and drops to a knee in front of her. "Is there any chance that you'd promise not to scream if I remove your gag? I would like to speak with you."

Hesitating, she nods her head in agreement. Shotoku removes the gag and gives her water. Makiko smacks her tongue and lips and drinks quickly. "Couldn't you have asked me that hours ago? How do you think it feels with a fissing rag in your mouth? Hands tied?"

"Language!" he chides. But, chagrined, he concedes: "Easy, easy, I'm sorry. You're right. I—" Their eyes meet for a moment and he looks down, embarrassed.

"Well?"

"We are going to cross the border. It's going to require some stealth."

"Hey Jirai! Jirai, right? Gimme some of that beef, will you? I'm starved," yells Makiko.

She looks at Shotoku again, accusingly. Jirai stops walking, but looks at Shotoku, tentatively. He nods and shrugs. Jirai steps forward and places a piece of the dried meat in her tied hands.

"Anything else, sweet pea?"

Gravely, she punctuates, "Maybe after your funeral, a little of that Talan wine." She flashes him an insincere smile, then bites into the meat, chewing and closing her eyes. Jirai looks at Shotoku askance.

"Charming, indeed." Jirai eyes him, takes a step away and turns in order to hide a broad smile and his approval.

"As I was saying, silence is our greatest ally. We can do this the hard way or the easy way."

"Pummel me into unconsciousness or … what?"

"Get your word that you will not cry out."

Her face reflects amused disbelief, "Are you mad?"

"Promise you will not alert the troops as we cross the border and I will trust you."

"Then you are a fool."

Thoughtfully, Shotoku nods his head and smiles, then offers, "Yes, but that does not change what you are.

Some will keep promises, stay true to themselves, despite what others may do."

Makiko pauses at this.

"Why didn't you hit the boy … back in Mujong? In the castle."

"He reminded me of someone. Someone I lost long ago." Shotoku smiles, remembering. "He shared the same reckless bravado."

"But he threatened your success," Makiko stresses, searching for the pattern in his behavior. "And now you trust me. Why would you take these risks?"

Shotoku returns her gaze, silently.

"What will my captivity be like? In Sterling."

"You'll be free to wander the castle grounds … given all that you require, but you will be a prisoner until your kingdom's aid is ensured."

"Do you guarantee my safety? Do you promise to protect me?"

Overhearing their exchange, Jirai approaches as if witnessing a horrific act. "Shotoku?" he barks.

"Swear that no harm will come to me, unto your life, and I will swear not to betray you."

"He can't do that! You can't," insists Jirai, making a concerted effort to cover Shotoku's mouth.

Avoiding Jirai, he answers, "I swear to do as you have spoken."

Observing that she has won some small victory, Makiko hastens to answer, "Then I, too, swear."

"No!" Furious, Jirai seeks Shotoku's eyes, but he evades. "Do you realize what we're getting into? Do you know what's coming? War, Shock. How? Saiak will never agree."

"His agreement isn't really required, is it?"

"Now? Like this you choose to rebel? You've done everything he's ever asked of you."

This piques Shotoku's ire and he glares at Jirai, "Really? How long have I been your friend against Saiak's wishes?"

Jirai acquiesces, "That's not what I meant."

"Unbind her and give her whatever she requires." Shotoku walks away.

Jirai complies and, with false sincerity, speaks to no one in particular, "Ok, yeah, sounds good. Right away." Then to Makiko, "I don't care if he does trust you. I don't. And I'll be watching. There's *my* promise to you, honey."

She only rubs her wrists and answers his words with a self-satisfied smirk. She doesn't understand her victory; only that if the word of this young prince invokes such fear in his friends, it will mean something much direr to his enemies. But what it meant to her—the rare warmth she felt radiating even to her fingers and toes—was what scared her most of all.

+++++

Thin light and boisterous voices escape from the tents of the encampment. A few of the tents are larger in size, while the smaller more numerous ones seem to be designated for sleep. The Mujong crest is dyed on the thick cloth of the tents and flaps in the light wind. Spires reach to the sky at the center and each corner of the tents. When soldiers appear, they crouch and run from tent to tent. All seem to be lingering in the large tents, enjoying the spoils of their find.

A few guards stand at the bridge, but they, too, are

sneaking wine to drink. A few times, the captain and his lieutenants walk about the camp, peering into the darkness in homage to vigilance. He eventually retires with a bottle of the finest wine he can find and dismisses his lieutenants to join the fun. They enter one of the large tents and a small cheer is given, the lieutenants more amiable with the men than their captain.

Emerging from the shadows outside the aura of light from the encampment, the dark figures of the Bright Guard slither to the edges of the large tents. Opening their gourds, the team members reach into the ash inside and remove sticks with hot, glowing embers at one end. A second gourd is then produced, which is pierced horizontally by a long hollow tube. Opening the gourd and dropping the ember inside, they slip the long end of the tube under the flap of the tents and blow into it. The smoke disperses invisibly into the festive scene inside the tents.

After several minutes, the drunken soldiers yawn and make themselves more comfortable on sacks of supplies, crates of provisions or, others being less selective and more drunk, on the ground. A few voices continue to relay stories, so the team continues until the last voice grows silent.

Shotoku, at the captain's tent, is being extra cautious. The captain sips wine, reading and looking over maps, and notices the revelry is beginning to fade. Shotoku continues blowing the smoke into his tent. He furrows his brow, but welcomes the quiet. Reflecting on his personal state, he yawns, finishes his wine and stands, but loses his balance, catching himself. He smiles and looks into the wine glass and then at the wine bottle.

He's only had a single glass, he realizes. Puzzlement crosses his face as he continues to breathe deeply. He reaches for his sheathed sword, wanting to take another look around the camp, but stumbles again and falls to the ground, passed out.

+++++

Makiko and Jirai sit atop horses in the darkness of the tree line.

"What are they doing? They can't defeat them all, drunk or not."

With affectation, Jirai jibes, "'The greatest victory is to defeat your enemy without conflict.' I thought you were the reading type."

"And you? Why did you stay behind? Too proud to crawl?"

"Don't read people too well, though, huh? Shotoku—and the ladies—know my style and how to get the most outta me." He winks at her and she rolls her eyes. "Shock knows who has what skills and how to employ them. He knows I'm better suited to covering with my bow." He pats his bow lightly, smiling, eyes scanning the terrain.

"You were pretty upset that he made me that promise. Why?"

He shakes his head, eyes forward, "Shotoku is in over his head already. He doesn't need to be making promises to every tart that comes along."

"Then he can go back on his promise. People do every day," she ventures, trusting a hunch.

Amused, he risks a quick look at her. "How I wish he would, princess." Thinking further, he chuckles and sighs, "Now that … is honestly funny. Ahhhh, oh my."

"He's that unwavering in his promises?"

"If he is going to go back on his word, it should be to break his oath with Saiak. Swearing off using lightning ... when he is so talented with it."

"What happened?"

"A long time ago, Saiak, ever the model father, dragged Shotoku and his brother, Zarushi, into battle. Perhaps you've heard of the unification of New Sterling?" Makiko's eyes move to the ground as she slow blinks in distaste at the recollection. "Yes. Zaru was younger than Shotoku, but headstrong. Saiak was slaughtering and burning a village in the north: my village." His eyes glisten in the dim light of distant mountain lightning. "Maji, one of Saiak's lieutenants, struck down my father ... shot lightning from his hands and burnt him to death. Then he moved to strike down my mother. I picked up my father's bow and fired, but the shot was weak and didn't pierce his armor. Just before he cut me down, Zaru stabbed Maji in the leg. Shotoku was equally incensed by Maji's conduct and conjured a powerful lightning bolt, much more powerful than Maji had used to kill my father." Jirai pauses, his voice grown thick, and adjusts his posture to distract Makiko. "But he missed Maji and struck his brother. His own brother. For me. He died at my feet. He died for me and Shotoku swore he'd never use lightning again."

"You're ... bound to him, then?"

"There are no bonds. Shotoku would never allow that. But that's what binds me even tighter."

"So you're not a complete rogue. You're loyal."

"I'm loyal to nothing, honey. You show me a reason to be loyal to something and I'll show you a person not looking hard enough."

"How admirable," she says, flatly.

"Well, you show me something admirable and I'll show you a person not looking hard enough."

"A world without hope?"

"Now you're getting warmer."

"I don't believe this cavalier attitude of yours," Makiko says dismissively. "If it were sincere you wouldn't ride with a principled man like Shotoku."

"Then he and you are a perfect match. He says the same thing all the time."

Makiko turns to face Jirai. "What do you mean by 'match'?" Self-conscious, she recovers. "You're a sparker, you know that?"

Distracted, he strains his eyes in the direction of the camp and his voice trails off. "Oh, don't mind me. I just take pleasure in razzing proper, young ladies like yourself." He turns his head suddenly. "Listen." Voices are heard up the pass from which the group came. A horn blows.

"More Mujongese. My kingdom has not forgotten me," she says with some pride.

"Time to go, ready or not. Hold to your promise now and ride." Jirai waits as Makiko considers. Then, following the tree line, she bolts toward the encampment. Jirai gallops to catch up.

+++++

The two guards at the gate are startled from their half-sleep by the horn. "Flash! What was that?"

Two riders gallop among the torchlit tents toward the gate, reining in their horses at the last moment in front of them.

"Halt," yells a guard.

Jirai's and Makiko's horses stomp in the light of the torches. "Shock, we need to cross the bridge now. There's a large force of Mujongese coming down the mountain pass," stresses Jirai, peering into the shadows. Having been hidden just outside of the aura of light and ready to strike down the bridge guards, the team emerges. Not having yet drawn their weapons, the guards think better of reaching for them in the lurch.

"Dismantle the gate right now. Move," commands Shotoku, and the guards rush to dismantle the makeshift barricade.

"But where are the others? You killed them!"

"And you'll join them if you don't hurry!"

Across the field from which they'd fled, the pursuing Mujongese force is seen at the edge of the woods. As with Makiko and Jirai, they must follow the edge of the forest toward the road, fearful of crossing the large, open field.

"How are we going to get through the barricade on the other side?" asks Char-ton, addressing Shotoku.

"Faster! Help them," he implores, then continues, "We do not impede trade, as the Mujong do, so there will be no barricades on the Sterling side of the river."

The barrier mostly cleared, the team remounts. "Alright, into the river with the two of you. Now!" On threat of their weapons, the guards eagerly leap into the river. "Okay, let's jump this thing. You first, prin—"

Makiko gallops by, jumping the barricade deftly, and turns to look back at the group. Arrows begin to whiz by on all sides, as the rest follow suit.

+++++

Shotoku takes the lead as they gallop across the long bridge. Slowly, the gate ahead becomes visible. Confusion and then shock rise deep inside him: a weathered, but solid wooden gate has been built on the Sterling side of the river. It is too sturdy to knock down and too tall to jump. In desperation, he moves his arms as he did in the mountains and conjures a large ball of lightning. Still riding, he draws back his arm and hurls it toward the gate. The ball strikes the gate high, seems to ooze into it and expand, bright veins of fire coursing through the organic material. The gate begins to glow orange, then red and finally white around the expanding blue-white ball. Getting closer, Shotoku prepares to reign in his horse, when, just in time, the entire area around the now shrinking ball crumbles in smoldering ash to the ground. He gallops through the smoke, followed by the rest of the group.

The guards on the Sterling side of the river have emerged from their guard shacks and stand astonished by what they have just seen.

"Saiak's orders! Don't follow," he yells to the guards, begging them not to pursue.

Confused, Makiko sits up in her saddle and yells, "Why are you still riding? We made it."

Jirai looks back without breaking stride, "Catapults!"

Ashen with dread, she looks back across the river and spurs her horse with renewed purpose. "But the fools will kill me, too!"

The confused guards on their side of the river, believing Sterling has been breached, disobey Shotoku, mount and chase after them.

+++++

On the Mujong side of the river, the border guards climb from the river and sprint for the catapults. The mounted Mujong pursuers arrive at the makeshift barricade and, realizing the border guards' intentions, scream to prevent them from firing at the princess.

Too late, the guards loose the deadly contents of their catapult.

+++++

Launching into the air, a large wooden box hurdles toward the clouds. A weak trail of smoke snakes from the lit fuse as each grain of black powder ignites the next, inching toward the contents of the box. It travels innocuously to its apex in the direction of the group, which follows the spire-lined road. Shotoku's party gallops far below the box with the two border guards in pursuit. As it descends, it appears the missile will overshoot Shotoku if allowed to pursue its course. Suddenly it explodes, scattering slag metal pieces in all directions. Attracted by the metal, the night illuminates in a cacophony of thunderbolts from the clouds. The diameter of the field continues expanding as the metal falls, but Shotoku's party manages to gallop away just outside the white-hot rain of electricity. The thunder is deafening as a thick dome of lightning sears the ground, a tornado of sound and fire. They melt the spires protecting the road and then start on the pursuing border guards. Lightning jumps between spire and horse, ground and sky. The epicenter is reduced to blackened cinders; tiny fires, melted spires, and scorched grass and flesh are all that remain.

Miraculously, along the road, a single guard rises

from the earth after all the slag has fallen and the thunder dissipated. Shotoku and his party stop and look back, breathing hard.

"Stay down, you fool!" yells Char-ton. Disoriented, the guard checks his charred gear and clothes, elated to be alive and deaf from the thunder.

"The spires are gone! The spires!"

Shotoku motions with his hands but it's no use, the guard is not looking. He stands and looks up as if to thank the gods, raising his arms in thanks. A single bolt flashes him dead.

Jirai looks up to the sky and gives it a not insincere sneer, "That's just mean."

Shotoku's eyes scan the horizon as he urges his mount forward. "That's Aurora."

SIX

Kingdom of Sterling

The huge castle at New Sterling rises from the vast plains in defiance of stormy skies. Blue paint glosses clay shingles atop long halls. Wide, well-manicured courtyards, gardens and rivulets are offset by strong, high towers dwarfed only by the spires harboring all life under their invisible protective domes. Once a grand monument to progress and enlightenment, cracks have formed beneath pristine veneers, and chips gather in the paint. The drawn faces of its people remain stoic as they pass, with only the flash of a fearful glance and the sadness that follows unrequited hope.

Shotoku sits in the gray light cross-legged with eyes focused on a rock near the pond. A small waterfall burbles nearby. All the shrubs and grounds are immaculately trimmed, frozen, as if murdered by a swift-moving plague. Shotoku is expressionless, but relaxed. Only the fluorescent throats of the dotted, glowing toads at the water's edge betray any movement.

A bent old man in a yukata approaches. "Shotoku! Shotoku, you're back." He turns to see Niwashi and smiles broadly.

"Old man, you're here! Sit, sit."

"Yes, yes." Slowly, Niwashi sits across from him and looks over the garden. The man's garment has extra wide, stiff shoulders with baggy sleeves and pants that conceal his arms and legs. A smile creases his eyes under a bald pate as he organizes his brown clothing beneath him and slowly sits beside the prince.

"I knew I'd find you here. You love this garden. In that we are the same. How did your mission go?"

"Strange, but successful. Ran into more inazuma."

"Wonderful! In the mountains?"

"Yes. Why do you say 'wonderful'? I have always been told they were a mindless, aggressive species. But they were not. Not this time. I mean, except when it shot lightning at me."

"Lightning? Were you injured?"

He rubs his hands together slowly. "No, surprisingly, but I'm not sure why."

"So they were violent."

"It's hard to explain, but I think not."

"How odd. Next you'll be seeing Iridian monks."

"Have you ever seen them?" overly eager, and then embarrassed. He begins to explain, "The tales of them have always seemed fantastical to others. But I'm not sure. I can—" He hesitates, but knows he can trust the old man. "I can do many of the things they did."

"I have heard only of their atrocities. I did see them, but not in battle. I heard they could perform many magical feats."

"But I don't think it is magic. Through my models, experiments, I can see how some of what the stories say might be possible. Okay, flying and disappearing: that is crazy talk. But … my talent for … you know … helps me see how some things may have been possible."

Niwashi's eyes glisten. "It's an important step toward manhood, unmasking the mysteries that surround us all. Someday, based on your knowledge, you may be forced to take a stand for a cause … one that others don't fully comprehend. That is what defines a man. Whether you pursue the truth, even to your own detriment, will determine whether your stand is just—or a path to darkness." Shotoku listens, contemplating. "How was the princess?"

"Oh, ah, Makiko," he says, casually. "Trustworthy. Seems of good stock."

"Stock? I was thinking of her general demeanor. But I can see what you were thinking of."

"No, I meant in, like, upbringing."

"So she is pretty?"

"Compared to you, old man. She has some confused ideas, I'll tell ya. But you know, on our way back, we discovered stockpiles of goods near the border. Why would that be?"

"I suppose for importation, no?"

"But Saiak says that Mujong refused to continue importing goods."

"Yes, that has placed much strain on the economy. I have to drink my own terrible home-brewed sake, now, instead of delicious Mujong wines."

"But the border gates were closed on *our* side of the river. I wasn't expecting that. Their side was wide open. And Makiko said that it is we who began the embargo, not them."

"Hmm. It sounds like you must educate her. Make her time here well spent."

"I don't understand. What I've seen doesn't make you doubt what we've been told … ?"

"My boy, be careful to whom you pose such questions. If something is amiss, unraveling the scheme might take some time. The fewer apprised of your findings, the safer. But we have the princess now. Perhaps with the alliance we'll resolve these issues."

"That's the goal. I'd better go meet with Saiak. He's expecting me."

"Yes, yes, go see our father. Tell him all that you have witnessed. He will have the answers, I'm sure. You can't expect a gardener to know such things."

Shotoku grimaces, "I can't talk to him like I do to you."

Niwashi looks away, an emotion surfacing then gone again, and places a hand on his shoulder. "Go, go, or you'll be late." As he watches after the boy, the hidden visage returns and his bottom lip quivers slightly, eyes softening. Then, angered by his weakness, Niwashi's face grows dark and he bites his lip. Deep in thought, he absently allows blood to dribble down his yukata. Then he rises deftly, walking away, leaving only a blood stain on the grass below.

+++++

Makiko is led through the labyrinthine stone

hallways of Sterling castle's highest keep. Surrounding and leading her are four guards dressed in long, heavy blue battle cloth and wooden breastplates. Entering a large chamber and halting, she eyes thick rugs and two terrific blazing fireplaces. Further into the great room, two men lean over a map of the surrounding lands. Their eyes are keen and their mannerisms betray intelligence. She is unable to hear what they say, but affects nonchalance as she appreciates the high, ornate vaulted ceilings.

Suddenly she interrupts, "This is nice. I'm glad to see you not stooping to shoulder the burden the common man bears. Does all this really shield you from culpability?" The men look up at her and exchange a glance. "For the tears of mothers weeping for their emaciated children? As the people grow weak and sick? As you invite war down upon the heads of us all?" She lurches forward shucking her escort.

Saiak's eyes grow thin as the young woman approaches, but his charismatic grin does not waver. His dark, short hair shines over a thin face, cheekbones and square jaw.

"Princess Makiko … no more doubts about that. I have heard of your … creative talents, shall we say?" He glances at Kurukov, whose look communicates redemption. Kurukov's spy network has done its work well. Saiak already knows much about enemies and allies alike.

"I believe you've met General Kurukov? He says you have a penchant for making up stories."

"We shall see about that."

"Indeed," Saiak answers euphemistically. "The

armies from the three states arrive tomorrow."

"You mean the other states you coerced into joining Sterling? I hope you don't get hit by a stray arrow. That can happen to an unpopular leader."

"They all have good reason not to betray me, as do you."

"I understand now, after speaking with your son, how an … unlikely leader rises to power. Lies and disinformation."

Dismissive, Saiak loses interest in the conversation and returns to the maps on his desk. "You have your truth and we have ours."

"No. There is one truth. And when it finds the ears of your people, your reign will burn in a flash."

Still looking at the maps: "Interesting theory. Wholly unnoteworthy meeting you, Princess. Keep to the castle or you'll find yourself in harm's way."

"I'm not worried. Shotoku promised that he would protect me." At this, Saiak looks up too quickly to conceal his surprise and meets her gaze. His nostrils widen slightly, betraying his irritation, and she smiles. "I see that someone's word here still carries honor. Even if he is a fool."

She turns and leaves the chamber quickly, almost running into Shotoku outside. She is flustered, but relaxes noticeably upon seeing him, before continuing away. After Shotoku enters, Makiko returns and hides in a nook close to the doorway.

Saiak approaches, drawing his dagger as Shotoku enters. Shotoku sees the weapon, but does not slow his pace, steeling himself for what comes. His father places a hand on his son's shoulder. "Well done, son." He lies the dagger on his chest, simultaneously. Shotoku waits in dread. Saiak whispers, "You defied me. Do you know what I have done to those who betray me?" He looks in his son's eyes a moment, then continues, "You went against me. You broke your word."

"I never prom—" he tries to protest.

"No. You'd keep your word to your friends, but not to me. Is that it?" Saiak seethes, still whispering. Kurukov can only speculate as to the exchange.

"Father, I thought it was best. For Sterling."

His father taps his shoulder with the dagger, backs up, suddenly, and yells, "And you succeeded." A false smile creases his face and he looks back at Kurukov. The old general seems untrusting of Shotoku's actions and, perhaps, his motivations.

Shotoku returns a proud look. "Yes, sir."

"How many casualties?"

"Just Devukai was injured. We used batons in our assault. I thought I would minimize political damage by avoiding unnecessary deaths. Unfortunately, two of our border guards were killed by the Mujongese as we fled."

"Border guards?" Saiak asks, as if this is strange to hear.

"Yes, at our quite tightly sealed border." Shotoku cannot help but add an accusatory tone. "Had I known, perhaps their deaths could have been avoided."

"They don't matter." Saiak looks back at Kurukov, "Have that looked into." He returns his attention to his son. "But no casualties? That is a feat."

Shotoku's sense of justice stokes courage. "They do matter. They had families, no doubt. If you could just be straight—"

"Whelp! If you think I will suffer a lecture from you after your betrayal, you know not how tightly you dance with misfortune." Saiak's eyes seem to ignite briefly and his teeth gleam, rendering a wholly terrifying aspect. Then his practiced countenance returns. Shotoku reflects, with surprise, that he feels no fear in open conflicts like this one, where the two sides are easily divisible. It is his inner dilemmas that sometimes rend his mind from his heart, resulting in inaction.

Saiak hesitates, then seems silently to make some unknown decision. "This will be useful in our bargaining with Mujong. Just when I think you've no more surprises—" In the pause, a father appreciates a son. Saiak moves to his desk, diverting eyes to paper. "But remember that alliances are made through fear. Fear is the root of all action. People are driven by their fears— fears of starvation, pain and death. These are the tools of the strategist. An army fears we'll attack one spot; they reinforce while we attack another."

Face flushing and voice a bit unsteady, Shotoku offers, "I thought this operation was necessary because of the failure of such tactics."

Saiak looks back to Shotoku briefly, ignoring the slur. "Defiant and still will not take up the Spark. You were such an apt pupil once."

Weary of this topic, Shotoku lets his gaze fall to the rugs. "You know my oath, father."

"Your brother's death was not your fault. How many times must I tell you?" Shotoku's eyes mist. "And to think it happened defending that orphan friend of yours, Jirai. What a waste."

"He is a loyal friend."

"Loyal? And do you think his loyalty has anything to do with your being a prince? Who else does he have?"

Shotoku looks up, smoldering. "He has no one, father. Fate made sure of that."

Saiak answers anger with his own grade of resolution. "Battle is imminent. We don't know if we can repel the inazuma. We'll need every skill. Every resource. You were young when you made that oath and I'm ordering you to abandon it."

"I understand, father." He turns to hide his scowl and begins to walk out.

"*And* the one you made to our little captive." Shotoku stops and turns his head enough to see his father with one eye. "Do what I say. In the coming maelstrom, you will need all your skills to survive. I won't always be there to protect you."

Shotoku exits the chamber quickly, failing to notice Makiko hiding in the shadows nearby, sympathy building for the young prince's impossible dilemma.

+++++

Shotoku makes his way from the main keep and across the battlements. He nods to several soldiers; he raises his hand to one or two and they reciprocate, moving theirs diagonally in a chopping motion: lightning upon the enemy. He puts his troubles aside for the moment for the sake of leadership and to convey hope to his men.

"Shotoku!" His reverie is broken by an older gentleman in battle garb. He wears a relieved smile.

"Douzen! I expected you at the meeting," grinning and then affecting a frown.

"I know. I'm sorry. I am not seeing eye to eye with

77

many of your father's and Kurukov's decisions these days. They have been forgetting to invite me to meetings, consequently." His look becomes grave. "I heard about your mission. Is my son okay?"

Shotoku has been dreading this meeting, and yet this man is practically a father to them all. He gives no quarter, makes the Bright Guard do what most would dismiss as impossible, and then he expects more. Now Shotoku has allowed his son, Devukai, to be injured. What kind of way was this to repay him? "He was injured, sir. I was there. As their captain, the blame is mine."

"Relax, son. Do you think I don't know the risks? He is a warrior by choice. I gave all my sons the choice to be whatever they wished. He believes in the way of the warrior and in that way lies death. Death for what you believe."

Visibly relieved, Shotoku says, "My father does not see it so."

"Just remember: I'm proud of the team and you." Shotoku resists, but gives a slight nod. "I trained you from a pup and many qualities that your father scorns, I see as your greatest gifts. He's right: you exhibit not the limited qualities of a soldier, but those of a leader. You are the finest I've trained … ever." Douzen looks at the young man before him and knows his mettle. He has seen him in the dirt, bleeding, seen him rise, even surprise him with an uncanny thrust of his sword, forcing him to put him down all the harder out of self-preservation. Douzen is adept at turning boys into soldiers and in detecting when they are at a breaking point. And he knows that a kind, honest word from a mentor will be remembered when they need it most. "A father's approval can be hard to win. He needs you, and the men look up to you despite your age. Take comfort in that and trust your intuition. The coming war will turn everything upside down. All a man may be left with is his character. Remember that nothing, no one, can corrupt you except yourself. Your choices are your own."

Shotoku absorbs this. "How dire is our situation?"

"The other three kingdoms have been razed. Until now the zuma have been random and uncoordinated, but something drives them now. They have emerged en force and linger in the lowlands."

"Strange for them to stay in the valley."

"I don't know what's happened, but they appear to be here to stay. They use our spires, not for protection, but like a lightning line. Like the spokes of a wheel they gather at the spires absorbing the latency in the skies."

"What protects us is feeding them? I wonder how that could be turned against them?"

"And they are hard to take down or even to get close to. I just returned from a reconnaissance. Those I saw attempting to resist the inazuma were fried by arches jumping from the short little bastards before they even got close."

Shotoku guffaws, "You're telling me." Douzen smiles to see his student's maturing confidence.

Just then a messenger approaches them. "General Douzen: Lord Saiak requests your counsel immediately."

Douzen nods, then focuses on Shotoku: "We'll speak later, lad. Tell my boy to take care of his captain."

Disappointed to see him go so quickly, Shotoku nods, accepting fate, as Douzen has taught him a good soldier does.

+++++

Still well within the castle's outer walls, Shotoku reaches the training grounds where the barracks lie. Members of his team are outside fencing and horsing around.

Devukai comes out to meet him with hope on his face, even though his arm is in a sling. "Hey boss. How's everything?"

"How's the shoulder?"

Trying to prove his toughness, the younger warrior moves to unsling his arm. "I can fight."

He stops him, reassuringly. "I know. Just take is easy. Let yourself heal. Your arm will be tested again soon enough."

"Starov! Chillson!" The two men cease fencing and run over to meet Shotoku. Char-ton, who was watching, also comes along. "How's the rest of my Bright Guard? Glad to see you're not softening. Thought I'd find you passed out in your bunks," he jokes. They ignore the jibe: to men of their aptitude, aspersions do not stick.

"Just teaching this whelp to fence," says Starov, the senior member of the group, referring to Chillson. Starov is short and stocky and seems of infinite constitution. He exudes the confidence won only by hard years on the battlefield, and his thick features mask cunning and uncanny intuition.

Chillson breathes hard and smiles at his elder's barb. Pale, but healthy, his ruddy cheeks and blue eyes glow under blond, short hair. Side by side, he elbows Starov.

"Didn't this whelp tag you a few times earlier? You must be rusting up, old man."

"Aye, like a kitten gnawing on a lion's ear. 'Til I brush you aside with my huge paw." He puts his hand on his head and pushes it.

Chillson laughs. "But what happened, Shock? All went well and whatnot?"

"Well enough, for your part. I have others to answer to. Sorry I couldn't bring you two. You were greatly missed."

"Don't plan on counting us out in the future, lad," says Starov, and he and Chillson grow ominous. Despite their difference in age, these two highly skilled swordsmen are like twins, nodding simultaneously, confident and deadly.

"I won't," promises Shotoku, his words enough for the members of his team as he continues past them and leans on a post next to where Jirai is sitting. He looks out at the gray skies.

Jirai looks at the same skies. "Went that well, huh?"

"Better than I'd hoped … and worse."

"You can't control life, least of all chaos like this. Hands on or off the reins, it doesn't much matter."

"I can't help trying to steer."

"That's why you're an idiot," Jirai jibes without smiling. "It's fun watching you try, though."

Shotoku gives a tired smile. "Are you trying to make me feel better? Any other constructive utterances?"

Yelling is heard from atop the battements and, a few moments later, a rider gallops onto the castle grounds via the nearby portcullis. Shotoku deftly mounts his horse and meets the rider. "A large group of Mujong troops has been spotted approaching from the south."

"How many?"

"Fifty, maybe. And bearing the royal standard." The rest of the Bright Guard mount and join Shotoku, exiting the castle at a gallop, but sticking to the wide road protected by lightning spires. The group of mounted Mujong troops approaches via the same road. Shotoku pulls up sharply, blocking their path.

"That's far enough!"

"A boy greets me? Where is my daughter?" Makiko's father, Kenshi, holds his powerful mount with disciplined control. His private guard surges before him, horses driving Shotoku's mount back, until his friends arrive. With equal aggressive posturing, their horses rear and snort and their forces and hostility mix, danger close.

"Unharmed; and this boy is the one who swiped her from beneath your nose."

"You ignore the question?" Kenshi notes.

"The Bright Guard answers the questions of its choosing."

"You were the ones?" His tone incredulous.

"Shotoku, son of Saiak."

"*You* are the Destroyer of Lunabi. I expected you to be older."

"An alliance is expected of you. One you would have offered before if you cared for the people of these lands. No harm will come to your daughter, I swear, if you join our alliance."

"Kidnapper and liar. Who would have guessed?"

Devukai urges his horse into the Mujong horses, incensed by the insult.

"I suppose name calling is a minor offense compared to starving my people," retorts Shotoku.

"Your father would know more about that than I, fool."

"I've seen the surplus left inside your borders to rot. Do not try that ruse with me. Do your people know how you squander supplies?"

"Of course, we produce far more than we need, but with exporting cut off by your father, I cannot reintroduce the surplus into our economy. It would erode supply and demand." Shotoku silently considers. "I offered to export for free, when I heard of your kingdom's hardship, but your father refused all aid and permanently barricaded the border gates. Your army grows, but the people starve. What are we to believe is the aim of such a strategy?"

"I've heard this before. The Mujongese all seem to know the script," Shotoku says, eyes fixed on the king.

Kenshi scoffs, "The truth is easy to remember, boy."

Saiak, Kurukov and Douzen along with several dozen Sterling troops arrive.

"King Kenshi, at last there can be peace. It is a great day."

Agitated, Kenshi ignores Saiak as Shotoku continues, "Our army grows to repel the zuma that have come into the valley. They have already destroyed many villages in the north. You cannot possibly be as ignorant of this as you claim."

King Kenshi's eyes flash. "Perhaps Sterling troops destroyed those villages. It wouldn't be the first time you've raised your hand against your own people, Destroyer!"

"Shotoku! Enough!" demands Saiak.

Shotoku, barely containing his rage, glares at the Mujong king. His horse, feeling his agitation, snorts and hooves the dirt.

"Kenshi, let us speak and agree to—"

Finally, looking at Saiak, Kenshi speaks loudly, "I've learned all I need from your boy. We're leaving."

Saiak glowers at Shotoku and then looks to the king, appealing. "But I insist—"

"You'll have your 'alliance,' but our troops will not integrate and will camp away from your fortress." Saiak dares to show satisfaction at this, pleased with himself. "And make no mistake. The sons and daughters of my nation are not for negotiating. I don't know why you showed such uncharacteristic restraint during your foray into our kingdom. But if the casualties had been greater, this would have been an invasion force." The king and his entourage circle to leave. "My patience is spent. Your next misjudgment will be fatal. I will send my forces shortly and, if my daughter is less than healthy, you will deal with them as an enemy instead of an ally."

Kenshi's horse rears and his forces make haste to follow him, galloping off under the gray skies.

SEVEN

Kingdom of Sterling

Shotoku lies on his bed staring at the ceiling. His expression is troubled as he tries to digest all that he has encountered in the last few days. Frustrated, he begins searching for anything to divert his attention. Casting his eyes about the room, they land on a small, onyx structure upon his desk. He sits up and walks to it, smiling and peering thoughtfully at its entirety. The elaborate cathedral is the culmination of months of work, heating and shaping the pieces with small arches of lightning, trying not to burn himself and failing. Concentrating, he even has conjured magnetic fields with his hands, passing them over bits and pieces to reorient their polarity.

He runs his hand though a pile of pieces on the table, looking for a particular one. Finding it, he moves to place it gently on the structure. As the piece draws closer, it is magnetically pulled from his fingers, adhering soundly to the greater building. He moves around his creation, appreciating it, lost in thought until he is jarred by the sight of Makiko at the doorway.

"Ah, I'm sorry. I didn't scare you did I?"

"No, no … Yeah, you're scary."

She grins and rolls her eyes. He leans, setting his hands on the table, but she doesn't enter.

"Nice room … big."

"I'd rather bunk with my men. Is yours alright?"

"Yeah, comfortable. Except for the nagging feeling that I'm surrounded by the enemy."

"Not anymore. We're allies now."

"I guessed that." She walks toward his window. "I saw my father."

"Do you think he should have allied with us?" Makiko looks at him. "That he did the right thing?"

"Why should that matter to you?"

"Because I'm not sure I would have done as he did."

"Well, that's grand testimony to your love for your daughter."

"I'd like to think that wouldn't matter, but I suppose it would."

Makiko lets a laugh escape, shaking her head, "Oh, you are a naïve boy. Yes, I think he did the right thing. We have not been completely ignorant of happenings in the north. It appears that an alliance will benefit all. Although it wasn't easy with your kingdom's current disposition toward us."

"And if it wouldn't have benefited us all?"

Feeling trifled with, Makiko rejoins, "Then I would have fulfilled my duty and killed as many of you as possible, or myself. Is that what you wanted to hear?"

"I'm sorry. I was—"

"A fool? Insensitive? An ungrounded—"

He shrugs, "What did you expect? I'm a kidnapping murderer, right?" He turns away from her and back to the structure on the table.

"What is that, anyway?"

"Magnetics."

"And what are 'magnetics'? It looks like a lot of them."

"It's a cut up lodestone, really."

"So they stick together, then." She walks over to his desk. "Wow, look at the detail." She moves to the desk in order to admire the elaborate square obsidian building with arches, cathedral ceilings, long windows and doors. There is an open courtyard in the center, with black grass and a fountain. "Where are the spires?"

"Fortunately, it's not real, so it doesn't need them."

"Bit of a dreamer, aren't you?"

"What sane person doesn't want to escape this world?"

Makiko reaches to touch the courtyard. "Is this supposed to be grass? What's it made from?" She touches the black grass and it leaves an impression. "Oh, sorry."

"It's just ferrite dust on a lodestone. Holds whatever shape you give it." He reaches into a small box on the table and removes what appears to be dark soil. "I just drop some of the metal dust and—" He sprinkles the dust on the place she touched and the indentation disappears, indiscernible from the rough, black ocean of grass.

"Interesting. And you created this?" She seems doubtful.

"Oh, this is nothing. Watch." Shotoku grabs a gray metal bar, small like a brush but triangular in shape. He sets one end of the bar into a groove at the base of the structure and holds the other end over a similar groove in a capacitor. Lining it up with the groove, but careful not to touch it, he drops the bar. A single spark jumps from the groove and suddenly the structure illuminates. Torches glow along the walls, stones, unnoticed before; luminescence and light pour out of the brightly colored windows.

Makiko's eyes go wide. "Incredible!" Shotoku laughs with pride, happy to share. She moves closer to the structure again. "But how did you—"

"Careful! It'll give a flash if you touch it. And those lights are hot … that's why they're glowing."

Taking heed, she stands straight again and her hands retreat. "How did you ever make the tiny shards that go into the lights?"

"Ever been to a blacksmith's? Little pieces of metal all over the floors. He lets me take 'em and I agree not to have him killed." Makiko gives him a wearisome glance and sigh. "Sorry," he offers.

She considers him more seriously and looks down as if remembering something. "You know, you look young for your age."

"Hmm. Thank you. Wait, uh … how old am I?"

"Well, you must be twenty-eight or thirty, right?"

"What?"

"Lunabi. You led the soldiers there. That was ten years ago, so—"

Understanding spreads across his face and he nods slowly, "I'm twenty."

"You lie! You were ten years old? Then you couldn't have … you couldn't possibly have been responsible for what happened there."

"No, not me alone. But many eager men helped me and I, uh … I watched. They were hacked down even as they clung to my horse begging." Makiko is silent, mouth slightly agape, breath thick. "Kurukov organized the assault, but Saiak made sure I received the credit for it. He wanted to make sure his boy had a fearsome reputation."

"And you perpetuated the lie?"

Quoting, Shotoku answers, "It inspires fear and that's a very useful tool. Very useful in conflict." Sadness shadows his face. "Besides, that's what I do best: nothing. Stand and watch without helping. When I do—"

Still in disbelief, Makiko says, "You didn't kill those people."

"He hit me. When I tried to help a boy. I mean … I didn't know what was going on. He never did what he was told." Shotoku stifles a laugh or cry.

"Who hit you?"

"I don't know. Someone from behind. Could have been a villager, for all I know. It was chaos," he says, voice disconnected. Makiko stares at him, measuring. Shotoku's eyes close as he relives the memory.

"I know," she confesses. "About your brother."

His head snaps in her direction, pained, and his emotions teeter between the quest for forgiveness and resentment over a secret betrayed. "Jirai," he utters finally. Then he collects himself, stands straight and grins weakly, acknowledging he's revealed something. He walks past Makiko toward the doorway.

"I have to go. I'm sorry I—" He tries to be glib.

"No, wait. I'm sorry."

"It wasn't a very appropriate discussion. I'll, ah, see you later." He disappears down the hallway leaving Makiko's mind aflame.

+++++

Amongst the beauty of the well-groomed gardens, Niwashi and Shotoku sit in an open-air pavilion. They sit on either side of a game board preparing to play and relaxing in the warm winds. Niwashi throws lodestones under the board, shakes it, and the ferrite dust reorients with the magnetic eddies, forming conductive strong points on the playing surface.

"Ah, the mountains are on my side again. It's not even worth playing." Shotoku folds his arms, grudgingly looking at the pieces on the board: soldiers, catapults, spires and inazuma.

"Would you like to reshuffle?" Niwashi moves to grab the board.

"Well, I'm no good with this. Is it fun for you just to catapult me to death?" He gestures at the board in frustration, but not angry.

"I always hope you will prevail somehow even against great odds. Then we could both learn something. You are an excellent strategist."

"I don't mind the odds being against me. Actually, I prefer it—winning is that much sweeter. Okay, let's play this out. I don't know how you beat me that one time. You remember? You had all those mountains. What happened to your lip, by the way?"

"I think you were just overconfident and played foolishly. I don't remember what moves I made, exactly." Niwashi ignores the question about his lip. They set up the board, placing their pieces in strategic formations, men, inazuma and catapults protected by spires. Shotoku frowns, calculating meticulously.

"See? I can barely fend off natural lightning strikes much less your catapult strikes."

Sick of his complaining, Niwashi gets up. "Try something radical, then, you big grouch. I'm getting some sake."

"It's barely afternoon."

"Then I am overdue, neh?"

Shotoku shrugs and nods, resolving to try fresh tactics. He reorganizes his pieces into three groups: a main force of catapults, spires and men, and two small groups of inazuma each with a spire and one man. Niwashi returns with sake and stops, standing.

"This is your new strategy?"

"Yeah, smarty. What's that supposed to mean? Why don't you just sit down and pucker up to kiss my victorious butt?" Shotoku looks over his shoulder back at the castle keep.

Niwashi sits down, looking back and forth between Shotoku and his pieces. "Looking for someone?"

"Ah." He returns his eyes to Niwashi. Then he confesses. "I feel bad about grabbing her. She's a good gal."

"Did you help her understand our situation?"

"You know, she and her dad claim that our kingdom has brought much of our fate upon ourselves, and I can't say I can think of anything to disprove them. When I was away, the things I saw … I just can't seem to make sense of it all.

"Make your move."

Shotoku does and Niwashi reciprocates.

"What do you know of the zuma? Really know?"

"You know what I do."

"So there are two races. No one ever told me that."

"I had not read that either."

"In the books we're not supposed to read?"

Niwashi flashes a conspiratorial grin. "Yes. That I showed you. Mind you don't reveal what you've learned."

"But the ones I met were tall and blue eyed."

"Yes, that's right, you said you encountered one."

Shotoku laughs and moves another piece. "Ah, haven't you been listening, old man? In the last few weeks I have been in close combat with the reds and made part of the family of a group of blues. The baby zuma on my head and a lightning kiss on the cheek and all." Shotoku emulates a creepy smooch and Niwashi's eyes smile from behind his sake cup. He spills a bit on his robe. "Totally different from the foreboding image conjured in that old book."

The old man wipes the sake from his shirt, "You believe the book is inaccurate?"

"It's not my place to challenge the wisdom of the sages who wrote it. Perhaps they just never discovered the other breed. What do you think?"

Niwashi takes a drink of sake and does not look at him. "I think you are old enough now to form your own conclusions."

"Some help you are. Who wrote the book, anyway?"

"Our elders. How should I know?"

"Well, one guy? Ten? One hundred?"

"Obviously, it's honored and time worn. Who are you to question?" Mocking Shotoku, Niwashi motions at the sky. "Perhaps the northern lights will tell you."

"Well, aren't you prickly." Shotoku interrupts his playing and stares at the old man, peeved.

"What does it matter? Remember the tale of Monk and Thunderbolt?"

"Of course. Every child knows that story."

"True or not?"

"Let's see. A monk tries to secure knowledge for humanity; and the angry gods smite him by sending Thunderbolt, familiar of Lucian, the god of lighting. But the wily monk tames the familiar and makes it his own. I guess it might be kind of true. The idea behind it."

"The point is, what does it matter whether it is true or not? Doesn't the story embolden you to succeed against all threats? To reach out and make that which was the gods' your own?"

"Okay, yes, I guess it does."

"And what if I now told you that that story is an allegory for what actually occurred? That a lone man, like you or I, did ascend into the mountains and did tame the laws of lightning? And that that man was a predecessor to the order of monks that evolved?"

"The evil order? The one that controlled lightning and tried to enslave humanity?"

Growing agitated, Niwashi rebuts, "The one that also built libraries and provoked the questioning and discovery of everything around us."

Confused, Shotoku responds, incredulously, "Are you saying they were good?"

"No. Yes. I'm saying … you're old enough to discard what you think you know and decide for yourself. With your heart."

"My heart?" Shotoku smiles and returns his eyes to the board. "Truth is based on facts. How am I supposed to find truth with my heart?" He looks up at the gardener as if he's crazy, and is startled. The old man's eyes grow black as night and dusk seems to swirl up around them. He grows broader and menacing.

"True or false? Black or white? Fact or fiction? Naught matters but what can be. And with the heart, the universe will bend and its enemies be shattered." Niwashi smashes the board with his palm, shattering many of the stone pieces.

"Hey, what's going on?" Makiko was approaching, but reconsiders.

Shotoku, indignant, says, "Crazy, here, just broke the game board."

"Everything okay?"

"I win. Go for a walk with him and teach him a thing or two. I'm going for a soak." Niwashi gets up, flashes an affected smile and walks away, sake in hand.

"What the hell, Niwashi?"

"Game over. Play another game. Many games to play. Life is a game. Play well or die. Laugh! If you're not laughing, you're losing! Might as well be dead …"

"Makiko, meet Niwashi," he says, embarrassed.

She laughs, deciding, "I like him."

Surprised, he admits, "Yeah, me, too."

"I was walking through the garden and heard you

two. I hope you don't mind."

"No, just relaxing."

"Huh? Well, the garden is … unbelievable. Elegant, but simple."

"Isn't it? I come here and think. That's how I got to know Niwashi."

"Have you known him long?"

They walk slowly through the garden until they come to a small bridge crossing a tiny stream flowing from a pond. Occasionally, lightning can be seen in the distance. Fireflies blink and float through the air. A servant weaves through the garden, agitating the glow pods in hanging paper lanterns. A white-blue light warms the trees while fluorescent mushrooms illuminate the pathways.

"Thanks," The servant smiles and bows slightly. "Niwashi showed up about a year ago. The garden had gone into disrepair since we moved in and he offered to help bring it back to life."

"Ah, yes, after 'unification' ended."

"After the monks were purged the various kingdoms squabbled for years over one matter or another. Saiak ended that rather effectively with his own campaign. You may disapprove of the means, but he did bring peace."

"Start a war to stop one, huh?"

"Look, I know. It's not … There must have been another way to handle it, but circumstances …"

"I know. I understand. But you must change the direction this kingdom is headed in, if you have any influence at all."

"I don't. The harder I try … everything just gets

turned upside down." He stops, looking her up and down. "You have a diplomatic air about you, though. All in all, I notice that you don't batter me too badly about our policies."

She shakes her head, unconvinced. "That's what we need: more diplomats."

"We do. If we had as many as we do soldiers, perhaps the soldiers wouldn't be necessary."

"Hmm, you may have something there. But I should batter you—after the way you treated me." She gives his shoulder a playful back fist.

"I know," he says, looking into the growing darkness. "I don't know what I'm doing." He sneaks a look at her that is laced with sadness.

Again, she is disarmed and drawn in by his honesty. She laughs. "Oh Shock, anyone who claims to know what he's doing is full of it. Do I look like I know?"

"I want to believe you do. Maybe that's all people need. I wish my ignorance had no ramifications, but I'm expected to lead these men. To know what they do not."

She nods her head, eyes off in the distance, "We cannot escape our stations. Do your best and I will do mine. Promise?"

"Of course, but no more promises," he sighs. Her words, although not lessening his burden, afford some comfort. "Everyone seems to get uptight when I start promising things," he chuckles.

Makiko returns a smile, then grows thoughtful. She turns her head away as she feels tears behind her eyes, heart skipping a beat. She opens her eyes wider trying to disperse the moisture gathering there. She never knew she was so susceptible to the charm of someone who always spoke from his heart.

A moment of silence lingers. "What do you think Niwashi meant, 'With the heart, the universe will bend'?"

"Is that an honest question or a quiz?"

"Would that affect your answer?"

She frowns, her turn to look him up and down. "You're so strange." Perhaps she could diffuse her emotions by labeling him one thing or another.

"Thank the gods you didn't call me normal."

"So you're at war with 'normal' too. You've got a war on all fronts, young man."

"What do you mean?"

"Against 'normal,' against the zuma, your father … How do you expect to win?"

He doesn't hide his apathy. "Oh, I don't. I *expect* to lose, but that acceptance casts out fear. As I am cut and pierced, I won't stare at the wounds in surprise. I'll fight like lightning and burn my enemies down. That is what Douzen teaches us: acceptance, even of death. It's the only way to give life to one's beliefs and bring them into reality with a ferocity that can't be ignored. That was the way of those who came before us."

"'One cannot live rightly with fear as his companion.' Something like that?"

"You've read one of the forbidden books?"

"In Mujong, they are not forbidden."

Unable to contain his enthusiasm, "Do you know any more quotes?"

"I can tell you I have a problem with the one I just quoted."

"Why?"

"It doesn't allow for love. That's what Niwashi was talking about."

"So, love will solve everything?" he teases, yet hopeful that she can explain.

"No, but you underestimate it, even within yourself. It is what drives us all."

"I still don't understand. My emotions are always misleading, telling me to do things I'll regret. My whole life has been about controlling my emotions and training to eliminate them."

"You can't lump them all together indiscriminately and eliminate them. I'm talking about the good ones, the ones that lead to friendship, laughter and … romance."

"You should see some of my friends' ideas of romance."

"Let me put it this way: when the time comes you'll see the difference between love and fear is the difference between lightning and the lightning bug."

He thinks, eyes softening as he peers at the lightning in the distance. "Wow, I think you just bent the universe."

She feigns anger, punches him in the shoulder, and he laughs. They walk a bit, taking in the beauty of the garden lights' reflection off of the pond.

"I heard there will be some guests coming soon," she says.

"Yeah, things are about to get very busy around here."

Makiko stops walking. "The fish are glowing."

Shotoku stops in front of her and turns. "You haven't seen luminescent koi before?"

"No, we don't have them in Mujong." She walks to

the bank and crouches to better observe the fish, moving some hair out of her face and behind her ear. She reaches for the surface of the water and the koi glow brighter, surfacing in hope of a treat. Light from the lanterns reflects off the pond. Makiko smiles and looks up at Shotoku. He tries to smile, too, but is smitten by her beauty, and his smile only half-forms. She senses his attraction and does not turn away. Their eyes portals, their spirits intertwine in a moment sharing joy, warmth, forgiveness, desire, respect and peace. They swim there a moment … an eternity. Still crouching, she raises her chin, eyes in his eyes, augmenting, wanting more of this bliss. Each second compounds the emotion in her stomach and head and she loses her balance, gently falling backward into a sitting position on the grass. He walks to her and holds a hand out to help her up. She takes it, her skin on his, and stands to face him. He does not let her go.

"What a beautiful night." She raises an eyebrow, daring him, but he backs away—his perception of her still too precious, exponentially higher than his own.

"No … ah, I can't," he releases her hand. "I mean, wow. I forgot about something. Um, I'll catch up with you tomorrow, alright? I'm sorry, I just have to—" He points at nothing as if it explains the reason for his retreat.

She stands, mouth partially open in disbelief. He hustles away, hitting his head repeatedly with his hand and muttering. She watches him until he disappears, and sighs. Looking down at the koi, she mutters, "Humph. Score one for the lightning bug."

EIGHT

Kingdom of Sterling

At his desk in his room, Shotoku moves to place a piece on a new model he's building. He leans on his desk, frustrated, and throws the piece in his hand back in the box. Walking to the window, frowning, he looks outside to the right and then the left. "Hmm … Ahh!" He walks back to his structure and tries to concentrate on it. Suddenly he starts to laugh. "I'm going into battle in days! What am I thinking about? A princess!"

Saiak appears at his doorway. "Something funny?"

"Father, ah, no. Just killing time."

Saiak walks over and takes a piece off of his structure. "Yes, I see. What is this?"

Shotoku raises his eyes from the floor in surprise. "This is going to be an electro-luminescent structure. I found that if you pass lightning through—"

"Very interesting. Does it have an application?"

"Uh, no. I mean, maybe. I hadn't really thought about that."

"You should. That's what we need. Not tiny glowing houses."

"Yes, I understand," says Shotoku, hopes dashed that Saiak might want to hear about his exploits into engineering.

Saiak turns away from the desk. "Against my better judgment, I am giving you a division. Douzen speaks highly of you, and your recent, rather intuitive, good judgment regarding the king of Mujong did not entirely escape my notice. You will join the Mujong forces as the ranking officer. They are captains, as well, but you will be the executive officer. Do not let them intimidate you. The Mujong are the most reluctant participants, so you must boost morale and inspire confidence. Can I count on you?"

"Of course, father," he responds, trying to hide his excitement. "You will not be disappointed."

"If recent performance holds, I expect I will not," Saiak offers, showing his son some well-earned respect. "Here are your orders. As you know, there will be a gathering tonight for the officers. Formal dress. After the preliminaries, you junior officers will be dismissed. The senior officers and I will have dinner and continue strategic discourse. Understood?"

"Yes, sir." Shotoku takes a step toward his father and receives the papers, and his father turns to walk out, but stops, contemplating something, and turns back around. Shotoku examines the papers.

"You're a good man, Shotoku. I know you know."

Shotoku looks at his father as his senses heighten, pining for the affirmation a boy so desperately wants. "And you're becoming a great warrior … of that I have no doubt." His father's efforts expended, he grabs his son's shoulder and walks out.

A son glows in the warmth of a proud father.

+++++

Shotoku walks across the gravel of the inner courtyard of the castle amongst several wooden barracks. He wears his formal military uniform with the jacket unbuttoned. Several squires of foreign nations with different colors and styles of crests tend to a few dozen horses. Some are relaxed, sitting in chairs talking in front of the barracks to which they've been assigned, while others run hurried errands. They begin to rise as Shotoku passes by, but he waves them back down. He hops up the steps to the barracks of the Bright Guard and opens the door widely.

"What in the wide, wide world of Aurora are you guys doing? Aren't you ready to go, yet?"

Devukai, happy and hopeful, jumps up, "Shock, err, sir, just playing some cards. You want in?"

Starov, Devukai, Chillson and Jirai sit at a table strewn with cards and coins. Char-ton, who was reading in his bunk, puts down his book. Jirai keeps his eyes on his cards, but flashes a look at Shotoku and grins wryly, "Yeah, Shock, how 'bout it?"

"So I can get skinned by Jirai? He cheats, you know."

Offended, Jirai speaks directly to Devukai. "Losers always whine about cheating." Still he doesn't look at Shotoku as they continue to play. "Where've ya been?

Haven't seen you in a while."

Shotoku ignores the question. "You boys look sharp. Should be some pretty tough characters here tonight."

"We saw most of them ride in. They look more tired than tough," Starov offers.

"They've been in battle and on the run for some time. Their main force is a day behind them. We'll learn a lot tonight about how to fight this new enemy." He takes a book from his jacket and hands it to Char-ton. "Char, I want you to read this over. I skimmed it, but feel you could make more sense of it."

Char-ton opens the book eagerly. "This is unbelievable. There are sketches of inazuma in here."

"It's very old, so be careful."

"Where did you get that? Who wrote it?" Jirai pokes at Shotoku.

"It doesn't really matter, does it? If we want to survive, we take the information we can get."

"I saw the seal. It's a book of the monks. Contraband."

"How did you see?" Shotoku shakes his head, "If he can see that, he can see your cards, guys."

"I don't know: No book … see the gardener … book. What's in it for him, anyway?"

"Maybe some just want the best for us."

"No, fiss on that. There's always an angle."

Shotoku is long used to Jirai making incendiary statements. Statements in which he knows Jirai doesn't even believe. It never ceases to entertain him. And he knows Jirai loves the old man as much as Shotoku does. He has caught them drunk together on many occasions. Shotoku knows in a way Jirai is saying the opposite:

thank the gods for that gardener and your relationship with him.

"Some folks are willing to take risks for others."

"You are hopeless. There's nothing and no one who lives how you talk."

"Well, we can try. And if that's true, I guess you could try, too. Does that upset you, Jirai?"

"It's not easy, but I try, too," Devukai jumps in.

Though apprehensive at Devukai's words, Shotoku nods his head in agreement. "I know you do."

Jirai looks from Devukai to Shotoku, his anger and disgust evident. He throws down his cards and gets up. "Now that fisses me off. You can sell that manure to Saiak or Douzen or these idiots, but Dev is just a kid. It'll be on you, when he goes down."

So passionate, so principled, and in such denial. Shotoku knows that Jirai is truly a wild tiger, living by his own rules, yet immensely capable. The sort of man who would betray his beliefs just to remain unpredictable. But this quality in his friend frightens him deeply, as well. What is at this man's core? What wouldn't he betray? Shotoku always tries not to react to his ostensible vices, but sometimes loses faith. They are best friends, everyone knows, but the fact that they may be more kindred than Shotoku cares to admit chills him. He knows from experience that Jirai would always watch his back physically, but ideologically, if Shotoku fell, would this man be there to help him rise, or drag him further down?

Jirai walks to the door. "You better back that up on the battlefield."

"Are you saying I don't?"

He opens the door and slams it behind him.

"Wow, Shock, you can sure clear a room," quips Chillson, uncertain what to do with his cards.

Shotoku moves to the table and grabs the flask by Jirai's cards. "He won't be gone long." He takes a swig. Speaking loudly and smiling, "I guess I'll finish his hand. Now, is it bad to have all kings? Let me get rid of my—" The door flies back open. Shotoku slides out of the way as Jirai strides over and sits in his seat.

"Get your hands off my booze and my cards. We can leave after this hand."

Everyone chuckles.

+++++

The six skilled men of the Bright Guard, dressed in black formal military attire, laugh at Chillson as he tells a story and they make their way across the battlements to the keep. They hand a flask to one another, passing by the tremendous spires that protect the castle. Lightning is seen near and far, accompanied by the rumble of thunder. As dusk falls in the distance, the northern lights rise, burning red and yellow rivulets.

Excited voices are suddenly heard from below. Someone yells, "Over here! In the garden!"

Jirai leans on the battlement. "What's all this about?"

"Look! Right there!"

They can feel the reverberation of thunder a moment before he hears it. It was close, almost beneath them.

"What the—? Lightning in the castle?"

Another sonic boom is heard and more voices yelling.

"I think it's coming from the garden."

The group strains, leaning against the battlements in order to see the entrance to the garden near the keep wall. At that moment, a figure appears sprinting out from the garden entryway. He is dressed in an amigasa, the trapezoidal straw hat of the warrior monks, and a jet blue cloak. He stops suddenly to confront his pursuers. His hands hold no weapon.

"A monk!" yells Char-ton, pointing.

From below again: "Spy! Spy in the castle! Close the gates!" The monk parries a spear thrust, which he grabs and pulls. Holding firm, the guard is pulled closer and the monk delivers a blow to the spear shaft, snapping it. The monk uses the shaft fragment to strike the guard in the head, knocking him to the ground.

More guards assemble, cautious now. Shotoku counts ten encircling him. The monk does not move, face hidden beneath the expansive hat. The wind ruffles the monk's cloak lightly. Currents of lightning trickle up and down his arms, sparks upon his hands. Suddenly the monk makes an aggressive move at the guards and they jump back, audibly surprised. One or two turn their backs and run a short distance away. The monk stands as before, unmoving.

"Did you see that? He's toying with them!" regales Devukai. Shotoku and Jirai exchange a quick glance, Shotoku's conveying doubt, while Jirai's reflects mild approval.

Embarrassed, the guards who did not retreat converge on the monk, but the staggered attack is what the monk had desired. A sword jabs at the monk's back, but he is already moving to the rear. Spinning, he knocks the sword aside with an armored forearm, while landing a back kick solidly into the guard's abdomen. The contact is accompanied by a discharge of lightning that travels up his leg, grounding in the guard in an explosion of light and sound. The guard is sent into the air and lands 30 feet away, smoldering, but alive.

Now outside the circle, the monk dodges and parries so that he never faces more than two attackers at once. Another guard is hit, clutching his shoulder and shuddering as he falls. His cry of agony is heard even upon the battlements. A sudden bright flash bursts from the monk's hands, making Shotoku wince and look away and fully blinding the guards in close proximity. Three more guards soon writhe on the ground.

Two swordsmen, having recovered their vision, approach aggressively, but the monk disappears.

"What the fiss?" comments Chillson in disbelief.

The monk reappears behind the two guards and they are both disabled before they realize what's happening.

Jirai taps Shotoku's shoulder and points. "Here we go."

On the other side of the field, Shotoku sees two bowmen take aim at the monk, while the remaining swordsmen distract him. They loose their arrows, but the monk holds up a hand and they slow in the air, stopping just in front of the brim of his hat. When he moves his hand away, the arrows fall to the ground.

Devukai nudges Jirai, affecting prescience.

The archers below look at each other in disbelief. The swordsmen in front of the monk, disheartened, turn and begin to flee. The monk moves his hands rapidly, thrusts them at the guards, and lightning leaps toward the men. A small bolt strikes each of the guards, causing them to flail and fall to the earth. Shotoku notices that none of the guards are truly hurt; they are in various stages of collecting themselves.

When Shotoku returns his gaze to the monk he notices that the monk's hat is crooked in his direction. From behind the thatched straw hat Shotoku notices pulses of blue light, and the monk points at him. His friends look over at Shotoku, lacking understanding.

When more soldiers flood onto the field, the monk runs toward the closed castle gate and jumps. For the monk gravity does not seem to exist and he rises up and up, clearing the castle wall. The soldiers cease their pursuit, when at his apex, in midair, the monk winks into nothingness … again.

+++++

Continuing on toward the castle keep, the group of men moves slowly, speaking in hushed but urgent tones.

"How are we going to handle that? Scientifically, I can't even explain it," says Char-ton plaintively.

"They are not our enemy, as far we know, right? The zuma are," adds Starov.

"Then what are monks doing in our perimeter? Don't you think it's a little odd for them to be snooping around a few days before a major battle?" Devukai walks backward in front of the others, attempting to engage them all simultaneously.

"They could be doing reconnaissance for Saiak, for all we know. Attempting to conclude anything from this incident is foolhardy." Jirai buttons his jacket.

"For once, I agree with Jirai," Saiak adds, emerging from the shadows. They are all startled by his sudden appearance and snap to attention. He continues speaking to no one.

"Even if they cared to mingle in our affairs, it's too late for them to effect a change." Then to the group, "At ease, gentlemen." The group relaxes slightly and follows Saiak as he walks. "We are still paying for our contentedness under their reign. If you come up against a monk, fight to the death. Don't let them take you. I've heard of how they transform men into subhuman creatures." They stop in front of the large wooden doors to the ballroom. Looking into each of their faces, he conspiratorially adds, "And boys, not a word of this to our guests. I've been keeping them occupied." He opens the baroque doors and orange light pours into the freshly fallen darkness. The room contains two dozen soldiers with variously colored formal uniforms conversing and drinking from flagons, but they turn to face their host. The walls are stone and lined with candelabras. A large ornate chair sets upon a raised dais. Opposite the throne is an expansive wooden wall set into a track, giving it mobility that would divide the room into two.

Saiak walks directly for his throne, but does not sit and addresses the gathering. Shotoku and his friends move to a table covered with flagons of ale and each take one in hand.

One man, informally dressed, stands alone. The broach of his cloak bears the crest of Mujong.

"Gentlemen, thank you for coming. Each of you has promised a force to defend our kingdoms from this new threat, and for that we are grateful. Some of your kingdoms have already been overrun by this dark army, but be gratified by the thought that this coalition will retake your lands and once again establish peace.

Tonight is a chance for us to share information, so that we can more effectively crush and drive before us this chaotic menace. Never before have our lands been so willingly unified." Saiak glances at the man from Mujong, who returns an impatient look. "Such a union bodes well for the future of us all. In this battle, our mettle will be tested." Saiak looks directly at Shotoku. "Let each of you hold faithful and true, no matter the outcome or loss of that which we treasure most. Faith and sacrifice!"

Some exchange worried glances, but everyone holds his flagon high and then drinks.

"Good speech," Devukai says, sipping his beer optimistically.

Jirai finishes gulping his pint and rejoins in an overly upbeat tone, "You do know that we're all gonna sizzle like bacon in a pan when we fight these guys, don't you? They—eat—lightning." He arches his eyebrows at the group, as if bearing good news. The alcohol has taken effect.

"You don't know that, Jirai," Char-ton answers.

"What do you think's gonna pop out if you do get your sword into 'em? Medical books?"

Char-ton looks around and shrugs, enjoying that thought and Jirai's humor.

Encouraged, Jirai continues, "I'm not thrilled about this marching into a fight thing, either. Call me a scoundrel, but I prefer sneaking up and slitting throats when they're not looking." Jirai mimes cutting his own throat, as if the others need teaching, and snickers.

The older generals congregate to converse while the junior officers from the other kingdoms approach

Shotoku's group.

"Do they have throats? I thought they didn't eat." Char-ton is honestly intrigued.

Jirai blurts, "I told you they did. I seen 'em."

"Shotoku, isn't it? I am Ian of Corville. This is Emerov from Yvan, and Mesapato from Kitan." Ian's eyes shine intelligently, taking in the group. He bows slightly, his blond hair well coifed over blue eyes. His white uniform is spotless. In dark red, tattered and slightly distressed, Emerov simply nods. The epaulets and numerous shiny buttons securing his coat thinly veil the fatigue of many skirmishes. Mesapato, unshaven, with wild black hair and a small earring of dark green glass in each ear, steps forward and bows—a man who tries to be magnanimous, but struggles with the weight of his kingdom's recent defeats. Still, he meets everyone's gaze with a wink and bright white smile: ever playing the robust, encouraging leader of men.

"It's an honor. I have heard tales of the accomplishments of each of you."

Humbly, Ian defers credit by looking down, while grinning politely. "We junior officers rarely get to meet, although our upper echelons have met on several occasions."

"I am eager to hear firsthand accounts of the enemy," Shotoku says, looking back and forth between the three young foreign captains.

Char-ton can no longer restrain his questions. "Ian, Chillson and I hail from Corville. Do the Spires of Sorrell still stand?"

Chillson steps forward. "And the Keep? The Keep of Mount Trepid? Impenetrable. Surely, our forces hold it still."

Ian's eyes falter. "It fell in hours. Walls do not deter the zuma. They climb like spiders and their fingers are like spears." Chillson's chest deflates in sorrow. "The spires serve the zuma now. They gather around them and take their sustenance from the skies … when they run out of flesh."

"What of the school? The library?" urges Char-ton.

"I honestly do not know," Ian replies. "But I have noted that the zuma want the spires. Need them to feed, especially in the lowlands. We destroyed many during our retreat in order to deprive them of food. So your building may yet survive."

Char-ton nods, somewhat encouraged, and looks at his captain. Shotoku places a hand on his shoulder.

"They swarmed us," Ian continues. "Gave very little quarter. We didn't even have time to organize before they struck. Came out of the mountains like a black line of death. Few who opposed them survived."

Starov interrupts, "Emerov, tell me of my home land. How did we fare?"

"Not much better," Emerov admits. "We did not believe the original stories that an organized army of zuma had emerged from the mountains. As a result, we did not adequately prepare. Every so often, we'd find a zuma exoskeleton in the mountains, but that's it. Never large numbers or any group maneuvers."

Starov nods, "It's true. I remember as a boy, finding 'em in the trees dead. Like they were trying to get closer to the lightning, instead of away from it. I did not understand then."

Mesapato is agitated by the decorum. For a

passionate man, the exchange of information only invokes the memory of so much recent pain. Not accustomed to being distraught, he struggles to find some distraction. "Jirai, correct? I remember you."

"And I you," replies Jirai, impressed by Mesapato's memory.

"My sister remembers you, too," he adds, angrily.

All turn to Jirai, waiting for his reply. He laughs nervously and scratches his head, praying for a mental escape route. "Mesapato, it was just one kiss. I swear. I was young and … a fool."

Mesapato bursts out laughing, "She doesn't remember you, you conceited fisser. Ay-yai-yai, did you see his face?" The men all chuckle and draw from their flagons, welcoming the break in formality. Spontaneously, they find themselves in separate conversations.

Mesapato claps Jirai on the back, who retorts, "You're hilarious, Pato," and looks around, embarrassed for once.

"You should have seen your face," Mesapato adds, grinning ear to ear. "I bet you think *all* the girls remember you!"

Playing along affecting narcissism, Jirai replies, "Of course, they do." Then he feigns disappointment, hugging his beer: "Don't they?"

As they talk, Shotoku keeps an eye on the representative from Mujong as Saiak walks over to him.

+++++

Saiak approaches the tall, blond ambassador from Mujong. He wears his armor in veteran fashion, some of it even notched from battles. He is young compared to the intensity of his gaze, hand resting on the hilt of his sword: a long, curved, single-edged blade with a small guard no bigger that a man's fist. It is an elegant tool of death, Saiak can tell, even sheathed. Saiak carries his flask full with untouched beer without spilling. He knows he must be tactful with him and easily discerns his posture and attitude as hostile. "I thought perhaps that no one from Mujong would come tonight. I'm glad—"

Finn snaps back, "I am here for one reason: to confirm that Princess Makiko is unharmed."

"I assure you that she is being treated well."

"You're not listening. I want to see her now."

Saiak returns his stare and grins darkly. "Power is necessary in order to make a demand. Something you lack." He knows he should show restraint, and also that power has loosened his own tongue of late. I must be wiser; just a bit longer, he cautions himself.

"I have been authorized to withdraw our forces by the king. Is that sufficient?" Some of the generals turn to listen; Finn's eyes continue to search the room. "Ah, there she is." He moves and Shotoku turns to see. Makiko walks across the ballroom to meet Finn. The expressions on the faces of the men who have seen her, compel the rest to want to behold what fixes their gaze. All eyes turn to her. She wears the ceremonial dark blue military garb of Mujong. A high collar wreathes her neck, contrasting with the pale skin under her short black hair. Long in front and usually concealing part of her face, tonight she wears it up, revealing all of the angular beauty she makes a habit of hiding. Silver embroidery adorns the tapering cuffs and extends down the hem of her pants into black leather boots. Mujong's silver crest covers a shoulder. As Finn moves quickly to her side, she casts a glance at Shotoku, who can't stop himself from approaching her as well.

"Princess. Are you alright?"

"Yes, yes, fine. It was good of you to come, Finn."

"How can you stand it in this den of snakes? Should I demand your release?"

"It hasn't been so bad. Shotoku has made sure of that. Here he is now."

"Wow, where did you find those clothes?"

"Finn was good enough to have them delivered to me."

"You, ah, look so different."

"Different? You mean spooky? Or ridiculous?"

"Well, beautiful." He glances at Finn, embarrassed, and then pleads with her in exasperation, "You know what I meant."

"Then, ah, just say that."

"He's quite the bold one, isn't he?"

"You should see him fight. He reminds me of someone."

Finn turns his head to Shotoku and looks him up and down, incredulous. "What happens when this battle goes bad? You have a contingency plan?"

"My team and I know what we're doing. Forward or back, we will perform as few can," rejoins Shotoku.

"He's sworn to protect me. And in battle, at least, he does not lack daring." She looks at him askance and smiles.

"Then my task is fulfilled. Princess, I'll take my leave. I'll see you on the battlefield, boy."

Finn strides across the ballroom and, without acknowledging another soul, leaves, cloak rippling in his wake.

"Your rakish boyfriend?"

"Hardly a rake. He is a great soldier. He is held in high regard by my father and his men. You'd be lucky to fight alongside him."

"I will be … fighting with him. Saiak gave me command of the Mujong forces."

"Good luck with that."

"I know. They'll loathe me. You don't think I can do it?"

"Finn has been in command of more troops and in more battles than most generals twice his age. Why would he listen to a pipsqueak like you?"

"Tease me if you like. The welfare of my men comes first. You could do worse than having me in charge."

Makiko just looks at him and smiles, eyes acquiescing.

Saiak interrupts the festivities. "Gentlemen, it's time for us to sit down to dinner. If you younger gentlemen would excuse us."

Servants on opposite sides of the room begin cranking the handle of a large gear. The tremendous wooden wall splits down the center and begins to recede into the walls. Behind it is revealed a long wooden dining table covered with succulent dishes. The ranking officers gravitate toward the table.

Shotoku looks for Jirai and sees him motioning and mouthing, "Let's go."

"So, Princess, you wanna get outta here?"

+++++

The night is thick and dark, but does not overcome the lightning and glow pods punctuating the castle walls in blue light. Makiko and Shotoku stroll out of the keep and onto the veranda. Jirai and the other captains tarry there as well.

"We're going to the Broken Spire. You coming?" Shotoku inhales audibly and frowns, looking at Makiko.

"She's not supposed to leave the castle."

Jirai dismisses him, "And you're not supposed to have books."

"Come on. It'll be fun and whatnot. We'll take the back way out," Chillson adds.

"Until my dad finds out."

"Who's telling? Besides, no one goes there anymore. Not since that lady was struck and killed in the area."

"Ooh, that place sounds nice," Makiko quips.

"You'll probably be dead in a few days. What do you care?" Jirai suggests.

"Well, when you put it that way—" Shotoku's tone affects optimism.

Jirai winks at Makiko and puts his arm around her waist. "Do I know this guy or what? Now I don't know if it's you, the suit or the moonlight, but this outfit is workin'." Shotoku raises his hand near Jirai's head and his hair begins to stand on end. Electricity dances between his fingers. Jirai dashes away, smoothing his hair. "Hey, that's not funny. I don't care if you shock me, just don't mess with the hair. Who has my flask?"

Hearing him, Starov quickly takes another drink. Jirai grabs it from his hand. "Starov, you hog. Ah, good. A little left."

Devukai runs up and rubs his hand on Jirai's hair and sprints away laughing. "I've had it!" He runs after Devukai, looking angry. They run down the stairs and Starov and Chillson follow to watch the action. Makiko laughs.

The group stops at a large, dilapidated iron door in the exterior castle wall. "This door hasn't functioned in years," Jirai explains, "but my man here can move it."

Without touching the door, Shotoku concentrates and somewhere inside gears and pins can be heard moving. He turns his hands in midair. A final click and he relaxes. Makiko, curious, looks at the others and the door. Shotoku squares off with the door and, several feet away, thrusts his hands forward in the air. The door lurches open, grudgingly, leaving a one-foot gap. "Hurry up, Shock. I'm thirsty."

"Shaddup, you pain," he says, making a second, more forceful thrust, and the door swings open all the way, slamming noisily into the outside of the castle wall.

Ian and Emerov exchange glances in disbelief and Ian speaks, "Do all of you have the powers of the monks?"

Mesapato claps Jirai's back again. "Ho, hoooo. I like my new allies."

"What the—? Keep it down, Shock." Acting upset and holding a finger to his lips, Jirai looks to the others, emulating disbelief and consternation. He allows a smirk only when Shotoku chases him through the door. Once outside, Shotoku uses his abilities to close and lock the door once more.

Shotoku and Makiko follow while Jirai and the others raise a commotion well ahead of them. Ian,

Emerov and Mesapato run to keep up, finding their second wind. They stay off of the pod-illuminated roads, but near the buildings that lay thickly around the castle's perimeter. The Broken Spire lies at the edge of the residential area that encircles the merchant district. A once busy road runs past its entrance, and a large broken spire rises from the center of the structure. Several smaller spires now provide protection for the establishment. Warm light glows from the windows into the night. Contrary to appearances, soft music and mirth pour from inside.

Shotoku opens the door for Makiko. A few patrons are present, but one large table is full of soldiers. Jirai and the others have sat at the table and are ordering drinks. Makiko and Shotoku join them. All loosen their formal attire and sip frothy brews, shoulders sag and some lean back.

Ian speaks eagerly, "So, tell us about the spy."

Devukai chokes on his beer. "You know about that?"

Ian just smiles, "I do now." He takes a hearty drink and Devukai looks around feeling foolish.

"It's okay, Dev. We would have told them anyway. Yup, we saw him, flying, disappearing … like a ghost," says Jirai.

"By whom do you believe he was sent?" Ian continues.

"Don't know. Ask Shotoku; he's infatuated with the monks."

"It doesn't matter. What could they have learned?" Shotoku consoles. "It's not like Saiak is a real innovator. We haven't produced any imaginative weapons in years."

Char-ton is quick to join: "Shotoku here is quite the scientist. I've helped him put together some amazing mechanical structures. But Saiak rejects them, one after the other."

Everyone looks briefly at Shotoku. Accusing, he points at Char-ton. "He's a medic! Can't keep a book out of his hands, even when they are illegal."

"You bring them to me," Char-ton laughs. "And I do love them." He glows a bit from the beer, maudlin. "And you. You are a good friend." He clasps and shakes Shotoku's shoulder. Makiko smiles.

"Come on. I just watch nature and try to emulate it. I'm sure science hasn't stood still in your kingdoms."

"Nothing. Metal is forbidden. Improper use has caused too many fatal strikes," admits Emerov.

"What about your kingdom, Mesapato? Surely—" Makiko says, expecting affirmation.

"What the flash is science? We grow crops and raise sheep. We do have a blacksmith that makes a lot of stuff, though."

Makiko looks at Ian, desperate. "I know what you speak of and I have seen the books filled with scientific discovery and history, but we haven't had the spare resources to pursue such findings. But we have plenty of catapults and weapons of war, all en route here to fend off the zuma."

"And what do you know of them?" asks Starov.

"Sadly, little."

"And the monks? What do your books tell you of them?" Shotoku asks, feigning only mild interest.

Ian continues, "That is the strange thing: the books

seem to contradict themselves. They tell of the monks leading this land out of darkness, building great stone monasteries and libraries, and making great strides in science and medicine. Then, suddenly, they began attacking villages and destroying whole cities. They claimed we were not worthy of their teachings. The people resisted and the monks went into exile. Most of the books were used for firewood and the buildings gutted for materials."

"Not all the books, though, thank goodness," says Char-ton, taking a swig.

"The history we know is the same. What I wouldn't give to have seen so many books in one place." Shotoku takes a drink, looking at the table.

"You can. We have an unviolated library at the foot of the Sayloon range in Mujong."

"Impossible," he says in hope and disbelief.

"And the stories we hear of monks are much different from yours."

Jirai leans back with his beer, enjoying an opposing opinion.

"Well?"

"The monks never burned a single building or hurt a single person."

The young men lean back, eyebrows arching in disbelief and exchanging glances. Mesapato and Emerov look at each other and burst out laughing. Most smile at Makiko's audacity. Shotoku's face is gravid and Jirai watches him uncomfortably.

"Do you know what impact such a truth would have on this world?" All play has left his voice.

"I do. I offer you no proof. No reason to believe me,

except a multitude of inconsistencies in the timeline and actions and philosophies of their legends."

Shotoku is somewhere else, his mind swirling … calculating.

"You … You believe me, don't you?"

"He does. I've seen this look, gods help us all." Jirai takes another drink and spills a bit.

"That's not all, but even your endeavoring, impartial mind could not find perch for what I would say next."

"Indeed, it may not be the best time, if you're going to blurt what I think you are." Jirai gives her his most foreboding look. He appears nervous, looking around the room, but she cannot resist.

"Saiak is mixed up in it somehow. There is a connection. Too much coincidence surrounds him."

"Saiak is in league with the monks?" Shotoku offers it as a question.

Suddenly from behind, Shotoku is yanked backwards to the floor. Pulled to his feet, he looks directly in the face of Rakko, one of Saiak's sycophantic young captains from the Sterling army regulars. Jirai is at his side just as quickly.

"You dare accuse Saiak. Your father and our leader. You're not worthy of him."

"What the fiss? You better just relax, Rock." Rakko's eyes are red and his breath reeks of liquor, but Shotoku knows he is wiry and fast, having sparred with him many times. He would not underestimate him even when drunk.

"Or what? You're not the only one with friends."

"As long as you're buying, huh?" Shotoku provokes him just a bit, the beer loosening his tongue. "Look, we were just teaching Makiko the true history of these lands. I was just repeating—"

Rakko pulls him closer and his hot breath makes him turn his face aside. "I heard you. Didn't we?" The two men nod, but do not smile, hands on their sword hilts. Both wear the blue and white insignia of the army on their chests.

"Look, the captains from Corville, Kitan and Yvan are here. Sit down with us. We'll be on the battlefield together in a few days. They'll be protecting your life and ours."

Rakko looks at them, eyes slowly adjusting.

Ian stands up in an effort to disperse tension. "Yes, I believe I saw you speaking with King Saiak earlier. Your council must rank high with him." Ian looks at Shotoku quickly. "Barmaid, some beers here for our friends!"

Reluctantly, Rakko releases his grip on Shotoku. His friends take the beers and sit at a separate table behind him. He moves to sit, but Jirai punches him square in the face and takes his legs out. Rakko hits the ground hard. On top of him, Jirai holds a dagger to his throat and dares Rakko's friends to save him. Makiko is taken aback and retreats. The other captains stand on alert, but the Bright Guard, having predicted Jirai's mood, remain seated, offering reassurances.

"Don't you ever fissing touch him again. You understand that, you pathetic piece of filth? Ever." Their noses are almost touching as he speaks and he seems not to notice Rakko has lost consciousness.

"Jirai!" Shotoku stands, compromised and embarrassed. Jirai is drunker than he thought to pull this kind of stunt.

He looks back at the other men. "Friends of his? Really? Then I'll have no qualms about killing the two of you, too."

The two men glare at him, but remove their hands from their swords. They exchange looks again and shrug. The men pick up their free beers and turn away from Rakko and Jirai.

Jirai turns to look at Shotoku, a wide smile on his face.

+++++

The group bursts from the tavern door as yellow light floods into the night. Shotoku follows, while Makiko has her arm around Jirai, providing subtle support. Their guests follow and make their goodbyes.

"I can't believe you hit him," Devukai says with esteem. "He's still in there asleep."

"I fail to understand why we must leave so early on such a splendid evening. And I do protest your sweeping generalizations, Shock. Contrary to appearance, those were fine upstanding ladies of culture, worthy of my most noble intentions."

"Yes, yes, but I feel that when you're with me, I'd best be a positive influence. The gods only know what you do on your own. Besides, you're getting surly."

"How fortunate I must be to have such a … thoughtful companion. Surely I won't escape your escort without a kiss at my door, Shock."

"Ah, no thanks. Makiko, can you handle that request?"

"What? I don't get to see two men kiss?" She feigns disappointment.

"He just hit a guy. That's not titillating enough? You know, one of these days you're going to get into trouble and I won't save you."

"I think that there is no lie you utter except that one. And, oh, how often. You can't resist saving me 'cause I'm so adorable."

Turning toward the castle, Shotoku's eyes catch the silhouette of a man near the edge of the tree line across the old road, silver sparkles near his hands. It disappears, though, just as quickly and he squints, mistrusting his eyes. Chilling him even deeper is the feeling that, just before the shape vanished, he could make out the form of an amigasa and the blue-white glimmer of two eyes observing him.

NINE

Kingdom of Sterling

Large groups of soldiers uniformed in a variety of colors representing the five kingdoms can be seen in the fields around the castle establishing campsites and building defensive structures. Large mobile spires protect the troops and inspire them to maintain order. Chains drag behind the mobile spires, grounding them and protecting the soldiers from strikes. Permanent spires are dotted throughout the parade ground as well. Troop columns stretch to the horizon as they march under gray skies.

Shotoku sits, legs folded, gazing at the pond. He wears his dark blue battle gear with a multi-layered wooden-plated breastplate. He breathes deeply. Taking his sword from its scabbard, he examines the blackened blade and the writing left by the inazuma. He stands and strikes the air with the sword, reversing his direction, swinging the blade swiftly upward. He continues to study the blade, curious. Niwashi wanders up carrying a walking stick and using it to momentarily examine plants and bushes. He uses it to point at Shotoku. "What happened to your sword?"

"That inazuma grabbed and burnt it or something. It seems okay, though."

"Ah, yes. You saved the zuma child," Niwashi says quietly, pride in his eyes. He seems to stand straighter today and looks stronger than Shotoku can remember.

"We go to war today. The zuma will be here by nightfall."

"It's okay to be afraid."

"Is life so grand that escaping it doesn't hold some appeal?"

"This world needs men like you."

"For what? To torture?"

"All your days will not be like these. In time, you may make a different life. One that you would not consider so readily disposable."

Shotoku looks down, sheathing his sword. "The spy came through here. Did you see him?"

"See him? I spoke to him." Shotoku freezes, eyes lingering on the well-kept grass. In a blur, he pivots, draws his sword and strikes at Niwashi's chin. The blade does not touch, however. In a lightning-fast motion, Niwashi has raised his stick and blocked the blade. The two men look at each other, unmoving.

"I've seen you faster. Thank you for not truly attempting to strike."

"What are these games? Who are you really?"

Niwashi pushes the sword aside with force. "I am

leaving and you should, as well. The monk you saw brought me a warning. The battle is lost and this castle will fall. Corville has joined the list of the fallen."

"What? Our scouts have reported nothing of the sort. You are mistaken. You're in league with the monks and the zuma?" Shotoku's voice rises in disbelief.

"Yes and no. I am a friend of the monks and the zuma, but not this breed of zuma. With the breed that you met in the mountains—intelligent and peaceful. There is too much to explain, but Corville has fallen. You can imagine how easily it fell with its protective forces massed here. Coincidental?"

"Does that describe the monks, as well? Intelligent and peaceful? If so, why don't they help? Why don't they share their knowledge with Sterling?"

"Listen! This battle is lost. The monks are too few now, they could not make a difference and we and Saiak have … history. I was told there are advance forces already within Sterling."

"Now I should trust you? How?" His eyes cannot conceal a deep pain at the old man's deception. "Was everything a lie?"

"Don't you dare say that. One of my missions here was to learn about you: the Destroyer of Lunabi. If you were like Saiak or something else entirely."

"I confided everything in you. You were my friend."

"You are everything Saiak is not. Come with me now and we can help you realize your destiny."

Shotoku looks at the castle. "Come with you to what? And let everything I've ever known be destroyed? What are you fighting for? I can't go. Too many people are counting on me."

"I assumed as much. I'm leaving. Keep those you care for close and make for the mountains in the south, if you do escape."

"I see the monks' reputation is well deserved: they are just as deceiving and underhanded as legend says."

"These people had a chance for truth once and chose Saiak, instead. I pray you're beginning to realize what a huge mistake that was. Farewell."

Niwashi turns and strides away quickly. "Niwashi, stop!" Confused and clearly tortured, Shotoku runs up and grabs his shoulder, turning him..

"How can you leave? How?" Tears are frozen in his eyes. He grips the cloth at Niwashi's shoulders, twisting it in panic. Momentarily stunned, Niwashi lays his hand upon Shotoku's softly.

"I … We'll try to come back … to help. Maybe … I don't know. Flee at the earliest sign of defeat. Your survival is more important than you know."

Shotoku nods. Tears in both of their eyes, Niwashi hurries away, leaving Shotoku alone in the garden.

+++++

Shotoku walks down the hallway distraught over what Niwashi has told him. He looks around nervously, but tries to conceal his state of mind from those he passes. He picks up speed, anxious to reach the safety of his room.

Entering, he finds some comfort and closes the door.

"Hiding from someone?"

Shotoku whirls, surprised.

"I give you command of a battalion and you repay me by taking that Mujong whore out of this castle?" Shotoku cannot speak; his confusion is evident. His chin quivers as he tries to regain his calm. "You don't even deny it."

"That would be a lie." I have my honesty, he chants, calming his nerves. In all this turmoil, I will keep that safe.

"Oh, that's right. How pathetically naïve. I told you a long time ago there's no place for that kind of idealism and, again, you disobey me. In front of everyone. In front of the entire kingdom!" Rage has consumed him, his lips curl and his son's apparent defiance only fans the intensity. He walks over to Shotoku's desk. "This is what I get? Toy houses?" Saiak swings his arm and it crashes down upon the structure, splintering it into pieces. Shotoku stands motionless, eyes distant and reflecting only disappointment in his father's reaction. "Report to your command immediately." Saiak moves toward Shotoku, threatening, but opens the door. Without turning to face him, he says, "Redeem yourself in battle … for the glory of Sterling. Make me proud one last time." He leaves, slamming the door behind him.

Shotoku walks a few steps and, shaking from the conflict, falls to his knees, surrounded by the pieces of what he built and his father destroyed.

There is a knock on his door and then it opens slowly. "Are you here?" Makiko enters, in her light battle dress. Shotoku gets up quickly, but does not face her and straightens his uniform.

"Is it time for me to join the men?"

"Soon. Were you going to say goodbye?"

"No. Why?"

"Come on, Shotoku. You like me a little, don't you?"

"You are a dream. I think of you constantly … your eyes, your face, your form. You're bold, true and wise. I want everything in this world for you. That's why I have to go … without a goodbye. I mean, we both know what awaits me. I haven't been right about much." He grows a bit delirious and laughs, "Anything, I guess." Staring at the floor, he abruptly sours: "But I'll make up for that and more in battle."

He tries to walk past her, but she stops him, "Oh, no, no, no. I know a thing or two about how to send a man off to battle and this isn't it. You'll heroically hurl yourself into the first ridiculous charging horde. Come with me."

She takes his hand and pulls him out of his room. She leads him to the highest of the castle towers and up the narrow staircase to the top. They walk out into the cool wind of the turret's battlements far above all the others. A spire rises from the center a hundred feet and branches out like an upside-down umbrella. Glass balls, meant to detect strikes by breaking easily under current, jingle as they lay hanging against the conical rod. The day is cloudy, as usual, and lightning is visible near and far.

"I used to love to come up here. This world can be beautiful."

"Look at me." Her short black hair moves in the breeze, lightning reflected in her eyes. She approaches, their bodies lightly touching.

"You are a tempting man, Shock. Don't you see I can't resist you?" He is lost in her eyes and the stress melts from his face. Their lips meet in a long, slow, deep kiss. Lightning tingles from his body to hers and she moans. He looks at her, savoring, mind not wanting to go and body begging to stay.

"Now you will come back to me," she orders. "Now you know what I want and now I can let you go."

A weight visibly lifts from his soul and he exhales, "Thank you."

They embrace one last time.

+++++

Shotoku, Jirai and the rest of his unit ride east across the encampments to the north of the castle beneath the protective spires. They rein in their horses and dismount when they near a group of tents bearing the standard of Mujong. Finn exits one of the tents and walks to meet Shotoku.

"What is it you command," asks Finn, sardonically.

"Any problems? Oddities?"

"None so far. I sent out scouts north and east of our position, but they haven't yet returned."

"Our knowledge of the zuma is limited. Have you encountered them in battle before?"

Finn hesitates, not convinced he should share information, but he relents. "Not in battle, but we know that they have a hard, yet brittle exoskeleton. Their blood is thick and caustic. Try to stay away from it."

"We ran into some in the mountains. They can roll fast and climb like lightning."

"I've not heard that before." Finn examines Shotoku more closely. "The princess trusts you, so I suppose I shall, as well. Your father assures us that they are without sophisticated weaponry. According to our allies, they used none in their initial offensives. This should give us a distinct advantage." They continue to exchange tactical knowledge, finally finding common ground.

+++++

A scout makes his way across the field of battle, over rolling plains which lead to several thick copses. He reaches the easternmost of all the trees and is apprehensive about leaving their protection. Straining his eyes, he surveys a good distance over the plains to the north and to the sheer cliff in the east that plummets a thousand feet to the great sea below. He feels obliged to make his way to the cliff's edge, but looks uneasily from the meager spire attached to his horse to the lightning coursing from the low clouds. Overcome by fear, he turns his mount and returns back through the trees.

+++++

In the west, the sun wins its eternal struggle to pierce the clouds of Aurora. Rows of soldiers beneath the pennant-bearing spires glisten: brilliant battalions steeling themselves to make their stand for humanity. On their flank, off the shore of the cliff, the shadows swell, erasing the setting sun's scintillations, augmenting the bioluminescence of the sea creatures great and small beneath the waves. The shore glows dimly with accumulated algae, contrasted with the jet black forms that scurry across the rock face. Slowly making their way, inazuma cover the sheer rock face, crawling over one another, deep behind the human vanguard and impatient for the darkness.

+++++

Men enter and exit the tent, relaying information and troop, weapon and ammunition dispositions. Shotoku and Finn examine a large map on a table. A young

Mujong captain enters the tent.

"Sir, our northern scout reports zuma preparing for attack on the other side of that far hill north-by-northwest."

"It looks like a direct assault, just as Saiak predicted. We shall go ahead with his plan, then, and perform an enveloping maneuver."

"Sir, the scout's report also claims that they have mobile spires and catapults."

"They what?" Finn looks at Shotoku, anger in his eyes.

"What of the other scout?"

"Our other scout reports no forces detected attempting to flank us."

"Then we must proceed as planned. This will make our flanking maneuver all the more crucial. If we can surprise them, we may be able to avoid catastrophic losses. Captain, get our forces ready to deploy as soon as the sun sets. Tell them to pack light, we'll be moving with haste."

Shotoku looks uncertain. Finn continues to give orders and he simply nods in agreement. "Commander, I am not sure of what use I am to you here. Saiak gave me command of you and your men, but I can clearly see that that is a mistake." Finn listens, expressionless. "I'd like to take my men and do what we do best. If you'll allow, we could re-scout this area here ahead of your forces—make sure there are no surprises."

"If you discover nothing, rejoin our force for the attack."

"Yes, sir. We'll fire off a red flare, if we spot enemy forces." Distracted, Finn nods and turns to answer a question from another soldier. Shotoku does not wait and exits the tent. Finn looks after him, opening his mouth, but says nothing. Then the demands on his attention resume.

+++++

The Mujong battalion moves at a light run from its encampment and the safety of the permanent spires. They follow a road cutting through the plains and skirting the copses whenever possible. Medium-sized spires are pulled by horses on noisy wooden carts on either side of the troops, their clanking metal chains dragging behind, grounding the spires.

+++++

On the western flank, Emerov leads the battalion from Yvan along the foot of the mountains, hidden from the view of the enemy. His men are weary from the forced march to Sterling, but they are seasoned veterans who will not give up ground without a fight.

+++++

Shotoku and his companions lead their horses through the trees, careful to avoid the juicy, fluorescent fungus layering the forest floor which might mark their passage. At the northernmost end of the copse they dismount and secure their horses. Crawling across an open field, they make their way to a high, grass-covered knoll. Slowly, they peek over the top. Spread across the valley is the black sea of the inazuma encampment.

"Zounds," breathes Shotoku.

"There must be 20,000 of them," adds Jirai.

"Look how they've arranged themselves around the mobile spires." Char-ton's eyes are alight as lightning strikes the spires repeatedly, almost as if the inazuma are drawing it down. They rest their hands on each other and the lightning flows down the spires and throughout their carnal network. "Look, they're starting to move."

The spires jerk into motion with great rava beasts straining at the chains. Their stout, powerful legs dig into the earth. Glowing red veins shine brighter under the strain, highlighting their plated hides, and their single-horned heads bow low. Everywhere the red lights of inazuma's eyes blink in the darkness. They bunch up and are disorganized, but move steadily forward, directly toward the castle. Lightning strikes continue to illuminate the enemy. Several large catapults and ballista lumber along in the rear.

"How will we defeat so many?" Starov looks askance at Shotoku, nervous.

"I want to know who is behind their organization. Our lack of information will be our undoing." The young prince curses beneath his breath, eyes searching desperately for understanding, but Jirai spots them first.

"There. Monks. Fissing monks are in league with them." One monk can be seen wearing their signature amigasa. He drives the unruly inazuma with lightning from his hands and spurs the rava forward. The inazuma struggle to stay near the spires, near their source of power.

Shotoku turns away from the inazuma and looks south. "Finn shouldn't be too far behind. Perhaps if they can flank them, we may have surprise on our side." Looking toward the horses, Shotoku continues, "We scout west one last time and—" He stops and elbows Jirai. "Wait. What was that?" The floor of the forest, covered with the glowing mushrooms, highlights the movements of something unseen.

Jirai is already leaning forward, squinting. "Yeah, the fungi … are blinking."

"Something's moving in front of it. It's on the bottom of their feet."

"Whose feet?" asks Chillson.

"Now, back to the horses! We've got to warn Finn."

"What about the flare?" reminds Devukai.

"Do it." Jirai launches a bolt from his crossbow into the sky, a long, fine metal thread trailing behind it. When it is struck by lightning, it sizzles in bright, red light across the sky for all to see.

+++++

Soldiers look out anxiously standing in formation as flecks of black and red rise at the horizon. A lightning storm seems to follow them in the sky. Douzen gives the order, "Load catapults and ballista!"

+++++

The Mujong battalion is holed up near a copse of trees erecting larger mobile spires for traversing open ground. Half the soldiers use the trees as protection from lightning strikes.

"Sir, look!"

Finn sees the red flare arch through the sky to the east. "Enemy at our flank! Close ranks and—"

Screams are heard from the woods; the soldiers stationed there run quickly, haphazardly from the trees, smashing into the rest of the battalion organizing in the field.

+++++

In the lightning flashes at the center of the battlefield, the inazuma loom closer: a black ooze blotting out the grass. Saiak sits atop his mount and gives Douzen the signal.

"Prepare to fire catapults! Fire!" Douzen raises his sword and drops it.

The catapults fire their shot into the air. At their apex, the fuses ignite small explosions in the wooden containers, which splinter, scattering metal shards over the enemy. Detecting the ion leaders, lightning rains down upon the inazuma. Some are killed or explode violently, but most are unfazed by the attack. Then the inazuma's own catapults fire. The soldiers watch the approach of the shot, surprised and horrified.

"Close ranks! Hold," commands Douzen, and the well-trained soldiers reduce the distance between themselves and the nearest spire. The shot explodes and lightning decimates hundreds of men, even those partially protected by large spires, which manage to absorb some of the bolts. Crying and moaning fills the air.

"Spires forward! Prepare to charge!"

+++++

"Draw swords! For Mujong!" Finn's men scream and charge on the heels of their captain.

Large black balls roll quickly from the woods, unfurling into inazuma that spring into the night sky over the soldiers. Their red eyes bright, lightning strikes several of them in mid-air, coursing through them and grounding in the soldiers below, melting swords and burning flesh. The unconventional attack surprises the men and they look to their intrepid captain for resolve. Finn is already recklessly deep in the enemy mass building a wall of inazuma dead. Out of fear and love, the Mujongese soldiers surge to protect their captain.

+++++

Soldiers continue jogging across the rocky ground moving away from the mountains. Emerov urges them on, "Move it, move it! Get those spires unloaded and assembled. You don't want to be late to the party." A nervous soldier tries to untie one of the ropes securing a spire. Emerov smiles reassuringly. "Easy, son. Nothing to worry about, yet." He looks up. "The enemy is— What is that?"

As the soldier follows his eyes, black objects roll down the mountain. Just before they roll off the ledge above, they unfurl and leap out, down upon the soldiers below—red eyes afire.

The young soldier realizes too late: "Flanking man—" He is pierced by the spear-like talons of the three-fingered inazuma. He looks at his killer as it opens its black maw and rips at his neck.

+++++

The Sterling soldiers charge in a straight line, but the wild inazuma rip through their ranks, rolling and leaping. Lightning arches off of the creatures, indiscriminately striking human and inazuma alike. This has no effect on the inazuma, but is devastating to the soldiers. Some manage to stab the dark figures, but the weapons also serve as leaders for the electrical arches. One resolute soldier stabs an especially bright-eyed inazuma and it explodes, killing several inazuma and humans. Explosions can be heard around the battlefield. Natural and catapult-induced thunder dominates the theater of war, deafening the defenders and knocking them to the ground.

+++++

Finn slashes repeatedly in a blur, splashed with caustic inazuma blood. "Push them into the trees!" Forward, dodging left and right, his men vigilantly struggle to follow. Their efforts bear fruit and Finn roars under the adrenaline, "Push them, lads. Let them know sorrow under the Mujong blade!" He sees panic in the eyes of one of his men looking past his shoulder and whirls, sword high. An inazuma flies through the air toward him, but then arches violently backward. It falls to the ground dead, Shotoku standing in its stead. Another inazuma bolts toward Shotoku when it's hit with two crossbow bolts, then another and another in rapid succession. It falls dead. Jirai smiles, reloading. The inazuma attack recklessly up and down the line of men, but humanity matches ferocity with discipline. The men inch slowly deeper into the forest, eviscerating their enemy.

+++++

Hopeful, Finn yells, "We can flank them—"

"No. They have twice as many men and are not going down easily enough."

A bright-eyed inazuma runs in their direction, but Jirai hits it with an arrow in the chest and it explodes, energy bursting out of its abdomen and chest. Everyone ducks.

"What's in those arrows, Ji?" quips Chillson.

Jirai continues to fire his crossbow at inazuma emerging from the woods. Several inazuma approach as Starov, Chillson, Devukai and Char-ton meet violently, slashing and spinning, keeping low to avoid lightning arches.

Starov has to drop his sword when one arch shocks him. "Damn, you sparkies." He reaches down and grabs his sword as Jirai pulls his bolts from the dead. The heads break off of one bolt and he frowns, but places it in the clip on top of his bow. Explosions and thunder from the central battleground roll across the plains. He looks up. "We're too late."

"We're lost. Take your men and retreat to Mujong. Our center has collapsed," Shotoku speaks slowly, straining to make sense of the darkness blotting out the castle walls. The inazuma are breaching the walls.

Finn nods, breathing hard, "What will you do?"

"We'll get the princess and my father."

"I'll go with you. I can't leave without her."

"Gather your men." Finn turns to a soldier: "Sound the retreat."

The soldier blows his horn and the Mujong forces look up in surprise and dread. Although near a spire, a lightning bolt flashes the bugler, dropping him to the ground smoldering. Shotoku looks up to see a warrior monk descending slowly from the sky. The soldiers back away, but the monk moves his arms through the air and lightning materializes, striking half a dozen men. They fall to the ground unmoving. Jirai moves laterally firing his crossbows, but the monk holds up a hand and the bolts fly by to either side. Using the distraction, Chillson attacks, but the monk raises his other hand and invisibly jerks his sword from his hands. Chillson falls forward and the monk grabs his neck. Chillson struggles, surreptitiously drawing a dagger and stabbing, but the knife stops at an invisible barrier, unable to get any closer. The monk curls his lips and opens his mouth, hissing at Chillson. In desperation, Shotoku launches himself. The monk motions toward his sword, but without the expected effect, and is forced to drop Chillson and parry Shotoku's attack. The monk somersaults high off the ground, motioning with his arms, and lightning bursts forth, striking Shotoku. Seeing the coming attack, Shotoku prepares himself, but this is not the friendly, communicative lightning of the blue-eyed inazuma. His flesh smokes as he is flung across the grass, tumbling awkwardly in pain.

Jirai yells at the monk in a fit of rare panic, firing all his bolts while chasing his friend's body. "Retreat, you fools!"

The Bright Guard surrounds the monk, but they move cautiously. The monk grins and, struggling with arms out as if lifting a huge boulder, draws a lightning bolt down to himself from the sky. From some distance, Shotoku rises, feeling the power the monk conjures. He stretches his senses and taps into an invisible storm of ions. Suddenly, he can see the pathways along which the monk intends to channel his immense power. He can see the death of all his Bright Guard as sure as his love for them. And, for a moment, his oath and his brother's memory are replaced by fury.

"No!" he cries, and a tsunami of magnetism bursts from Shotoku in all directions. Only by chance, most of his allies and all of the Bright Guard wear metal and are blown like paper across the fields and forests. A hundred-foot circle around him is cleared of all but inazuma, the monk and a few Mujongese wearing wooden armor, whose metal items have all been blown off of them. They turn to him in surprise, while he bares his teeth, trying desperately to control what he has unleashed. Tears burn on his face as he looks at the Mujongese, reliving the death of innocence. Control slips away from him as the air crackles and ignites, lightning, the breadth of the dome of destruction he's created, riddles friend and foe alike in the flash of an instant, their screams drowned by the resulting thunder that knocks anyone nearby unconscious, including Shotoku.

+++++

Across the battlefield, all living creatures turn and squint, their eyes widening in awe of the spectacle of Shotoku's might.

+++++

Saiak's mount rears; he smiles, his hopes realized, and yells, "I knew it. I knew he had power, but not like this." His eyes are wild as the possibilities take hold of his heart.

Douzen is dumbfounded. "Gods, help my boys. Such power …"

Saiak gallops for the castle, throwing caution into the wind.

+++++

Finding their legs, the Bright Guard brave the scorched earth, collecting their captain and retreating. The surviving inazuma do not follow, seeking instead to recharge around the humans' abandoned mobile spires, although many feast on the dead human bodies.

The soldiers run south toward the road. Several panic, trying to cross the open ground, and are struck by atmospheric lightning. Shotoku and his men mount and follow the tree line at a gallop.

+++++

Shotoku strides breathlessly into the ballroom. "Saiak! Saiak! We're overrun. You need to signal—"

At the opposite end of the room, Saiak turns to face Shotoku. Beside him are several figures wearing amigasa.

"Father?"

Jirai looks at Shotoku. "Oh, I don't believe this. I knew it. I always hated your father."

"Still alive? I guess you're better than I thought."

His son walks slowly forward, the pain in his soul flooding his being. "But … you couldn't want this to happen. All those men …"

Makiko enters behind Shotoku. "No, it's just what he wanted and what my father feared: an ambush."

"Clever girl. You know, it just got too hard playing politics … trying to bring the kingdoms together, bribing some, coercing others. Now there won't be any kingdoms. They'll all pay the price for their inflexibility."

The monks spread out, cavalier. One with silver rings and scale mail cracks his knuckles, a smile barely visible under the brim of his hat.

Ire begins to overcome Shotoku. "Do you think for one moment that I'll allow that to happen?"

"Allow it? You have facilitated it. I should thank you for your unwavering trust. You barely questioned my bidding. And you *will* join me in the end," Saiak predicts. "Your power spike on the battlefield today was … impressive. The Kuroshi were skeptical of your abilities. Not anymore."

"Was anything true? Our history? About the zuma?

The warrior monks? Why would you propagate so many lies? Why!"

"So that this day would come."

"Join you? My only reason to live will be your destruction."

"Yes, yes, I know. I knew since Lunabi. Always self-righteous, self-aware and trying to do the right thing. I had to knock you out to keep you from interfering."

"You hit me? All I wanted to do was save Zaru."

"You and he were going crazy, attacking our own soldiers."

"They were killing children."

"On my orders."

The silver-ringed monk takes off his amigasa. Jirai and Shotoku both are shocked to immobility. The silver-ringed monk is Maji.

"You," spits Shotoku. "Saiak, you've bound your fate to this murderer? The one Zaru was trying to stop?"

"And instead you struck your brother down. I have savored that day. That day your father chose our path and your destiny was written … one filled with suffering."

Saiak is not happy with Maji's words, but his eyes waver only a moment. "Zarushi's death—that was unintentional."

Jirai glares at Saiak, renewing his grip on his crossbow.

"Do you wish I'd died?" Shotoku begins walking forward. "Maybe that was it. Well, here's your chance."

Jirai strides past him bringing his crossbow to bear. "No, here's our chance."

Shotoku draws his sword and, encouraged, follows Jirai. The monks edge forward to meet them.

"No," insists Saiak, "this isn't what I want."

"Shotoku, no!" yells Makiko, but Shotoku and Jirai do not slow their pace. She runs to the partition mechanism in the center of the ballroom and pulls the lever. The doors begin dividing the room, cutting them off from Saiak and the monks. Char-ton and Devukai attempt to grab Shotoku and prevent him from closing with the monks.

Shotoku slows to glare at Makiko, but, unwavering, Jirai runs shooting around the door which is quickly closing. His aim is true and Maji is forced to hold up his hand, skewing the arrows upward and over their heads. Falling behind the closing door, Jirai leaps, rolls and comes up firing. Overconfident, only at the last instant does Maji detect the headless arrow, narrowly averting his face. Maji and Jirai exchange visceral countenances just before the doors shut.

Shotoku screams at the doors, "For what? For what?" He looks at Jirai as he stands, still being restrained by the others. "For what would you sacrifice everything?"

"Revenge," Jirai breathes.

"Shotoku, come to Mujong. We know this wasn't your fault," insists Makiko.

Char-ton and Devukai continue holding Shotoku up, but he just stares into the distance, disembodied.

"Bring him," she says, turning to Finn.

"Princess, we have to go." Finn pulls on her arm; he is ready to force her if need be.

"You'll take care of him, Jirai? I can count on you?"

"Don't be stupid," Jirai snaps.

"Meet us in Mujong," she pleads, trusting Jirai to see it done. The Mujongese leave hastily.

"Let's go," orders Jirai.

"To Mujong?" asks Devukai.

"No," Shotoku blurts, their words rousing him back to consciousness. "To Mujong? And how do you think we'll be received there?"

"But the princess said—"

Shotoku is replete with fury: "We'll be hung, you idiot! It is our kingdom that single-handedly felled the peaceful nations of these lands. Ours that beguiled all with lies. Ours that exacted suffering by embargo. We will be eviscerated and deserve it! The blind are not forgiven by the cliff they walk off of, or by the rocks below which crush the life from their bodies! What excuse do you intend to use? No … but the rules have changed. The hidden enemy is now seen. And nothing will shield their heads from the strikes we will visit upon them."

Shotoku strides away. Jirai briefly regards the group with a look betraying grim satisfaction and angry resolve, then pursues Shotoku. They follow their captain as the dark veil of future deeds covers the once cavalier aura of the Bright Guard—the responsibility of vengeance in their capable hands.

TEN

Kingdom of Sterling

Starov, Jirai and Shotoku lie flat on a stone ridge under gray skies above a lush valley. Several dozen inazuma lean on each other in a swirling, uneven circle touching a large spire near the road.

"I count forty zuma and one monk," says Starov, sounding hopeful.

"Their eyes look dim," Char-ton adds.

"They should be. We've destroyed all the spires for a mile and there hasn't been a storm in two days."

"One?" Shotoku asks in order to be sure. They all squint.

"Just one," confirms Devukai, but he looks unsure. "Can we defeat them? Are they even human?"

Char-ton admonishes, "They're human. They want us to believe they are something more, some kind of super-zuma. But they bleed just like us."

"Let's just do this." Jirai knocks an arrow and cocks his crossbow. "We've passed on two monk-led parties today alone. We need to test our theory."

"They will not be as easy as the human-led groups," Char-ton cautions. "Have you forgotten our encounter?"

Shotoku, white knuckles on the hilt of his sword, is not listening. He knows he is too eager, but does not resist the certainty of hate that warms him. Of late, this is the only emotion that gives him pleasure—lying alone through the long nights, sleepless, no longer musing about bravery or what is right. Only how to kill. How best to dispatch the enemy, be they human, monk or inazuma. In his heart the frost found a home when he gazed at the cold corpses of those he'd seen fall—those who had lent their swords to protect Aurora. The only path he can sense toward a vague notion of salvation lies through more death and the suffering of those who orchestrated this grand deception. He is broken and knows it, but lacks the mental legerdemain to repair himself. He tries, but reason cannot heal his heart.

He works hard to maintain appearances. "This is the group." Feigning light-heartedness he pushes Devukai's head: "If this whelp's youthful eyes see no other monks, I guess today we begin monk slaying. Let's go. Make sure you don't have any metal on you. If I can sense it, they can, too. Chillson. Devukai. You lead the feint from the trees on the opposite side of the opening. We will attack a few moments later. Signal when you are ready."

+++++

On the opposite side of the spire, a blue light blinks twice in the trees, and Shotoku blinks in return. A volley of arrows sink into the inazuma at the spire. Several sag and die, uncomprehendingly. The monk hisses and its eyes pulse. The inazuma leave their spire and run, some rolling, for the copse from which the attack came. The monk trails behind, spurring the attack with bolts of lightning that elicit modulated, plaintive roars of the inazuma. With these lightning whips, he directs the attack. Using the distraction, Shotoku's team moves low and quick toward the monk from behind, rising once they achieve the cover of the spire and hurling large wooden javelins. Jirai fires his crossbow bolts devoid of metal tips.

The monk does not fall. At the last moment, he spins in a defensive arch, arms and one knee swinging, lighting sprawling from his appendages. The arrows dissolve in ash, but not the javelins. While most are blunted by the heat, they knock him back, off-balance, his protective bolts fizzling. Then a late-arriving spear skewers his leg. They can see his eyes burn bright red, even through his amigasa. They rush to surround him, leveling their weapons.

Along the far tree line, the unguided inazuma are being slowly defeated, led by Chillson and Devukai. The two youngest of the Bright Guard, a sword in each hand, they jump and spin in an effort to stay ungrounded and, yet, avoid jumping high enough to be stricken by lightning from the sky: a fighting style for the young. Their swords slice through the crenellated shells of the inazuma. The lightning of their enemy occasionally leaps to a sword which they readily drop, quickly drawing a third or fourth weapon. The spinning youths risk a grin, heads often beneath their knees as they cut down the creatures like lightning bamboo.

Surrounded, the monk kneels in pain. Shotoku removes the monk's amigasa. "You see. Just a man," says Shotoku, peering at his blackened face. "Although it appears they would like you to believe they are zuma." They exchange glances, reassured.

"You are the boy. I feel the hunger in your soul for the Spark," breathes the monk. Shotoku senses the invisible waves of churning magnetic poles between them like his body in wild seas. "Your father has joined his spark to ours. Your brother, as well."

Jirai inches forward, his jaw clenched, jabbing the monk with his crossbow. "Watch your tongue, you fissing fool, or I will skewer it with another kind of bolt."

The monk is forced to place a hand on the ground to regain his balance, but he continues taunting, "We are the flow to which all things return. Your resistance is pathetic. You cannot stop it. Time cannot stop it. You all will return to the flow … to us. You can't even stop a single one of us."

Starov steps forward and grabs the monk, lifting him from the ground. "We got you, laddie, and we'll get the rest of your ilk."

The monk laughs, but his breathing is labored and he hisses a cough. "Not one. One of you, instead."

Suddenly, Shotoku feels the buildup of charge around Starov and the monk. Before he can speak, he sends a counter-polarized protective burst at Starov as he is blinded, lightning from the sky striking immediately in front of him. The Bright Guard is cast backward through the air in a shockwave as the thunder blots all noise from their worlds. Silently, only his heartbeat in his ears, Shotoku can make out the monk rapidly receding into the distant sky, riding the bolt into the thick clouds. Cursing, he gets up and checks on Starov, who is not moving. His eyes water, stinging; he blinks, realizing that the two of them are laced with soot. Jirai and Char-ton join them.

"You shielded him, Shock. I saw a wave push the lightning away from him. Like you did at Sterling," Char-ton says, checking his pulse and listening to his breathing. "He's alive. Because of you." He looks at Shotoku, uncertain and bewildered. Then he starts laughing, eyes filled with wonder and glistening. "That was some serious science! Yeow! What else can you do? And did you see that guy fly?"

"I cannot let myself use it, Char-ton. Please don't ask," Shotoku says, closing his eyes.

Char-ton looks confused, "But you just did. What's the difference—?"

"That was defensive. When the situation is life and death, it just …seems to serve my will, but that is *not* control. Didn't you see the Mujongese that died from the bolt in Sterling?"

Keeping low, Devukai and Chillson join them, worried about the senior member of the team. Jirai splashes water on Starov and he begins to stir. Shotoku stands facing the new arrivals: "He's okay."

They relax visibly. "We have prisoners," reports Chillson.

Javelins and bolts skewer the dead and wounded, some writhing in shock and pain. Shotoku wrests a wooden-tipped spear from one of the wounded inazuma, places both hands on the shaft and plunges it into its face, which implodes on impact. Devukai and Chillson stop in shock. The young prince turns to them in a rage, "I'm sick of this. Letting them go."

Char-ton runs over. "Shock, what the fiss?"

A struggling inazuma, pierced by a javelin and flailing in the air over the ground, tries to turn and fire lightning at Shotoku. Shotoku walks straight up and puts a foot on its back, forcing the thickening shaft deeper. The inazuma looks out, glowing eyes on the horizon as it sinks to the earth, eyes fading to black.

"Shock! This isn't what we agreed." Char-ton grabs his shoulder and he reacts, a bolt arching from his hand to Char-ton's chest. The medic is thrown off of his feet, partially caught by Devukai, who looks on in chagrin.

Shotoku is shamed by Devukai's reaction. Although the act was unintentional, he continues unapologetic, yelling so that all may hear, "Remember what is going on. All of you. Protect your team. Look at Starov! Do I really need to remind you? All of the dead in Sterling? How many died today? Kill the enemy. Kill them all. That is the new order."

"They're intelligent and they're starving. In our valleys there isn't enough natural lightning," Char-ton insists.

"Not enough," Chillson guffaws, in spite of the mood, "that's the problem with this whole planet."

"That's why they should leave," reinforces Starov, in the light of his near-death experience. He walks over and dispatches a wounded inazuma.

Shotoku walks toward one of their fallen Sterling soldier allies, pointing to him and then to Char-ton. "Do you really have the luxury of a clean conscience after you let Sterling, your kingdom, lead thousands to the slaughter?" Char-ton only glares at him. He takes his sword and finds another gasping inazuma and, raising his blade, chops its head off.

"I think we understand, Prince."

"I don't think you grasp what's happening at all, Char-ton." Char-ton meets his gaze, but with disappointment, not anger, in his eyes. "Do it now," he yells, threatening, and strides away.

Char-ton looks after him, searching for a wisp of hope, a small act of contrition, and is left wanting.

+++++

Saiak stands looking out over the plains. Red circles of light can be seen dotting the grasslands; some overlap where the numbers of inazuma and spires are most concentrated. Kurukov approaches.

"They hit another of our units. This time in the Verato Valley. Now they're hitting our units with monks."

"How?"

"They're using wood. By shunning metal, they're avoiding detection."

"How do they know that the monks can sense metal?"

"Could the Iridian monks be helping them?"

"It's not their style to kill every zuma. They embrace all living beings and abhor killing. No, this is more … my style." Saiak can't resist smiling. "Shotoku. It has to be."

"You believe he has developed his abilities. If so, he could undo everything—"

"Abilities? He has none, nor the discipline. I tried to

develop them at one time, but he swore off using his talents when his brother died."

"What a waste."

"Domination is almost complete. Only Mujong remains and we march on them within the month. I don't want these rebels interfering. Take a company and blend it with a few zuma units. That should add some intellect to the zuma. And have Maji deploy the monks. I want these dissidents rooted out and my son found."

"And if it is Shotoku?" asks Kurukov.

"Then bring him to me. I will break him."

Kurukov smiles and walks away.

+++++

Devukai and Chillson are sitting around a fire. An assortment of haggard men and women sit in small groups, some soldiers and some civilians. Char-ton approaches the campfire, reading a book and making notations.

"I've been studying the zuma's anatomy and discovered several vulnerable areas that we may attack. Hey, does anyone want to see this?" Chillson moves next to Char-ton.

"Whaddya got?"

Char-ton indicates various stabbing and slashing movements on his own body. "Under the third rib, about here, is a soft area leading to what seem to be vital organs. Again, here on the back and also on the thigh."

Chillson stands up and takes out his dagger. "So here. Here?"

"No, it would be more like this."

"Gotcha. Here and here."

"I believe so."

"I know this. Hold on." Chillson changes the order of strikes, shifts his feet.

"Wait, I know that, too."

"It's Oozeshin."

"What's that?" Devukai rises, intrigued.

"It's a martial arts form. One you probably haven't learned yet. You know, sometimes when Douzen shows us a series of empty-handed arm movements to memorize, they don't seem logical. Sweeping your hands around together like a snake … who attacks like that?" Chillson's eyes brighten: "But when you put a sword in your hands later—"

Recognition dawns on Char-ton's face as he remembers the lesson. "Yes, it all made sense. He was teaching us to use a sword without holding one."

"Exactly. This is the same. Oozcshin: old, mysterious series of movements and whatnot. I learned it just out of respect for the old ways. But they were teaching us to fight zuma!" Chillson delights in his discovery.

"I thought those movements were just punches and kicks and stuff." Devukai tries to mimic the others.

"Well, we've always known there are multiple interpretations of the movements, but never guessed at anything like this," says Chillson in awe.

"It says in the book that they're energy points. Junctures in the flow of energy which can dictate polarity. Depending on how you apply pressure to them, massive amounts of ions will gather to stimulate healing … or disperse in a whirlwind … depleting energy."

"This is awesome, Char-ton. You're a genius! What else is hidden in there?"

"An excellent question. This is going to require thorough research." Char-ton drifts off, the mere suggestion of required reading as enticing as a favorite meal.

Chillson and Devukai grin widely, "Bookworm!"

Shotoku and Jirai ride into camp and dismount. Their clothes and faces are dirty. Jirai goes to Devukai and Chillson sitting at the fire. He ladles some brown soup from a pot over the fire into a bowl, sits and eats.

"Where have you guys been?" asks Devukai. "You've been gone for two days."

"There aren't enough ladies on these missions, I'll tell you that," quips Jirai, and Devukai cannot help but laugh, prying a smile even from the clutches of his exhaustion. Jirai chews, savoring the food.

Shotoku walks over to a table with a map on it. "Starov? Starov, where the hell are you!"

Starov rolls off his bed pack and gets up hurriedly, wiping sleep from his eyes. "Sorry, I just got in from patrol."

Shotoku impatiently pretends not to notice. "I want you to take a company and lead an assault on a new group of zuma we spotted north of here." Shotoku points at the map, but Starov is barely awake and stares blankly. "Starov! You're pathetic." Shotoku straightens from the map, frustrated. "Is there anyone here willing to seek and destroy the enemy that uprooted us from our homes?"

"I'll try, sir." Jirai looks at Devukai and laughs quietly, still chewing. Shotoku hesitates.

"Good. Gather some men and I'll brief you."

Disbelief and anger register on Jirai's face. "Shock.

May I speak with you?"

"I know what's on your mind, Ji—"

"Right now. Over here." He indicates a location away from the others. Shotoku strides over to meet Jirai. "You need to ease up, pal. Everyone's exhausted—" Shotoku returns to the map, waving Jirai off. "Don't fissing walk away from me!"

"Someone needs to do what must be done. They are down there preparing to destroy the last vestiges of human civilization and you want to what: sleep?"

Jirai sits back down, smirking and returning to his food. "None of us are any less committed than you. Everyone is doing what they can."

"I'll do it myself, if that's what you really think. And if you don't mind, I'll accept the service of those willing to sacrifice for Sterling."

Jirai looks to Chillson, smiling. "Service, yes. But when you mention 'sacrifice' before a mission, it makes me and the sheep a little nervous."

Shotoku steps in close, looking down at Jirai. "That's enough! You think this is a joke? Get the flash outta here!"

Without looking up, Jirai dismisses Shotoku. "Go flash yourself." Shotoku's anger is tangible. Jirai eats, unaffected by their proximity. In fact, he appears entertained by it, wanting to see what his friend will do next.

"Shotoku. I'm ready," says Starov, standing. "I'll need twenty volunteers. Brief me on the mission."

"Yeah, brief him on the mission." Jirai barks it like an order, mocking his captain.

Shotoku continues to hover: "I don't think our paths

are the same any longer, Jirai. Why don't you go and find your own."

"Thanks for granting me a freedom I already have."

Shotoku stops, restraining a reaction, and walks over to Starov.

Chillson is uneasy at the exchange; it isn't often these two come to words. His worry is growing for his captain and his disappearing humanity. He studies Jirai and, even through the grime on his face, can see he is near the breaking point. What will become of Aurora if the Bright Guard cannot hold? What hope for mankind? And if it is time for the group to part ways, whom will he follow, and to what terrible fate?

+++++

The next day, Shotoku sits on the rocks, eyes closed, feeling the electricity in the air, sensing the waves and flow. He can see without looking the rich veins of lightning, where to scoop and how to collect the invisible, charged particles. He can feel the magnetism in the rock face and the leaders that waft like smoky tendrils through the air from the iron spire he drove into the ground twenty feet away. He stands and moves his arms, assembling enough potential to reach the spire. It gathers in him and he finally thrusts his arms forward toward his target. Lightning materializes extending from the spire to his hands and the superheated air emits a small thunderclap. He smiles.

"You're getting better."

Shotoku turns to Devukai, unreceptive of the compliment, sick of lies that lead people astray and kingdoms to war, including the polite platitudes of acquaintances. "What is it?"

"Jirai is gone."

"I know. He left in the night." If Shotoku is worried about his friend's departure, he conceals it well.

"We have prisoners."

"Why the fiss do you have prisoners? What are you thinking?"

"They surrendered. They're men."

"Men who have sided with Saiak. Against the people of our kingdom."

"Sir, I—"

"Take me to them."

+++++

Shotoku approaches one of the four prisoners. "From where do you hail?" Chillson, Char-ton, and Starov stand guard.

"We are from New Sterling."

"Oh, that's what you're calling it now. Before that."

"Kitan."

"There, you see. They were the first to ally with the invaders. They deserve no sympathy."

"The monks are the rightful heirs to these lands. They are gods. We should serve them."

"Gods? Why? Because they can do this?"

Shotoku lifts his hand and the prisoner rises in the air, hanging from his handcuffs. He writhes in pain. "They can do much more. Ah! You know nothing of their ... powers."

"You mean this?" Motioning again, Shotoku tosses the man against the rock face and he slides to the ground. As he rises defiantly, lightning bursts from Shotoku's hands. Fire and smoke erupt from the man and he falls, unmoving. Devukai can hardly keep himself from gagging. He looks at Shotoku, the esteem that was there replaced with fear. Shotoku looks at him. "Kill the rest. Don't make me tell you again."

His friends only watch him walk away. "He's gone mad. He is consumed. I never believed it could happen to him of all people."

"Can you really blame him?" Chillson kicks some fulgurite, shattering it, and glances up at Char-ton, questioning.

"Can you honestly say that is our captain? The man you knew a few months ago? Saiak has destroyed him, after all."

Devukai's eyes glisten. He fears that what the medic says is true; yet his world is too firmly intertwined with his captain's morality to undo. "Don't say that. He's saved all of our lives before and … and we owe him for that." Hope and anguish burn in the youth's eyes, producing a volatile disposition.

"We owe him, kid," admits Starov. "But men's hearts change when confronted, sometimes forever. You whipper-snappers don't think much of us old guys, but getting though these conflicts, soul intact, without prejudice … without giving up hope, still able to feign a light heart—these are high accomplishments. Not everyone makes it."

"I still believe he'll come back," says Devukai with a touch of defiance.

Starov just smiles, not without pride, "Well, look at you, boy-o. Unfortunately, I'm too old to waste time on circuitous routes." He exchanges looks with Chillson and Char-ton and they nod. "We're leaving. Tonight. And you're coming with us."

The news is almost more than he can take, but the young man hardens. "I will stay. Someone has to."

Char-ton begins to protest, but Starov stops him.

Chillson tilts his head back, reconsidering the young man. "He's old enough to make his own fate. The way you would take is precarious, but no route is without risk. Good luck, Devukai."

The men say their goodbyes, not without affection, and part ways in the night.

ELEVEN

Mujong/Sterling Border

Makiko, eyes scanning for motion through the thick forest, quietly ties the leather reins of her mount to a tree. The gray day combines with the thick foliage to deprive her senses. She strains her eyes in an effort to discern the dun inhabitants of the woodland. The soldiers behind her match her actions. The twenty leather-armored and cloaked veterans move with practiced purpose. Accustomed to irregular warfare, most trackers and hunters even in their spare time, they know this environment as a second home. That, she imagines, is why they have been assigned by her father to protect her on this venture. He tried but could not dissuade her from going.

A light sweat beads on their skin even as their breath turns to fog under the pines. They move slowly forward, finding a keen sense of hearing more valuable than staring into the maddening maze of timber.

The wind picks up, bending the branches and conjuring the soft flirtations of the foliage above. Makiko blinks slowly, allowing herself a moment to slacken. As always, her mind unseals her memories of Shotoku and the cool burn which the recollection of his intensity of spirit invariably stokes. She is shaken from her reverie by voices on the wind. Alarm resounds, then stern voices boom upon the fickle wind: men preparing for battle. Then the wind fails and silence returns. Makiko signals quickly, but the men need no urging. They race through the forest deftly dodging under and around the uneven landscape.

At the edge of the forest, they witness a ragtag band of human soldiers springing a trap on a horde of inazuma. Using the tree lines and portable spires, they envelop the creatures quickly, dispatching them with great effect. Bowmen fling arrow after arrow at the solitary Kuroshi, who flees into the sky, witnessing the destruction of his host.

Makiko and her men fell a few of the creatures with their bows as they approach. Strong and confident, a man in his fifties approaches her band. "Who is your commander?" he bellows. The men point to her. "Indeed?" he answers, surprised. He reexamines the woman before him, knowing well the inner strength it takes to rule men. "You are the Mujong princess, are you not?"

She nods, "Douzen, correct?" They both turn their heads when shouts arise from across the field.

"The Bright Guard! The Guard lives!" The soldiers congregate, trying to catch a glimpse.

"Douzen! Where is the one called Douzen?" yells Chillson, just as his eyes find his general.

"You young pups," Douzen utters, disbelieving his eyes. "You young pups!" he yells as the two soldiers meet full force, hugging, faces cracking in pure joy. "Starov! Char-ton!" He continues to search the crowd, concern creeping in beneath the mirth. "But where are the rest? Shotoku and my son? Where is Devukai?"

Makiko steps into their circle, surprising the team. "Yes, where? Tell us now."

Eyes jump from face to face, but no one speaks. Finally, Char-ton breaks the silence, "He is much changed. You would not recognize him."

Douzen speaks, triumphantly, "He lives? You say he lives?" He walks in a circle, aimless, but energized.

"Douzen, do not trust to hope. Revenge has swallowed much of him."

Makiko's voice is frantic and thick with emotion, although her countenance does a courtly job of concealing it. "He is volatile. He was shaky even as I left you that night. Take me to him," she demands.

"We were hoping to join Jirai."

"Him I have seen," says Douzen. "Drunk. South of here at a little bar in the mountains a few days ago. Claims he quits, the self-serving fisser. I couldn't reason with him. He won't be of much help, I fear."

The men exchange knowing looks. "We must retrieve him. Princess, Shotoku continues to resist to the east. Finding him should not prove too difficult, but I warn you against what you will find," Char-ton says.

"No one can go east," Douzen insists. "The way is shut. An army approaches from that direction."

Makiko shakes her head, "No, we cannot abandon—"

"He has abandoned us," says Starov, purposefully cutting her short. "He is lost. I have seen it before." Makiko's face turns red with anger, but Douzen interrupts.

"Lost? No, no, no, he is not lost. Don't you know your prince? Why do you think I wax jubilant?" They just stare at the old general. "You don't understand. Jirai does." Douzen looks to the skies, considering. "Perhaps that is what Jirai is doing …" He hesitates, then patiently explains. "When they were young, Jirai was not well liked, as you know. An orphan … cocky, with no one to protect him. One day, half a dozen older boys were picking on Jirai, again, and Shotoku intervened." Douzen meets all of their gazes. "He told the boys that he had taken an oath to protect the people of Sterling and was obliged to help Jirai. The oldest boy scoffed and knocked him to the ground, but Shotoku kept getting up, saying he had made an oath. Again and again, he punched Shotoku's bloody face. Jirai even tried to get in the way, but Shotoku pushed him back violently. 'An oath to protect': he said it so many times, the other boys started to want this young boy as their leader. They realized that he was made of something more. They didn't understand it. I suppose it is still hard for most of us to comprehend. But the boys saw it and their spirits turned. Their spirits … turned. Finally, one of the other boys hit the bigger boy in the jaw and they all lit into him, united by a single spirit."

Everyone looks at Douzen, weighing his words.

"One brave man inspires a thousand. One man …

rare. One man who believes, changes hearts. Fights the odds and wins. Ignites the uncertain masses and casts his uncomprehending enemy down. That man who runs toward the enemy when all others flee. Shotoku is that man. Young, yes. Misguided, perhaps. But he will find his way. I trained him, I punished him. I have seen him at his worst." He nods his head and smiles, reassuring his listeners. "Makiko, it is time for us to prepare Mujong for a fight. I shall accompany you, bringing my forces, and help make ready your kingdom. The way to the east is closed and an army comes for your lands. Tell them what you know. Starov, take your men and resurrect Jirai. He may have given up, but he will never give up on Shotoku." He turns and walks back to his troops. "Those are my orders. Take heart. If he lives, gods flash it," he stops to deal a finishing blow to an inazuma clawing at his leg, "we may have a chance after all."

+++++

Kingdom of Mujong

Lights glow from a group of small wooden buildings high in the mountains near the border of Mujong and the Great Southern Sea. Jirai's eyes slide over his cards, then rise to read his opponents' expressions. He grabs his stein and drinks its contents without looking, spilling a bit on his shirt. He smiles, revealing his bright white teeth, achieving the antagonism for which he'd aimed. The two other men at the table are not having as much fun.

Bright, red paper lanterns cover the ceiling of the tavern, but only the few over the card table and bar are lit. By dim candlelight, a few other patrons conduct their affairs in the peripheral darkness. Jirai faces the exit with the bar at his back. He tries to focus on the play, but cannot seem to ignore a blinking light from the darkness on his left. He finally looks over and sees a hooded figure smoking something, its bright embers glowing with each inhalation. The thick, salty odor of a stew simmers somewhere mixed with the sharp tang of the pipe weed.

Somewhat miffed at the distraction, he returns his attention to his fellow card players and reveals his hand by laying it on the table. "Let's see 'em, boys." Unhappy, but gracious considering their poor luck, his opponents lay down their cards. "Haha, you know I thought you guys had me there. You play a pretty straight game here. You might want to learn to bluff." They return a somewhat puzzled look, and Jirai can't help but feel the generosity that springs from playing a hopelessly outmatched opponent. "Why don't I buy you fellas a drink. It's your money, anyway." They perk up at this suggestion and Jirai moves to the bar. "Barmaid, two for my friends and two for me." As he receives his beverages, the smoker emerges from the darkness, approaching the bar. When he pulls back his hood, he turns out to be a she. Jirai, struck by her beauty, is at once paralyzed and invigorated. He makes a clumsy effort at affecting nonchalance.

"Buy me a drink, too, sparker?" Her look is pure daring.

He looks her up and down, depreciatingly: "Something wrong with your money, firefly?" He diverts his eyes, coyly, but cannot erase the gold of her hair, the red of her full, smiling lips or the flash of her emerald eyes.

"I don't have any money."

"Okay, I'll play. Give her one of anything."

"Two," she corrects him as she slides down the polished, wooden bar and turns to face him. "Two Crowns, please," she says to the barmaid, who looks at Jirai.

He nods, arching an eyebrow at her, "You like the hard stuff, huh? I've never seen a woman drink this stuff. Except my grandma."

As the woman offers them the shots, his new companion slowly moves her cloak back, revealing one shoulder and then the other. She wears a tight, maroon one-piece in a V pattern on top of dark blue around her lithe torso. Her shirt tucks into form-fitting black pants which disappear into tall boots. Woven into the material are fine filaments that glisten. Jirai does a double-take when he notices they glow like living veins.

Sparks dancing from the shots, she grabs one and downs it, her eyes returning to Jirai. "I'm not Grandma," she smirks.

Try as he might, he can't suppress a smile. Grabbing his shot, he toasts her, "No confusion there."

+++++

Cheeks flush and the knot in her hair now slightly disheveled, the woman smiles broadly, listening to Jirai. They sit at the table where he was playing cards. Shot glasses litter the marred wooden tabletop, upon which she also props her feet, hands behind her head, eyebrows arching in disbelief at another of his tales. The barmaid slumbers in the corner, the bar now empty of other patrons.

"You are so full of it," she smirks. Jirai challenges her with a cocky, quizzical look. He lets his eyes follow her long legs to her torso and up to the exposed nape of her neck. The long curved sheath of a sword dangles from her hip. She places her feet back on the floor and walks over to the bar to grab another bottle of liquor. She irons her outfit with her hand as she returns, smiling, embarrassed but amused at her unkempt appearance. She leans in close to him as she pours them each another. "You almost hit a monk with your bow?" She reaches down, "This bow?"

He wiggles. "Midori, that's not my bow!"

She whirls and returns to the bar. "Ha, you'd like that wouldn't you?"

"No?" he offers, unconvincingly. "You like this?" he asks, showing her his crossbow. "This clip feeds it the bolts. Below there are two triggers. Pumping one trigger, via this series of gears, quickly knocks a bolt, while the second fires it. Multiple shots."

"Are you as good as you think you are?"

He nods, "Yup," and lets his bottom lip bulge. "Sometimes you just have to own a skill, you know? With the monk, though, that one had no metal tip, you see? Couldn't detect it," he adds, winking at her. "That's the trick, my little firefly," he says, dropping the bow back into his lap.

In a lightning flash, she turns, hurling a shot glass through the air at Jirai. He doesn't move. He doesn't flinch. So when the glass shatters midair and the bolt lodges in the wall behind the bar, she can't help but inhale sharply. He throws his crossbow on the table.

"You shot from the hip?" she asks, still in disbelief. He shrugs and drinks his shot. "Gods, you're fast." Frowning, she wrestles with her emotions. She finds herself hesitant to return to her chair, looking him up and down. He has somehow changed from a temporary distraction into something exponentially more attractive. "Where are you from?"

"Sterling … or what was Sterling. I am of the Not-So-Bright Guard." He giggles at his joke.

"Sterling? And what are you doing here?"

"Oh, I abandoned my friends. I answer to no one. Do what I want, when I want. Besides, things gettin' crazy."

"I don't care much for rules, either," Midori nods, "but you're a liar. Maybe you enjoy belittling yourself. But your admittances are lies. You're hiding behind this motley act you put on."

"It usually takes people a lot longer to figure that out." Jirai whispers, "If you let people know what you're thinking, you get predictable." His voice grows boisterous: "I don't like that." The barmaid stirs and Jirai snickers, taking a sip from his stein. "One guy I know has a talent for snaring my falsehoods."

"One of your abandoned friends?"

"Shotoku is always going on about honesty. Sees right through my claims. Annoying." Something changes in her demeanor when he mentions Shotoku's name. "What?"

"*That* is your friend? Shotoku of Sterling? Saiak's son?" Jirai follows her with his eyes, cautious. "I have been looking for you." She walks into the darkness and returns holding a satchel. She removes a quiver of bolts. "Try these next time you start some static with the monks."

Jirai examines the bolts; they have long, magnetic, aerodynamic heads that spin around a copper shaft. It's his turn to ask questions. "Who are you?"

"An ally. You must help me find Shotoku and your friends."

"Whoa, whoa, I just told you—"

At that instant, a sharp crackling sound is heard outside. They look to the door as light begins to shine through the cracks. More crackling sounds erupt from either side of the tavern and Midori stands as if frozen. "Midori, get behind the bar. I got this." He backs up, grabbing the new quiver and pointing his bow at the source of the noise. "Dori!"

Holes burst from the side walls and doorway and three amigasa-wearing Kuroshi step through the apertures. Midori stands in front of the door and pleads with the monk, taking a step back and holding a hand toward his face. Jirai moves to take a shot without hitting Midori, when she draws her sword high and fast. Calmly, she sheathes the sword again and turns to close the distance with the monk on her left. Uncomprehending, Jirai sees one side of the monk's amigasa dangle and fall to the floor as he clutches his neck. Falling to his knees, the monk looks at the blood on his hands. Jirai can hear a sickening whistle as blood spurts rhythmically from the cut in his neck. She killed him with her drawing stroke, Jirai realizes, sobering. As he falls face down, dead, the other Kuroshi reassess the situation.

Then the tavern ignites in lightning. On the left, the monk throws a bolt at Midori, but she channels and redirects it back through her body, catching him square in the chest and knocking him back outside. From the right, the Kuroshi fires hastily bolt after bolt in her direction, but they find ground too early, scorching chairs and tables. Producing several small knives, she flings them quickly at her new opponent. Jirai fires shot after shot from his crossbow at the same monk, but he keeps a hand extended in his direction and the bolts veer wide. Gesticulating, gathering the resident energy, she fires several lightning bolts which, thanks to the ion path produced by the knives, wind their way directly toward the monk. Compromised by fighting two foes, he manages to fend off one but is impacted by the other two and falls to the floor, smoking. Two of Jirai's arrows finish him off.

The last Kuroshi reemerges from outside as Midori, via their metal frames, magnetically rips the lanterns from the ceiling. She arranges them, forming a wall of glowing red paper between the two of them and obscuring his view. Just before the lantern wall, he breaks stride and is barely missed by her emerging sword. Better than the others, he catches her arm and delivers a strike to a nerve cluster in her wrist. The lanterns rain down around them. The pain in her wrist is exquisite; then she is countering, moving with the inertia of his attack. Hand to hand, he strikes hard and fast. Wrist locks and elbows, she fights to keep her center of gravity, but he is at least her equal in speed and strength.

Jirai, out of regular ammunition, struggles to knock one of Midori's bolts. The monk gets a hold of her hair and twists as a visceral sound escapes her. Jirai panics, redoubling his efforts at the sound of her suffering. As the monk bends her backward, she swings one arm around. He falls for her feint, blocking with his free hand as she back-fists the arm at her hair, snapping her wrist quickly and striking the nerve cluster at his elbow. He howls, but brings his other fist down on her face. Midori falls to the floor barely conscious.

One arm hanging useless, the monk draws his sword to finish her. Raising it above his head, he is unaware that Jirai's new bolt is en route to where he stands. As it travels, wind resistance causes the head to revolve around the copper shaft, building a straight tube of charged ions to the target—ions which search desperately for a conductor. When the bolt strikes the monk's chest, he is lifted off of his feet and pinned against the tavern wall. Here the electricity finds ground and the tube of ions ignites. Lightning illuminates the room again, charring the monk into a corpse and creating a sonic boom that extinguishes all but a few of the remaining lanterns.

The bow still in his hand, Jirai's heart pounds in the aftermath of the tremendous power he just unleashed. Remembering Midori, he rushes around the bar, sliding on one knee to her side. Tiredly, her jade eyes open to see his angular face, usually guarded, but now disarmed and boyish. Even in the dim light, they easily read each other's faces: fear, hope, and abandon. In pain, her mouth rises and his descends. As his lips timidly meet hers, she manages to slowly snake her hand behind his head, granting more vigor to the exchange.

More noise from outside prompts them to rise and reorient their senses. Starov pops his head through the opening. "What in the devil is going on here, Jirai? Good heavens, look at the fissing place." Midori and Jirai relax visibly. Char-ton and Chillson follow Starov inside, smiling when they see their friend. "And who is this unlucky girl? You haven't taken a shining to this one, have ya?" he adds.

"This is Midori. A monk," he says, expecting incredulity.

"Do not worry. I am an Iridian and I have been sent to find the Bright Guard and train you all for what lies ahead."

"Train us to do what?" asks Char-ton.

"To fight monks. If you don't learn how to put our kind down, you stand no chance at all. We have fighting techniques and weaponry to share with you. You are all welcome."

Char-ton and Chillson exchange a knowing glance. "We have seen a book detailing the fighting forms. You can teach this art?"

"We can and we will. I will take you to our home, but I was told expressly to retrieve Shotoku. Where is he?"

The team shares distraught looks, then Jirai speaks, "Ah, I … I know where he is. I will get him."

"How will you locate him?"

"Easy, I know his habits. Go with Midori. Dori, tell me where to go and we will meet you as soon as we can." He packs his things, preparing to leave. "Oh, thanks again for the arrows. She's not kidding about the weaponry, guys. Just ask that guy behind you." They turn to see the sizzling monk on the wall and blanch. Jirai unpins the corpse from the wall which tumbles morbidly to the floor.

"Don't take on any Kuroshi, Jirai. I won't be there to save you," she teases, but her tone contains an edge.

"I won't, firefly. I—" he says, placing a foot on the monk's chest and yanking out the lighting arrow. He starts to speak, again, but cannot. He does not want to leave and cannot be his usual cavalier self. The team smirks at him and then at her, figuring things out.

Her eyes soften with the unspoken compliment, and she helps him out: "Just shut up, fool." She takes out a map and points. "Meet us here, okay?"

"Right. Look after this riffraff, will ya? Starov, follow me."

They walk into the cool night air high in the mountains. Starov is struggling to match his pace, when Jirai whirls. "Take care of her. On your life, Starov." His face is resolute.

Offended, he retorts, "Hey, she's a monk. How do you know we can trust her?"

"If she wanted you dead, you'd be dead already."

"She doesn't seem—"

"Sometimes wild things don't appear wild until challenged, and then"—his eyes drift to the horizon as he relives what occurred only a few moments ago—"savage." His eyes return to Starov's. "On your life, my friend."

"Of course. Do you really need to ask?"

"I don't know. I'm not thinking straight." He jumps on his horse. "Safe journey," he yells, finally riding away.

Left in the darkness, Starov can't help but shake his head. "So that's what Jirai-in-love looks like," he says, chuckling, and watches his comrade disappear into the night.

+++++

Kingdom of Sterling

Shotoku, a young captain and a dozen troops crouch amongst the trees, observing a moving force of men and inazuma.

"They're mixing up their forces."

"Yes, we'll have to hit them fast." Blinks can be seen from a copse north of their position.

"Our forces are reporting a group of close to sixty, half and half, men and zuma. He can see two enemy monks. Tell him we see the same. Confirm they are stationary. Looks like they're bivouacked for the night."

"Confirmed. We'll have to move fast. That's a lot of open ground. I wish we had a better vantage. Jirai had a flare for that."

"Well, he's not with us anymore, the selfish fool." Shotoku lets the comment slip, not even believing it himself. The men sneak an askance look. "Sorry everything isn't perfect, Lieutenant. We'll just have to make do." Shotoku gives his junior officer a diminishing glance and turns to the soldiers behind them. "Stay out of sight and move down the tree line to that point. Fire arrows first, then attack the men hand to hand. Move!"

The soldiers move quickly and quietly. Thunder booms from the north. "Looks like a storm. We'd better get this done."

"Give the signal," orders Shotoku.

+++++

Arrows fly at the encampment, striking multiple enemies, but their reaction is quick and they form a defensive perimeter around the spire, minimizing their profile. Arrows begin to fly back at Shotoku's men.

"Fire the leader arrows and then attack."

The lieutenant pulses the light signal, and arrows with long metal filaments fly above the enemy. Lightning flashes from the latent skies, but the humans crouch and inazuma stand to absorb the energy.

"Sir, maybe we should … nothing's working."

"Too late."

The group to the north has begun to clash with the inazuma–human perimeter. Bolts arch from the inazuma and the enemy men fall back to a safe distance.

Shotoku feels the advantage slipping. "Attack!" They jet from the trees, crouching with their chins as low as their knees. Two men are struck by lightning as they approach. The rest of his force safely gains the protection of the enemy spire and they stand, hurling themselves upon the enemy. Flesh sizzles as men tangle with the creatures. Shotoku and a small group flank the inazuma and set into the humans in the center. There the battle is more evenly matched. Shotoku cuts down a few men as he searches.

"There! Monks!"

Devukai, Shotoku, the lieutenant and his men fight their way toward the monks. Shotoku gets close to them first and readies his black-bladed sword. Slowly backing up, the monks hiss to one another, "It is he."

"You boys look like you've heard of me."

The two monks hiss and fly back through the air toward another copse of trees. The inazuma, deprived of their masters, attack wildly and seek the sustenance and comfort of the spire.

Devukai reaches Shotoku, but the others have not yet broken free of the battle. "Let's go, they're not getting away this time." Devukai and Shotoku move low and fast into the copse of trees pursuing the monks. They reach the northern edge of the trees, but do not see the monks. Shotoku concentrates. "This way."

He takes off again, Devukai on his heels. East, the trees grow thicker, but Shotoku can sense the magnetic eddies from his prey. Soon his senses become blurred by interference. Continuing toward his last feeling, he and Devukai come across a great stone building in the center of the forest. Still majestic, but crumbling now with overgrowth and dilapidated spires, the huge building is a beacon for lightning strikes. They open the metal door, making an awful racket. Walking inside, they are astonished to see row after row of books.

"Unbelievable. Who knew such a treasure still existed?" Devukai strays to read the bindings.

"Focus."

"Look: the spires from the roof lead down the walls all the way to the floor. What do you think these large cylinders are?"

"Do not touch those. They could still contain a charge. I used the same devices in my structures."

There is a sharp sound from deeper in the structure and they both listen. Shotoku signs to Devukai and he nods. Shotoku moves into the building, keeping as far as he can from the cylinders. The rows of books end and the way opens into a large chamber with a fifty-foot vaulted ceiling. Gigantic stained glass windows form a honeycomb-patterned dome high above with a diameter half the width of the chamber. Colored light exposes the chamber's contents. Paper litters the floor and innumerable scrolls lay within the walls set in tiny cubbies. Chairs and tables are scattered throughout the chamber, and stairs lead to double doorways at all four ends.

"I don't like this. There's too much magnetism here. I can't get a read."

Devukai, overcome with zeal, throws off Shotoku's caution and runs into the room. "Are you kidding? Look at this stuff. This could teach us who knows what."

"Dev," Shotoku cautions.

Nothing happens, and Devukai continues to rifle through the papers. Shotoku takes a few steps further into the chamber.

"These look like plans … What do you call them? Schematics! It's science, Shock. Look at the science!"

Devukai looks at Shotoku, his boyish features untarnished by the months of hardship. He smiles at Shotoku, whose own face softens just a sliver.

Shotoku feels the storm coming before he sees and hears it. The stained glass dome bows and sags, cascading fiery droplets of melted glass upon them. A dozen monks shoot through the new aperture, raining lightning and thunder down upon Devukai and Shotoku. Devukai is hit right in front of Shotoku, who dives to attract and deflect the bolts. The younger man falls to the ground, while Shotoku stands, shielding him. Too many bolts to channel, he falls to a knee. Never has he encountered such current. Falling, his hand lands on a metal girder flush with the floor that helps to ground the structure. He directs all current into the beam and a visible pulse travels the tract, slamming into a monk unlucky enough to be standing on it. The monk tries to avoid it by flying, but is blasted into the side wall, instead. The rest of the monks walk slowly toward him, motioning, blasting until Shotoku collapses. The monks cease as Shotoku and Devukai lay smoldering.

Devukai gasps, burnt and shaking. "No, no, noooo." Shotoku's face is panicked as he takes his friend into his arms.

Devukai strains to breathe. "I, *huuugh*, let you down, *huuugh*. Alwayssss, did, *huuuuh*." Shotoku grabs him, loosens his armor.

"No, no, you never did. That's not true," he says as he hugs and rocks him, his breathing labored.

"Wanted to be like you. Make you proud," Devukai struggles.

"Quiet, my brother. I'll get you out of here," Shotoku says, eyes searching, darting, desperate for a miracle as the young soldier's fate becomes clear.

Devukai smiles at his words; peace on his face. "You called me brother," then his eyes glaze as his body falls limp. Shotoku sinks, his chest to Devukai's as he shivers with pain, anger and despair.

"I told you not to waste time on him. He was too naïve to last long." Saiak emerges from behind the monks. "Douzen's son dies. His father won't be far behind."

Shotoku lays Devukai on the ground, forehead on his chest. He rests it there a moment then sits up. He turns his head halfway to see Saiak behind him out of the corner of his eye. The monks stand on all sides.

"You've performed some incredible feats in the past few months, but, in the end, you are no match for me.

183

Perhaps someday, under my mentorship …" Saiak circles Shotoku seeking his face, but Shotoku turns his head, evading. "Shotoku, I've worked for so long … sacrificed. I didn't want to make you suffer, but the pain has borne fruit after all. I began to doubt it would, but I see you now and know the truth. You are finally ready to join me."

Shotoku's eyes search for something, but find nothing. Nothing to assuage the pain or the guilt. Tears mix with the grime on his face, his will spent, uncertainty prying at the door of his heart, rending it and allowing suggestion to slither in.

"What do you want me to do?"

"Turn around." Shotoku turns, remaining on one knee and staring at the ground. "Do you still tell the truth? Tell me you'll be loyal and I will believe you. We will be allies."

Shotoku starts to shake. Saiak waits and soon his son's shaking becomes an audible laugh, growing louder. Saiak smiles, too, slowly building to a laugh himself. "You'll believe me. You've never accepted me at my word. Ha, ha, ha …"

"I'll need someone I can trust," confides Saiak. He cannot help but feel joy at the chance that his son will join him. His son, the most truthful, stubborn and principled person he has ever encountered, standing by his side.

Two monks move closer on either side of Shotoku. His laughter ceases and he looks up to meet Saiak's gaze for the first time, expressionless, mirth replaced with the chill of a grave in winter.

"I will keep my promise to you. My promise of

vengeance." Shotoku rises like lightning, his knife blade flashing, cutting Saiak's chin as he falls backward. The two monks grab and hold him fast and he strains against their grasp.

"You will never know trust! Only my rage … it will all be for you! Ahhhhhh!" Saiak gets up off of the ground, eyes alight but uncertain. "Raaaaaaaaaaaaage!"

Shotoku's arms glow brighter and brighter until pulses of electricity pass down and into the monks restraining him. They rise, out of control, into the air, the pulses bursting and sending them into the walls. The remaining monks hurl lightning at Shotoku, but he absorbs the bolts into his arms, straining under the current. He doubles his efforts, but succumbs, kneeling, face contorting.

Saiak checks his throat and chin, panicked, astonished at what he has witnessed and at how close he has just come to death. Nausea threatens to overtake him as he realizes his son is lost, and his lips struggle to affect a fatalistic smile. "You are defeated. Your ideals a failure. Even your friends have deserted you." His tone is derisive and bitter.

Shotoku continues to strain under the current as the monks continue to surge lightning into his body. He remembers the face of Jirai, his best friend, who left him. He should have known then that his path had gone astray. Tears burn his face, boiling in the heat of the current.

At that moment, the doors on the west side of the chamber explode inward. The monks cease their attack as Jirai strides into the chamber, leveling two crossbows unlike any before seen. Arms extended and crossed, the bows fire bolt after bolt as Jirai fans them in opposing arcs. Behind each arrow is a metal filament and upon striking the target they flash, becoming lightning from his bow to the victim. Taken off guard, the monks try to dodge or fly, but do not escape Jirai's marksmanship and are blasted about the room like paper. Saiak runs and dives through the doors on the opposite end of the chamber as Jirai kneels next to Shotoku.

"That comment about your friends just fissed me off. Take my hand."

Shotoku looks down at Devukai and then up at Jirai, eyes flooded with sorrow. He does not take his hand.

"Leave me."

"We need you, Shock. I need you. I've never seen a man use principle like you ... forge unbreakable bonds from nothingness. I'm so proud to call you my friend. Now get up, not for yourself, but for all of us."

Jirai supporting Shotoku, they back out of the room. The monks shake their heads and try to stand, but their confidence has waned. Jirai and Shotoku reach the exit and he points his free crossbow.

"Tell your friends about me."

He fires a salvo at the charged cylinders around the room. A few monks manage to levitate off of the ground before they explode. The long, high walls of the great stone library, having been perforated by the explosion, begin to crumble under the extreme weight. The monks look up in trepidation as huge blocks rain like wordless gravestones. They cast lightning indiscriminately, impotent and weak in contention with the dense masonry.

Outside, Jirai forces Shotoku onto his mount and

jumps on behind him. Shotoku's eyes deadened, he looks back at the ruined library as it becomes the tomb of a young soldier and friend. In lieu of reckless anger, a cold, desolate wind, a hopeless force, lays barren that place inside him where fury flourished, its strong roots expelled from the choked dust of his heart. Purpose replaced by a vacuum of impetus and the unredeemable certainty of having blighted the life of every human he has ever touched.

TWELVE

Fulguris Mountains

Shotoku awakens, thick-headed. Light reflects from the brown swirls which decorate the beige stone in the ceiling above. He remembers his ordeal and sits up suddenly. Dizzy, he leans back on an elbow, pain raking his body, newly healed skin stretching. From his pillow, he turns his head and sees a face, resolving slowly.

"Ready for action already? Not quite, aye? There'll be time for that. Just enough, I think." Niwashi looks on the young man, pleased and relieved.

"Where am I?

"You are awakening … and just in time. You will have much to prove here. You are at an Iridian monastery."

"Devukai?"

"He's gone." Shotoku closes his eyes tightly and

Niwashi draws closer, placing a hand on his shoulder. "You made it and for that I am happy." Shotoku winces and looks at the old man, studying his face and finding truth. He appears years younger. "Important people want to see you." At Shotoku's silence, he rises slowly with a consoling demeanor. "When you are ready, I'll be outside."

Shotoku stares at the ceiling, his face a reflection of the stone. Jirai's face suddenly appears above his own.

"Hey, boss. Feeling better?" He sits down in a highly-polished, ornate wooden chair. Its angle of recline is slightly obtuse and the black lacquer worn in areas from use. He crosses his legs, relaxing. "Quality furniture they have here."

"Jirai, what's been happening? Where are the others?"

"Midori, the female monk, took them somewhere. They don't want to see you. You know I met her when I got sidetracked in a little town we passed on the way here. They had the nicest little tavern with beer from the north and girls from the south. You know, that's a rare find these days. I couldn't help myself … and chance brought me Midori," he muses, appreciatively.

Shotoku covers his face with his arms. "What have I done?"

"You killed a lot of people and zuma with them. Nothing I wouldn't do—they all had it coming. Except you have this conscience anomaly."

"I broke faith with the team. They trusted me to do the best I could. To see them through this."

"Would you like to name someone who might have done better? You brought them as far as you could.

Farther than most."

"Except Devukai, you mean."

Jirai purses his lips and looks down. He stares for a few moments at the floor, expressionless. "Yes, except Devukai." Jirai smirks in remembrance of something and then it fades, his jaw clenching. "We will never forget him, will we?" His eyes return to Shotoku. "That's pretty fissing good for wartime, in case you failed to notice. The plains are littered with dead citizens—the dead you were helping to minimize with your tactics. Effective, is what I call it, and if someone needs an apology they can rot in hell."

Shotoku's expression remains grim. "Any word on Maki?"

"I heard she was okay. I also heard that Mujong counterattacks have met with massive losses with little effect. They won't last the month."

"Ji, I wanted to say … about what I said before—"

"Words seldom reflect reality, Shock. Most people are liars and you have to learn to question what you hear. Except with you. When you kept every promise you made to me, you showed me how different you were. You were baffling." His eyes slide to the swirling patterns in the ceiling, tracing them with his fingers from afar. "Deliberate, where most are just … drifting. Showed me what was possible and damned me at the same time." He stops and Shotoku lifts his arms to look at his friend. "I could see what was happening to you: you needed to be human for a while. To deceive and be cruel. I knew you'd be back. And I felt I could do more elsewhere. That's why I left. Anyway, you have a nap and just relax," his tone sarcastic in an attempt to disperse palpable emotion.

"Why? What am I supposed to do?"

Jirai turns and walks away, waving his hand and dismissing his friend. "All I can say is that this is the last rest you'll be getting for a long time."

"Why? Why did you come back?"

Jirai hesitates at the doorway, then turns his head. "All the times I fell … that your father told you to cut me loose … Did you ever abandon me?"

+++++

Shotoku exits the stone building in which he was convalescing, wincing in the light of a rare day of bright sunshine. Niwashi walks with him, appraising his condition carefully. The complex is Spartan but immaculate, with well-groomed stone pathways and shrubbery. A monk tends to the greenery and another sweeps a stone pathway. Shotoku watches them guardedly, in slight disbelief of their peaceful proximity, when he almost runs smack into a tall, sleek, black inazuma. Frightened at first, he immediately realizes this is an inazuma of the kind he met during his retreat from Mujong. Its blue eyes shine, even in the light, as it ranges freely across the grounds.

"Zounds." Shotoku looks to Niwashi. "A few months ago I scarcely believed you when you said they existed."

Niwashi only smiles. "They're beautiful, aren't they? Nothing like their red-eyed cousins."

Shotoku's eyes fill with tears. "What sort of man believes all the lies ever told him and not the truths?"

"You are young and the young trust others a bit too hastily. On top of that, you are idealistic and act as you wish the world would be, but that makes you the mortal enemy of many. Few have the will to stand fast." He places his hands on the young man's shoulders.

They continue walking and Shotoku struggles at times, stopping and placing his hands on his knees. Niwashi is unable to discern whether this is out of physical or mental pain.

The architecture of the building resembles the clear lines and angles of the library Devukai and Shotoku so recently destroyed. The memory makes him clench his fists in sadness and anger. Finally, Jirai joins them and Niwashi leads them into a grand hall of wooden timber and heavy oaken doors. Ornate spires rise from the structure, the beauty of their artistry surpassing their functionality. Blown glass hangs intertwined with glowing vines over skillfully wrought iron. They enter the building and find a group of monks meeting over wooden tables. Scrolls and mugs of various liquids are atop the tables, and a fire roars in a great hearth whose stonework bears the same cinnamon swirl of light and dark browns he found in his chamber.

The monks notice them enter. One imposing figure, closest to them, turns more slowly to them, but speaks first.

"Shotoku, I am Zensou. A long road you have taken to get here. Your troubled past has not escaped our notice … nor your recent actions, but you will find peace here, as long as that is what you bring." Shotoku only stares at Zensou coldly. "Perhaps you have met some of my brothers before. This is Still Thunder, and this is Spark Hand."

"I wouldn't know. You monks always manage to

conceal your faces beneath amigasa. So I am supposed to believe you are not in league with Saiak?"

"Correct."

"Then who are the monks helping him?"

"They are the Kuroshi. We were once joined with them, until we were all betrayed by the people of these lands and excommunicated."

"Excommunicated? But why?"

"We ourselves did not know. Someone was attacking villagers, so we sent our best and strongest to hunt them down. Koro, my son, and two others were sent, but the attacks only worsened. Then Koro was killed. When we found his murdered body alone, the burns indicated that he had been murdered by monks: his two companions. We returned to our monasteries to find rebellion. The Kuroshi and Iridians fought and many monks died."

Shotoku listens, closing his eyes already guessing at the answer: "And the two who led the betrayal?"

"Maji and Saiak."

Jirai walks up and grabs a mug of brew from the table, raising it as if to drink. His hand shakes, however, his lips curl in anger and he throws the mug to the floor. "I can't even drink, I hate those two so much," he seethes.

"Thanks to the staged attacks on the inhabitants of the lowlands, the Iridians were marked as enemies. After sharing so much with the lowland peoples, we had no choice but recede into the highlands."

Shotoku, looking down, shakes his head. "I will make it right. I will do whatever it takes."

Silent Thunder scoffs, "Does this whelp honestly

think he can right the wrongs of the past by a solitary act of revenge?" He looks from Zensou to Shotoku. "You have bought into every fabrication, every machination of your father's. You have done nothing right from the beginning."

Jirai is not in the mood for criticism. "Hey! Silence, Thunder. He said he'd try. What have you done?"

Silent Thunder smolders at the remark, as Shotoku speaks: "I think you would find me much changed, Thunder. I'm sorry, Zensou, but I don't bring peace and I am not looking to make it. I thank you for helping me, but we will be leaving as soon as possible."

"Peace-loving people do not turn their backs on the needy, and I have seen no one as needy as you in some time," Zensou says. "Shotoku, you will never be complete again, never be able to do honor to your brother's name, until you set down the blame for his death."

Shotoku stares at the floor, his heart and mind a maelstrom. "I made a vow never to use it."

"I know. And you see yourself as a man who killed his brother. But I see a man who saved an infant. A man who cares more about his men than himself. A man who wants to see a just world." Zensou looks at Jirai. "And a man who accepts others' faults, but not his own."

Jirai rolls his eyes, but keeps silent, reluctantly acquiescing.

Shotoku's body shakes under the memories. "He was innocent. I couldn't stop it. He looked up at me as I held him." Shotoku's own face rises, tears running down his cheeks. "Looked up as if to ask why." Spark Hand, becoming emotional himself, turns and walks a short distance away. "Why I had done such a thing. Now you're asking me to abandon my word, but it is the only thing I can keep." His breath becomes heavy as he grows angry and makes a fist. "I keep it. I keep it, so that people can count on something in this world, if nothing else. My word is all I have."

Zensou says, quietly, "And yet you are a good man without it. You made that promise to yourself and, therefore, may release yourself at any time. I do not ask you to break your word. I ask you to forgive yourself." Shotoku's gaze wavers … questioning … wishing. "A man once told me that he thought you could do it." Zensou looks past Shotoku. "A rickety old man who believed your heart would one day heal this wound."

Niwashi walks in slowly from the doorway, grinning. "All I said was you have a good sense of humor. That's how I knew you were special. People of good humor always heal up eventually. Give me your sword, Shotoku." He does and Niwashi shows him the fluorescent inazuma engraving. "Do you know what it means?" Shotoku shakes his head. "'Protector of the Innocent.' It is the highest honor the inazuma give." He smiles, returning the weapon, and Shotoku regards it, trying to believe that that is who he is.

Zensou continues, "The world needs your gift … to combat this spreading darkness. Will you let us teach you?"

Shotoku looks at Jirai. His usual smirk has been replaced with quiet surety. "Do what's right, Shock." Shotoku can only look at his friend with wonder. "And don't ever stray."

This is Jirai. His spirit revealed. Unselfish and

without pride.

Shotoku turns to Zensou, confidence soaring where before there was only uncertainty. His head rights itself, his shoulders broadening, and, with a nod, he reveals his will. "Show me."

THIRTEEN

Fulguris Mountains

Shotoku stands on a grassy hill below light-gray skies. He mimics Spark Hand's movements. "From me you will learn how to control and unleash lightning with perfect timing. You will feel the eddies of ions, learn to project and attract. Resistance to current causes heat and pain. The trick is to let it flow and to do so quickly. Nature is fickle, as much an enemy as a friend. It can deceive you with a low-current feint and then fry you with its real attack." He walks over to a well-groomed garden with rows of different plants. He touches a few of the varieties as he speaks: "This is crackleweed. Sparkthorn. Lightning bamboo: very dangerous. All these are tremendous sources of energy you can use during battle." Shotoku smiles, enjoying the idea. "Now stand in this crackleweed." He is uncertain as he roots his feet in the plants and static causes them to adhere to his legs. Sparks snap at his pant legs. "Now amp up," orders Spark Hand.

"What?" Shotoku can feel the plants filling his body with a lethal charge. "I—"

"Do it before I attack you!" His face dire, Spark Hand draws his sword and inches toward the lightning bamboo. Shotoku hesitates and the monk charges him, yelling. Shotoku moves his arms, emitting a tremendous bolt, scared of its magnitude. The monk throws black dust into the air as he rolls away and the lightning bends, chasing the dust to ground far in Spark Hand's wake.

"I could have killed you," Shotoku yells at the monk.

"Not likely. It's a little countermeasure we like to use." He approaches Shotoku and nods, holding out a fist. Shotoku opens his hand as the monk spills black, metallic sand into his palm. "A little of this goes a long way and can turn a lethal charge into a waste of energy." He smiles, "No pun intended. That's a little monk humor."

Shotoku grins, begrudgingly, "Hilarious."

"You saw how much more powerful your bolt was, though, did you not?" Shotoku grins, impressed. "Now observe." He leads him to a tree stump several feet away. "Here is a natural bolt." Spark Hand motions with his arms, undulating them like water, drawing on the waves to which he grows more and more attuned. A bolt springs forth, striking the stump, but it only chars a bit of the wood and ignites a small fire, which quickly dissipates. Next, he walks over to the lightning bamboo and crouches low, throwing out his arms palms up and fingers squeezing an invisible force. His arms shake and glow as he rises. Suddenly, Shotoku can see the blue aura as tendrils of energy from the bamboo are sucked toward his forearms. Shaking, Spark Hand releases the power which streaks through the air. In a terrific boom, the stump explodes. Shotoku is knocked to the earth as he is showered with splinters. Picking them off of his shirt, he crawls over to the smoldering pit that has replaced the stump. "You okay? Sorry," says the monk. "See the difference?"

He returns an absurd look: "Ah, yeah."

"Do you know why it explodes?"

"No," he says, getting to his feet with the monk's help.

"The explosive force unleashed is nothing more than the simplest of elements: water."

"But how can that be?"

"The lightning superheats the water or sap in the tree. The water rapidly turns to steam and, if trapped, will rend the material that contains it. Even stone walls have been known to explode with great force when stricken."

"That's true. I knew that this happens, but not that it was moisture rather than the lightning itself that causes the destruction." Then he realizes something and smirks at the monk. "It was you at the castle. Months ago."

Spark Hand smiles and bows, "In the flesh."

"You were invisible. How did you do that?"

"Ha, I will teach you, but it is quite inefficient. It allows you to hide only. Motion disrupts the effect."

"Amazing." Shotoku walks, examining the garden, looking at the monk and smiling, and exploring the new ideas igniting in his mind.

+++++

Silent Thunder attacks Shotoku again and again, relentless in his speed, technique and ferocity. His clothes smolder while fresh cuts and straining muscles sear with pain. They battle in a room in which metal bars are built in flush with the floor and crisscross the walls. He tries to mount an attack, but his air strikes are drawn into the beams harmlessly, while Thunder attacks using the beams to conduct strikes into Shotoku's legs and feet. He leaps, trying to avoid the beams, and falls against the wall: another setup by the monk. A giant surge of lightning enters his shoulder, blowing him across the room. Shotoku moans on the floor, panting and sweaty.

Silent Thunder lords over him, unsmiling. "Your father was much better at this."

Shotoku can't help but wince and smile. "Gee, thanks."

"It is vital that you learn to condition your bolts to navigate even the most complex of magnetic environs. You think you can really beat him?"

Shotoku stands slowly. "At what, Thunder?"

"In combat."

"Am I going to fight him?"

"What are we doing here, if you are not?"

Growing irritated, he snaps, "I don't know, Thunder. Maybe he'll give up. Maybe he'll see you and quiver like a glow jelly. Maybe he'll settle for a game of Spires."

"You have his temper."

"Fiss, you're chatty for a guy with Silent in his name. Are we done?"

"Hardly. We go again, but this time you strike me."

This gives Shotoku pause. "So you're gonna let me strike you? Finally the good part," he quips, but his adrenaline increases as his fear mounts.

"Yes, if you can. Do you think that we would inflict that which we ourselves would not endure?"

Despite its being Shotoku's turn, Silent Thunder hits him with bolt after bolt as he struggles to mount an offensive in a room fraught with magnetic vagaries. Finally, Silent Thunder sends a bolt through a beam that Shotoku redirects without resistance through his arm, then his body, discharging it with a forceful back kick to the monk's chest. Taken off guard, Silent Thunder flies through the air and hits the wall, but he regains composure and, using magnetism, lands deftly on his feet. Shotoku's face wears surprise, but the monk only looks him up and down, reassessing. For the first time, he grins, says "Good," and attacks, lightning illuminating the room. "Again!"

+++++

Shotoku enters a room filled with glass vials, bookshelves and instrumentation. A balding man with pepper-gray hair busies himself adjusting various knobs around a rotating iron bar which stops and starts in quick jerks. Shotoku is at once fascinated by the device. He approaches slowly behind the man, who doesn't notice until he is practically on top of him. Startled, the man falls, casting several sheets of paper into the air.

Shotoku doesn't react, just stares at the man and back to the device. "Are you making the bar move with magnetism?"

The man is appalled and embarrassed at having

fallen, but quickly swaps his anger for the boy's enthusiasm. "Why, yes. Do you know magnetics?"

"Only a bit. But why? What is the point of this?"

"Well, what is the point? My boy, great things could be achieved by this."

"Like what?" asks Shotoku, truly interested.

The man is clearly flattered, but composes himself and gets up from the floor. "I am Terrus, and I am considered something of an expert in lightning and magnetics around here. And you are?"

"Oh, Shotoku, Prince of … er, nothing."

"Ah yes, of course. Niwashi told me you'd be coming by." Terrus composes himself, comfortable in having categorized the boy and reestablished order to the world. "Now, you are here to learn, not quiz me as to the purpose of my devices. Here you will study the rules of lightning, its properties and methods." Shotoku smiles, liking Terrus immediately and ready to listen to his passionate teachings with the eagerness of lightning seeking the ground.

+++++

Zensou and Silent Thunder stand in a small gazebo high upon the mountain. Smoke rises from a few braziers filled with fragrant embers of cedar and sandalwood. Zensou searches the horizon, troubled by his friend's words.

"This cannot continue, Zensou. He is too dangerous."

"And so we abandon the challenges that enter our life?"

"He melted the practice room! Do you know the power that it takes to summon enough current to get past the spires and through the roof? He is an unknown and could be turned so easily," Silent Thunder warns, eyeing the back of his master's head, knowingly.

"Are you going to invoke my son's name? Now whose heart darkens?"

"I will not let history repeat itself."

Zensou turns, eyes soft. "Thunder, I know you mean well, but I can't deprive anyone of a chance to succeed or fail. You should know that." The monk diverts his gaze and clenches his teeth. "I will sit with him. In the end, if he chooses a dark path, you may do your worst."

Shotoku approaches slowly, not wanting to disturb his venerable teachers. "You sent for me, Zensou?"

Silent Thunder flashes him an unwelcoming visage, turns, cloak ruffling in the wind, and leaps off of the cliff. He rises a moment later, rapidly ascending on a bolt of lightning. He quickly recedes into the distance.

"Please sit, Shotoku. Do not mind him. He's a bit upset you destroyed his training room."

"Yeah." He rolls his eyes and frowns. "I told you I cannot control it."

"That is why we are here. It is not enough simply to learn the weapons of the warrior; you must also learn the mindset. Even ordinary people will acknowledge that they cannot effectively obtain their goals if they are fearful of the consequences. The consequences of one's actions, especially the dire ones, need to be predicted. This is so that when they arrive, the person may immediately surge forward. He is not shocked, but unfolds another aspect of his plan. A warrior enters the battle already cut; in his mind he has even seen his death. And when this fierceness is beheld by his enemies, it shakes them to their core."

"So you eliminate the fear of death?"

"Exactly. All fear springs from the fear of death. Social failures, loss of one's trade, all these threaten what enables a healthy existence. Loss of money leads to lack of food and starvation. A loss of social standing by breaking of the law can make you an outcast and greatly impede your existence. Explore your fears and you will find one behind them all: the fear of death." Shotoku considers. "There is one other thing, Shotoku. Worse than a forced physical death is the one you succumb to when your conduct deviates from the conduct you esteem. Betray your ideals and you will soon find yourself slamming into the cell walls of your own guilty mind. And no man lives long in that confinement."

Struggling with these concepts, Shotoku asks, "How can you destroy an emotion? What about fear for the fate of those I love?"

"Yes. You may even have to give your life to protect them, but what more can you do? If we may agree that life is not inherently good, that its prolongation is not our greatest accomplishment, then what does it matter when we die, but only … how."

"I do not want them to suffer."

Zensou hits him on the head. "You are not dead, yet. That is but a possible outcome we must accept. Death is the losing of this game called life and well-laid plans shall lead us to more fruitful outcomes. How to inflict pain is not all that you shall learn here and has little to do with what we are about." Shotoku waits, listening. "When the barriers of your life fall, life becomes simple again. Like when you were young. No longer do you question whether or not you should do the right thing, because fear is a thing of the past. 'What *is* the right thing to do?' becomes the only relevant question. This is your new dilemma. What will you do with your life? Should you become a farmer? Should you avenge your brother? Should you fight to protect another kingdom? Why? Should you even try to make sense of it all?"

Shotoku rolls his eyes and sighs, "I thought you said it made things simple."

"Ahh, but this is where the quest for knowledge begins. Where it becomes an obsession. The more we learn, the more the world takes shape and truth emerges. It is why we build libraries and fill them with all that we learn. We give it to others. Sacred, hard-won knowledge. And this knowledge gives us the power to make wiser decisions. That is why we celebrate the most learned of warriors: because they can make the truest choices, where the ignorant can be manipulated by their masters."

"Like I was manipulated. No wonder Thunder hates me." Zensou tries to object, but he stops him. "No, I can admit it. In part, because that is not me anymore." He laughs, lightly. "It took me a lot longer than my brother. He was six at the battle of Lunabi. Zarushi was the brave one. He didn't hesitate to try and help the people being exterminated. What could he do? He was a skinny thing." Tears in his eyes, he smiles sadly. "Maybe he just didn't belong in this world."

"How can you say that when his memory carries so much for you? The bright burning of the defiant burns unforgettable."

"I wouldn't know. I've done nothing my whole life but the bidding of an evil king. Never resisted. Never cared enough to discover the truth."

"Few learn without having to endure misfortune themselves."

Shotoku sees Jirai chatting with the female monk. She laughs, but regards him patiently, enduring some silliness.

"I may choose death if you keep talking."

Zensou stares at Shotoku gravely before bursting into laughter. "Good! Now let us set peace aside and, if we wish to lament fate, let it be for the fate of our enemies."

+++++

Thunder and lightning punish the mountainside as Aurora unleashes one of her storms. The strikes melt rock and sand into glass, producing razor-sharp stalagmites that occasionally bristle with translucent shards that claim the life of the unwary. Several inazuma climb the steep rock faces, getting closer to the lightning strikes. The sky glimmers green, blue and red with the stirring, ever-present flow of energy. They raise their arms and the lightning strobes, their silhouettes dark in the swirling lights of the blue night. From afar, the eyes of the inazuma dance, resembling a caravan of glow ants.

The inhabitants of the Iridian monastery disappear inside to safety. As rain begins to fall, Shotoku runs into Jirai and the female monk by chance and they duck into the main hall.

Entering the warmth of the empty hall, they relax and are immediately drawn to the massive fireplace.

"Have you met Midori?" Jirai asks.

"No. It's a pleasure," says Shotoku, pausing before

sitting, but Midori just smiles at him as she adds a log to the fire, her green eyes equally brilliant. Her long, blonde hair is held up in a complex knot and pierced by what resemble several metal chopsticks. She wears a blue long-sleeve shirt that reveals her shoulders and is snug on her body and a short blue skirt over knee-high boots. Small knives are sheathed on her arms below the shoulder and a long, curved sword is at her hip. She looks altogether feminine while simultaneously deadly.

Shotoku sits as Jirai disappears, returning a moment later with three mugs. They all take a seat, Shotoku wincing as he sits.

"Gee, Shock, you've looked better. Tough training, huh?"

He sneaks a glance at Midori and she returns a knowing smile. "You could say that. Oh, I'm going to enjoy this, though," he says, eyeing the lager. They clink their mugs and drink deeply. The storm rages outside.

"Bad storms up here," says Jirai, looking at the ceiling.

"Thank the gods. It's the only way I get a break." He leans back and sighs, enjoying the brew, taking another swig. "What have you been doing, anyway?"

"Well, we don't all wield lightning. Dori has been training me and the lads to fight monks with conventional weapons. Very knowledgeable lass."

"Your friend has quite the ego," comments the monk.

Jirai laughs, reveling in her attention. "Why go through life unnoticed, I say. Right, Shock?" Shotoku only laughs and shakes his head. The storm grows louder outside and they are forced to raise their voices. "She's the one who gave me that crossbow that saved your arse. The lightning one."

His eyes brighten, remembering the monks in the library. He nods and yells in an attempt to be heard over the lightning, "That was amazing." They look at each other nodding, somewhat disconcerted by the racket outside. They finish their drinks and Midori grabs them for a refill.

"She reminds me of Makiko. Her eyes. I think of Makiko's eyes all the time. They were like a harbor in a storm," says Shotoku, melancholy with the memory. Jirai smiles.

Jirai and Shotoku look at each other, trying to speak a few times, but cut off by thunder. Shotoku points in the monk's direction and back at Jirai, trying to ask if they are romantic, but Jirai doesn't understand. With a questioning look, Shotoku points again, first at her and then him, then presses the tips of his fingers together to affect kissing. Again, Jirai just looks puzzled. Finally, in frustration, Shotoku pretends he has a woman in his arms and kisses the air. Midori comes around the corner and sees Shotoku's pantomime. Disgusted, she sets the mugs on the table and, pointing at Jirai, looks at Shotoku questioningly. She lowers her face down to his and Jirai gives Shotoku a worried look, askance. She gets closer, dropping her lips to his neck, and sparks crackle and snap as she kisses him. He winces and looks at his friend as Midori sits, arching her eyebrow in silent affirmation. Shotoku smiles and mouths, "Okay," taking another drink.

The thunder outside sounds like it is rending the mountains from the earth as the storm continues.

Shotoku tries to yell over the noise to Midori, "Great place for a monastery! Prime location!"

"What?" she responds. Jirai screams something inaudible and Midori starts laughing. Shotoku and Jirai soon join her.

"I love this place!" yells Shotoku, laughing, unheard by anyone.

+++++

The next day, Zensou and Shotoku stand under an overcast sky amongst the smoking rocks of the mountains. Fresh glass cools, created by the innumerable lightning strikes. They walk, trying to avoid the razor-sharp protrusions. Shotoku thinks he feels something touch his hand and, when he looks, blood laces his fingers and drips onto an invisible glass shard he missed.

"Fiss. I didn't even see that." He stops, afraid of what else he may have missed. The cut is not bad, but the point is made. He adds fulgurite to his list of foes. He is about to wrap his hand when Zensou stops him.

"Not today. You'll want your hand bare." Shotoku looks at him, puzzled. "If you're going to beat the Kuroshi, you'll need to learn to coordinate everything we've taught you—"

"Okay, how's that different from what I've been doing?"

"—in the sky."

"Oh." He considers, then shrugs, "Okay, I've seen the way you jump. Seems simple enough."

"This is different. Reach out and see the magnetic eddies. From the stone, the trees, the skies." Zensou closes his eyes. Shotoku extends himself, as well, concentrating. "Find a good, strong lead and let it course through your hand. Can you feel the texture?"

He stops, dubious. "Texture? No."

"You must feel as quickly as the current … the speed of light. Heighten your senses, feel everything. Let no sensation go undiscovered."

Shotoku tries again. He dives deeper, forgetting the warmth of the wind, the smoke of the glass, the sweet smell of the rain. Time seems to slow as his heart beats and his mind accelerates. Suddenly, something bursts, assailing his senses, thousands of pin pricks like his whole body has fallen asleep. He rapidly breaks off concentration and dances uncomfortably. "Eeyada! It feels like I have sand all over me—through me."

"You do … and you do not."

"Zensou, how is it that you learned all this?"

"Shotoku, how is it that you did not?" They exchange a smile. "Now, grab the … 'sand' and hold on. We're going for a ride."

+++++

Hundreds of yards in the air, Shotoku and Zensou swing and sway through a lightning jungle, leaping from invisible leader to leader. Growing accustomed to this new sensation, Shotoku starts to see the world differently. Where he saw lightning before, now he also sees a system of transit, a means to propel himself across the land at great speeds.

Zensou's cloak flutters in the wind, a blur a good distance ahead. He challenges himself to catch the monk. Potential leaders flash kinetic in the wake of the passing humans coursing through the skies. The student chases his teacher, gaining altitude until he jumps and, unable to find another leader, plummets toward the earth.

Panicking, struggling to find a rich corridor of energy, Shotoku tumbles. As he nears ground, fresh leads are more ubiquitous and he finds traction, maneuvering to avoid the fulgurite and landing on a grassy patch near the monastery. He breathes hard in excitement and lies laughing as Zensou lands beside him. His exhilaration is brief, but it reminds him of how precious life can be. Zensou stands over him smiling.

"Saiak doesn't stand a chance. How many are you?"

Zensou looks into the distance. "We were once many, but now we number eight."

"Eight? Holy fiss. How many monks do they have?"

"Dozens, perhaps. That we've seen."

Considering this, Shotoku looks around. Several inazuma walk past them. One rolls down the mountain in a ball, then extends its body, hands pushing off of the earth, legs dropping as its torso rights itself. Without an arrest in its inertia, it transitions gracefully into a walk. "That was amazing. They are so agile. Can they fly, as well?" Shotoku asks.

"No, they are dexterous, but that skill seems to elude them. They can, however, deprive you of your electrical abilities. They can suck up all electricity around them," answers Zensou.

"And the ones sitting over there. What are they doing?" Several are bent over, fingers upon black sticks, sitting next to a makeshift thatch-covered stand. "They look like they're playing flutes," he guesses. Several sword blades lean against the wall, some blacked, others still raw iron.

"They are engraving the blades. With their fingers they burn their language into the blades they make for us. The blades are blackened—stronger than an iron blade—into what is called black steel." An adult inazuma, judging from the rougher surface of the creature, grabs a sword from the wall. He looks out to another inazuma, who looks up to another, twenty feet or so up the mountain. Their eyes pulse and the highest inazuma raises his arms, summoning lightning from the sky, channeling it to the next, and so on. The one in the stand directs the full power into the iron blade. It glows white-hot. They continue to channel, the highest inazuma tenaciously harvesting the bounty of Aurora. Signaling, they terminate the connection and the sword blade fades from white to red to black.

Recognition dawns on Shotoku's face. "My blade. When I saved the zuma child, an adult burnt my blade and engraved it."

"A rare gift for a lowlander. Terrus can tell you more about their ways, Protector of the Innocent." Zensou smiles and Shotoku dares to believe he sees pride in his face as well.

"Dozens of Kuroshi, you say. Zensou, isn't there some way we can beat those odds?"

"Against so many, I fear not."

Shotoku stands up, disliking his teacher's answer. "But with the right strategy—" Impatient with this subject, Zensou turns to go. "Then why are you teaching me?"

Zensou looks him square in the eye, his face one of empathy and calm. "Because it's not your fault. No man should carry the burdens of his youthful missteps. And your talents … you deserve to bring them to fruition."

"But I misled them. My people and my friends. Like

my father misled me." He sees Jirai approaching and looks at Zensou.

The monk blinks slowly, comforted and sure. "And, yet, some remain true. If you choose to pursue Saiak, however, I cannot help you find the way." He walks away, cloak rustling over the thick grass as Jirai approaches.

Shotoku looks off into the distance. Jirai munches on a glow apple. Standing next to Shotoku, he looks in the same direction as his friend and takes another juicy bite. "Hey, Shock. What are we looking at?" Shotoku turns and Jirai smiles at him, purposely exposing chunks of apple in his mouth, a trace of fluorescent juice on his lips. Shotoku bugs his eyes, looks away and laughs.

+++++

Jirai leaves Shotoku at the doorway of the monastery's observatory. Shotoku protests, "Hey, I know Terrus. Met him days ago."

Jirai just waves a hand in goodbye without looking back. "That's not my scene. Catch you later."

With consternation, he enters the room, quickly intrigued once again by the delicate instruments and vials, but then realizes he is not in the same room as before. This one is dominated by a large telescope aimed toward the star-filled sky. The northern lights dance across the night in blues, reds and greens.

"Big, isn't it," says Terrus, emerging from the back of the room. "Have you ever seen a telescope before?"

"What's it for?"

"For viewing the moons, stars, atmospheric activity … solar activity."

"Solar?"

"Our sun."

"Yeah, I know it means the sun." He examines the gleaming dials and numeric settings on the scope. "And you learn what? We—Aurora—have some relationship with these objects?"

"Oh this is a treat. What does the sun have to do with us? Everything, dear boy. Its eddies affect Aurora's lights, our atmosphere, magnetics, crop cycles ... tell us when to avoid travel, predict lightning storms. The solar discharge of energy is to blame for all of our woes here on Aurora." Shotoku just stares blankly at Terrus. "Our sun bombards our planet with waves of energy, sometimes small, sometimes large. This directly affects the frequency of lightning storms. If we observe the sun, we can predict fair or poor weather."

"That is amazing. You're serious?" His mind turns at the possibilities. "But doesn't it happen too fast? How much warning time is there?"

"A perspicacious question. About a day. Just enough time to take significant precautions."

"Fascinating. The world is so ... complex. The animals, the weapons, the weather." He glances around the room: "The devices you are creating." Terrus nods, an expectant look crossing his face. "I have *so* many questions. Why does lightning not hurt at low intensity? Why does it break glass, but not metal? Why do lodestones repel some metal and attract others?"

Terrus's eyes brighten and a smile burgeons. "Sit down. I will explain everything."

+++++

Shotoku stands up and pleads with the scientist, "But why, then, do we burn up, while these 'electrons' flow freely through metal?"

"It's the amps, not the volts, that kill us."

"But what does *that* mean?"

Frustrated, Terrus grabs a book from a shelf and hands it to Shotoku. "Clearly, you have a fertile and keen mind, but you need to revisit the basics." He walks over and looks into the telescope. "You know, just today I witnessed one of the largest flares I've ever recorded. I wouldn't go outside tomorrow, if I were you. I fear that we are revisiting a solar cycle that occurred a hundred years ago."

Shotoku looks at the book. "Basics? I've never even seen a book on the topic."

Terrus stops cold. "Hold it right there. You've never studied electricity?"

"No. Why?" A tall, blue-eyed inazuma enters through a passage on the opposite end of the chamber. Shotoku stands. He has become somewhat acclimated to their presence, but also has vivid memories of them tearing humans apart.

"Ah, Sprite. Finally you show up?" The inazuma's eyes begin to strobe. Terrus eyes him mischievously. "He says he knows you, Shotoku. Have you met?"

"No, I don't think so. You understand what he says?"

"Roughly. We've managed to figure out many of their words. Hold on Sprite, hold on." The doctor grabs a small device and begins tapping. Each tap produces a small spark of electricity.

"What are you telling him?"

"He says you are his … ah … father?"

"Gee, I think I'd remember that." Sprite walks over

to Shotoku and then behind him. Shotoku turns his head, watching out of the corner of his eye. "Ah, what do you think, doc?"

He shrugs, "This is a first for me."

Suddenly, Sprite grabs hold of Shotoku's arms. Shotoku struggles, but the inazuma's strength is too great. His mind reels and his sensations are flooded. Then the inazuma places his chin on top of his head. Wonder fills Shotoku's face as he begins to understand. "Sprite? Sprite? Is that you?" Sprite releases Shotoku, eyes flashing, playfully.

"He says 'yes.'"

"Well, he was just a baby … a few months ago."

"Yes, that makes sense. He's not fully grown yet. They reach full adulthood in about six months."

"I saved him from a rava. Sprite!"

Shotoku holds up his hands and wills lightning toward Sprite. Sprite holds up his hands, as well, and they exchange charges.

"No, stop! Not in here!"

Shotoku laughs, "I can't believe it. You got so big!"

Terrus struggles a moment, concentrating, and then laughs. "He says, 'You got so small.'" Sprite's eyes flicker rapidly and he turns his head back and forth.

"Doc, can you teach me to talk?"

"I'll teach you what I know. Let me make some copies. Will you come back tomorrow?"

Niwashi enters. "Ah, there you are. I knew he'd find his way here, Terrus. Scientifically minded, is he not? Shotoku, they'd like to see you in the main hall as soon as possible."

"Okay. Thanks for the book, Terrus. I'll be back.

Sprite, no rava hunting today, huh?"

Sprite leaves the room as well, but it is the young man who retains the scientist's attention. Niwashi looks at him and then after Shotoku. "He is an extraordinary young man. He stood here and grasped everything I shared with him regarding the electrical sciences, built upon it … intuited what I was going to say. But he lacked basic terminology. He's never studied formally?"

"He was my charge for the last year and I tried to inspire and steer his ideas. As you know, however, books were not allowed in Sterling, and I do not know the sciences as well as you."

"What an asset he could be."

"Yes. But he has a narrow path to negotiate. Damned narrow."

"Do you think he'll succeed? Much less survive?"

"Should he? After what he's been through? Raised by a father like his? If he does succeed, he'll be like no man I've ever met."

"You know Zensou. He will not budge." Terrus shrugs and gives Niwashi a matter-of-fact look.

The gardener walks to leave the room, but turns at the doorway, looking at Terrus askance. "Then, old friend, perhaps it is time to change sides."

+++++

Shotoku and Jirai enter a large circular theater of cinnamon-stone with an ornate stained glass dome through which light pours. The colored beams illuminate the fixed stone tiered seating that orbits the room. The eight monks sit and stand amongst sculptures of inazuma and men laboring together to create buildings. Paintings reveal geometrical formations of monks and inazuma, drawing great bolts of lightning from the skies and using it to mine the mountainsides. One especially baroque painting shows a structure of pure glass. He wonders if it is real or imagined. Finally, he moves to the tall glass stalagmite in the center of the chamber. In it are carved the iridescent words "knowledge" and "determination." These are the Iridians and they are no mean force, but he has not come this far only to hesitate now. The young men walk down the stairway leading to center stage, where Zensou awaits them.

"This council has been convened today to weigh the case for war."

"It has ever been our way to seek peace." Silent Thunder stands in the first row above Zensou and looks out at the others. Niwashi and Terrus enter the theater, but remain near the entrance, unconsciously wishing to avoid being noticed.

Jirai glares at the speaker without turning his head. "That's not what I heard. I heard you fought like demons before you were excommunicated."

"There was a short time when there was some ... infighting against other monks. But those were deviants of the true order and we fought in self-defense."

Jirai rolls his eyes and feigns exhaustion, sitting and putting his feet up. He stares at the ceiling, searching for patience. "So self-defense is okay? Who's the self-defense line drawn around? Just monks? Oh, wait ... just half of you, wasn't it? Convenient. Why don't you just draw it around yourself? Or since you're fond of extending it, why don't you just include all of the human race?"

"There is just so much a person can do."

Jirai is quick to retort, "Great. Draw up your make-believe groups, categorize by height, color and shape and make sure it doesn't disrupt your partitioned little life. Meanwhile, the innocent are suffering."

Zensou attempts to put a halt to the bickering: "You would have us break ourselves upon a tide that cannot be held back."

"You're damn right I would! I thought life was secondary to you, but it seems you've forgotten just what that creed materializes into: danger," flares Jirai.

"They are right, Jirai. Stop," says Shotoku, quietly. He looks away at the floor in surrender and acceptance. "It does mean danger, and acceptance of it." He regards the monks. "They have done their bit for the lowland peoples. This burden belongs to Sterling. To me." He makes eye contact with each monk, finally resting on Zensou. "And when I place fear aside and open my heart to what is right, I understand what I must do. It is right for me and no other. And I do not hesitate to do it."

Upset at Shotoku's words, Jirai stares at him and then turns to the monks. "Look, just say you're scared to fight and we'll accept that, okay?" Thunder smolders at the insult, but Spark Hand restrains him. Jirai rests his crossbow across his lap, lazily pointing it in the direction of Thunder's feet. Midori gives Jirai a disapproving look, but turns her head toward Zensou, trying to read the room.

"I'm leaving and I don't ask any of you to follow. You have all taught me so much and I don't know how to repay you, except to do my most to end the threat to these lands. To see you in the lowlands again … it could be a true renaissance." Shotoku's eyes again fan the room. "It will be better for me alone. To find that place of war in a man's soul and forget life and what could be. And to become the embodiment of sorrow to my enemies." Spark Hand fidgets, looking to Zensou, seeking the smallest reflection of the righteous flame that burns in this young man.

Sympathetic, Zensou tries to reason with Shotoku. "We have spoken and it has been decided. We are extending you an invitation to stay—here with us. To live as an Iridian. To live in peace."

By the looks on some of the monks' faces, he can see that the vote was not unanimous. Zensou has used his influence to gain him a place at the monastery. It makes what he has to say more difficult. "You honor me, but you know what I must do. You all are truly a beacon to follow, and I am sorry for any part I have played in your banishment." He bows slightly and leaves, cloak coursing through the air in his wake.

Spark Hand stands. "Well, I will be fissed if he's going alone. With some of us, there may be a chance." Several eager young monks stand, as well.

"Chance for what? They are too many," insists Thunder.

Enraged, Spark Hand points after Shotoku: "And yet the brave ride out to meet them."

Frustrated, Zensou shows anger for the first time, "Do not speak to me as if teaching a lesson, Spark Hard. I lost a son to the cause of the lowlands. And I will lose no more of you. With only Mujong left to resist, there is little we could do. The foolish boy will be crushed." Not even Zensou is content with the words he utters, but his duty transcends personal desire. "I forbid any of you to go." Jirai sits listening in disbelief.

Midori begs, "But, Zensou, we can't just—"

"We can and will. Perhaps he'll come to his senses."

FOURTEEN

Kingdom of Sterling

Iigh above the castle walls, abutting the main tower of the keep, a veranda adds a warm touch to the cold stone walls. Beams as thick as the trees they once were form a lattice of support below. An immovable two-beam railing skirts the edges, painted dark red with detailed inlaid wooden carvings of flowers at the midpoint between each post.

Saiak stands on the castle's veranda surveying the vast, dark army in the fields below. The tiny dots of the inazuma's red eyes glow as they stand surrounding the spires like spokes on a wheel, hands upon one another as they recharge. Maji, in battle dress and an amigasa, stands next to Saiak.

The thick boards do not creak as Kurukov walks across the balcony and stops behind them. "The search goes on, but we haven't been able to locate Shotoku."

"I don't like it. Maji: take some of your best men and find him. Destroy anything you see along the way. Eventually, we'll obliterate something that he cares enough about to come out of hiding." Face still hidden, Maji nods and leaves the veranda.

"The rebel attacks have lessened. Perhaps you've broken the boy."

"But Mujong is as tenacious as ever. Any news from the sun-gazers?"

"None of value, but that doesn't stop them from outrageous demands. Their requests for iron ore and glass have no end. They build huge telescopes and point them at the stars. What is this all about?"

"Their goals are more important than you realize. Even a slight increase in solar activity can make the difference between a fast and deadly zuma and a slow, dumb one. Pick the most demanding gazer and hoist him up the main spire, though, for good measure."

Kurukov smiles and nods, "My thoughts exactly. A charred corpse should quiet them down."

"We need to be ready to move at a moment's notice. I want hourly reports from the gazers."

"Aren't we throwing away the element of surprise by sending Maji?"

Saiak looks at Kurukov for the first time. "Only if he fails, and he never has. His talents are unmatched."

"But if he is bested, our advantage will be lost. The monks have great knowledge—"

Saiak returns his view to the grasslands and speaks dismissively, "It won't matter. I eliminated the monks as a threat long ago. Only a handful survive." Saiak smiles, "And I taught that traitor, Zensou, what happens when he denies me what is mine—I killed his son. Mujong will fall and I will be king of these lands. Thank you, Kurukov, but you may leave the battle planning to me. Don't you have a sun-gazer to kill?"

"Of course, sire." Kurukov turns and leaves the veranda.

"Maji? Bested?" Saiak scoffs at the impudence. "His skills are like few I have ever seen. Nothing can stop us now."

+++++

Kingdom of Mujong

"Archers!" Between two copses, Finn stands at the head of a phalanx of fifty Mujong soldiers in gleaming silver breastplates, helmets and swords. The swordsmen kneel as the archers, directly behind them, lift their bows. The line bristles with sharp, wooden, headless arrows. Makiko stands next to Finn, face grimy, but eager for the fight.

Several dozen hunched, black, red-eyed inazuma hop and roll toward the Mujong, dim and hungry, followed by two dozen men and five Kuroshi monks in amigasa.

"Fire!" The arrows fell many inazuma, but they continue to barrel forward. "Swordsmen!" They rise again and, well disciplined, wait. A short distance away, portable spires have been erected. Just before Finn orders the attack, Makiko runs down the line of soldiers, allowing her sword to touch each of theirs, and then leads the charge into the enemy.

"For Mujong!"

Inspired, they charge forward, twice the men they

were. Finn curses, charging. The two forces clash at the spires. Electrical energy discharges in all directions, but much of it is absorbed by the strategically placed spires. All suffer shocks when they strike the inazuma, but it barely registers on many of their faces. These are hardened veterans, and the inazuma soon waver. One of the monks joins the thick of the fray, driving the inazuma forward. He cuts down men with surprising agility and channels extra power to the creatures. Makiko attempts to flank one of the other monks, but is detected and forced to battle for her life. Finn fires a wooden arrow, but the monk motions and the arrow incinerates in midair. He and a contingent of troops rush the monk attacking Makiko and, for the moment, he is distracted. Then, just as suddenly, Finn is slammed by a bolt of lightning and sent rolling across the earth. Seeing their captain in jeopardy, the troops rally and finish the inazuma scourge, but the monks pose an altogether more dangerous threat. The New Sterling men, however, lose heart at the loss of their inazuma allies and turn to run. The Mujong are surprised to see the Kuroshi pursue their fleeing force. Mindlessly running across the battlefield, the monks and Aurora herself cut them down without mercy. They writhe violently, sickeningly illuminated before falling to the earth.

Makiko helps Finn up as they catch their breath, witnessing the grisly scene. At a distance, slowly, the five monks turn to face them again. She is unable to hide the despair in her voice: "Finn, we can't beat them. They know our tricks." Finn turns his head to her, still collecting himself and wincing in pain, his eyes wild and unsure. The Mujong reform their lines. "Finn, we need to retreat." Rivulets of electricity dance over the bodies of the monks as they take their time approaching. Unhearing, Finn raises his sword, readying to signal the attack.

The monks halt their approach, cloaks blowing the breeze. Beneath their amigasas they gather the lethal potential to dispatch the remaining Mujongese. Makiko and Finn exchange a final look of respect and affection. Then a gleam appears in Makiko's eyes, growing as they turn to see what new horror has come to manifest.

The monk in the center conjures a lightning bolt from the sky, grabs a hold of it and rises into the gray. Tumbling in midair above the Mujongese, he wrangles several bolts into one and hurtles downward wielding their combined destructive might. The super-bolt explodes in the center of the Mujongese, burning, disintegrating. A sonic boom follows, leveling anyone surviving the strike.

Makiko and Finn pick themselves up from the ground, stumbling to the tree line as the monks send bolts through the surviving soldiers. Noticing their escape, the monks flick tiny blades through the air which stick in the trees around their retreat. The trees erupt in fire and heat as they send bolt after bolt in their wake, aided by the magnetic knives.

Quickly emerging from the opposite side of the small group of trees, Makiko and Finn have no recourse but to traverse an open field. The monks stand at the edge of the glen and watch. Makiko's heart sinks when she looks back and sees one of the monks raise his hat, revealing his face: Maji. Tears fill her eyes as she helps Finn. Trying to stay low, they fall often, eventually crawling. Finn rolls over and faces the sky, gasping and still smoldering. "Finn, get up. Finn!" she pleads.

"The clouds," he says. "Look."

She looks up. "What? Come on." But then she sees something.

Maji sees electricity course over the surface of the skies from afar. Strikes approach, flash, flash, flash, in a line as if a single potent cloud is racing on the wind. Is it gaining speed? thinks Maji, as the power of the cloud becomes tangible. He frowns as his armor magnetically pulls at his straps, and his eyes widen as he is stricken by realization. The force of the entire storm appears to be bearing down on them.

The amigasa-wearing Iridian monk lands at the feet of the Kuroshi, bringing the full latency of the skies to bear. Four Kuroshi are hurled back through the forest, two bouncing hard off of tree trunks, bloody and unmoving, while two luckily miss the hard timber and rise slowly. Maji manages to repel himself magnetically from the earth, but careens burnt and disoriented toward where Makiko and Finn lie in the grass. Maji gathers himself, disbelieving he has been knocked down, and rises quickly. The other two monks hobble out of the woods toward him, fleeing the Iridian. The stranger turns calmly, rising from the crater he has created, face hidden under his low-brimmed straw hat. The two monks eye the newcomer cautiously as time slows. Silence followed by the soft low rumble of thunder from afar. One Kuroshi slowly adjusts his stance, legs widening. In response, the Iridian pivots his heel almost indiscernibly. In a sprawl of light, blinding flashes sear the air; tendrils of death light the pained visages of the Kuroshi. The two try to return fire but do so in haste and off target, bolts careening off into nothingness as their skin blackens and their bodies glow a molten hue. Then they are crumpling to the ground, smoldering, death replacing the life in their eyes. Only a moment since the flashes, thunder ripples the air sending shock waves, blowing clothing, hair and dirt away from the fallen corpses. The newcomer drops his extended arms to his side and straightens, stepping over the enemies he once feared.

The monk approaches until just out of attack range, cloak blowing in the wind. Finn and Makiko watch from the ground. "Maji."

"You Iridians will suffer for your meddling," promises Maji.

The monk removes his amigasa slowly and Shotoku's face is revealed. Shock and fear flash across Maji's face before he hides his reaction with a sneer. Makiko and Finn evince awe and wonder. "I do not have the honor of being an Iridian."

"Your powers have grown," spits Maji.

"Don't bother surrendering, Maji. I'm gonna kill you no matter what you say."

Maji bares his teeth and raises his arms slowly, visibly drawing lightning from the air. "Big words … just like your Mujong whore."

"Amp up, you son-of-a-bitch!"

Light, bolts, heat, wind and silence dominate an exchange whose brilliance and fury Makiko and Finn's eyes are unable to behold. Finally, the cacophony of thunder lays the grassland flat.

The opponents peer at each other, both smoking with the grass around them catching fire. Maji tries to conceal the pain in his side and the hint of fear in his eyes. Shotoku stands strong and undiminished. They clash again, this time with hand and foot. Shotoku suddenly stops Maji cold with a magnetic push to his metallic armor. The monk looks at his armor and back at Shotoku's, lowering his brow and sneering. Shotoku smiles and invites him to attack. He does, but now Shotoku pulls magnetically. Anticipating, Maji counters and a magnetic push-pull volley ensues. They dance and strike without touching, repulsing knives, pulling legs and causing imbalance: they look like awkward dueling children.

Maji affects a stumble and draws Shotoku in for an attack. He quickly regains his feigned imbalance and strikes fast and hard upward, only a blur. But Shotoku is not there; he leaps over his enemy in an arch, firing bolt after bolt. Hammered, Maji is forced to roll awkwardly away. Shotoku lands nimbly behind him and offers his own smirk. Maji looks Shotoku up and down, approvingly. "Who trained you? You did not learn this on your own."

"I guess you thought you had it all figured out."

"Meddling Iridians. I'll hunt them down when we're through with the lowlands. Yes, I will look forward to that."

"I could die here today and be happy, if I could just kill you and avenge my brother. My father and the rest of the war be damned."

"You are his son, I can see that. You may as well join us and accept your nature."

"My nature you will never understand."

Before Maji can react, he's hit with two lightning

bolts from the woods, thunder booming. Using the latency, he summons a bolt and disappears into the sky, leaping from bolt to bolt away. Jirai emerges from the trees, looks at Shotoku and then his crossbow. "I mean, I really love these things. Shock, did you see that? See?"

"I would have liked to finish that." Shotoku makes his way to the tree line where they are joined by Finn and Makiko.

"You don't talk while fighting, Shock. Haven't I taught you anything? Ya talk when you have them tied up. Besides, he was just sitting there." Shotoku's face remains peeved. Jirai shrugs, expressing consternation at having to explain. "Easy shot."

Shotoku turns from Jirai to Makiko, but lowers his chin, allowing his amigasa to better conceal his face. Makiko wants to approach, but hesitates at his reaction.

"Shock!" She embraces him, her relief washing away the strength that held her upright. Shotoku allows her just a moment before breaking contact. Surprise registers on her face. "You're not going to face me?"

"Makiko, you should know … some things I've done."

Her face is sad, but reassuring. "We all have. It's war, Shotoku." She begins toward him again. Hesitantly, he raises his face to hers, eyes fragile, dark hair blowing in the wind.

"Can you forgive?"

A few quick mutual steps and they embrace, holding each other tight. They press their lips to each other's tears, smiling, shutting out the world if only for a moment.

A horse, then others, are heard galloping through the

woods behind them. Char-ton, Starov and Chillson approach, horses breathing hard, and dismount, but Makiko and Shotoku refuse to let each other go. "Jirai, you almost lost us!"

"That's not as hard as it sounds," Jirai jibes. Shotoku slowly removes his amigasa. Char-ton sees Shotoku and hits Chillson to get his attention, surprise on both their faces.

"You're reckless. You rode across open fields! Open fields!" Starov looks at Makiko and Finn in exasperation. Then his eyes turn to Shotoku. "Oh … Shotoku." He straightens, composing himself, and scrutinizes his former captain.

"Well, I could tell there was a battle going on, and this guy always needs a hand."

Wide-eyed and still in shock, Finn interrupts, "You are a changed young man, Shotoku. Your power is extraordinary. You saved us." He looks at Makiko, her arms still around Shotoku. She gazes at him, appreciatively. "I was wrong about you."

"I wasn't," Makiko adds.

"But they did betray our kingdom."

"They did what they were told without questioning why. Isn't that the mark of a loyal subject? You are lucky to be in the service of a benevolent ruler. They weren't."

"We didn't come here just to bail Shock out of trouble … again. We rode as fast as we could." Jirai glances at Starov, who frowns. "Terrus said to tell you, Shock. That you'd understand. He said there has been unprecedented solar activity. That tomorrow night we'll feel the surge and the zuma will be reinvigorated—not to mention that anywhere but inside will be extraordinarily dangerous for humans."

Char-ton continues, "On the way, we saw Saiak's forces moving for Mujong. Rava, catapults, humans, zuma and monks."

Shotoku closes his eyes and drops his head. Then he raises it again, but his dismay has changed into a smile. "Ha, ha, ha, he thinks we can't win."

"The foundation of Saiak's new dominion and whatnot. We can't beat that many," states Chillson.

"Thinks he's got it all figured. If I could only get close to him, I might be able to end the attack before it begins."

"It's not so simple, laddie. Twelve of the monks broke off from the group at a gallop in the direction of Mujong. We believe they mean to infiltrate Mujong ahead of their main forces."

"We overheard plans for an attack tomorrow; then we had to maneuver away. Their entire force was striking camp, moving with haste," Char-ton adds.

"Tomorrow?" Finn's pride is pricked by the implication that Mujong could be so easily overrun. "They don't have enough time. Even at a forced march all night and day. They'll be out of position, tired and hungry. This could be the opportunity we've been waiting for."

"No. Even with an exhausted force, you'll be destroyed."

"Why?" Finn balks, incredulous, his experience making what he hears suspect.

"If what I have heard from Terrus is correct," Char-ton interrupts, "the size of the projected solar storm means that there will be lightning of tremendous frequency and magnitude. Humans will not be able to endure it, even with portable spires. The only safe haven will be in the castle."

"How do you know that? We'll be safe within our spired walls."

"Perhaps that is the mission of the twelve," Starov says.

Shotoku nods gravely, "To somehow impede the spires' effectiveness."

"But how are twelve monks going to destroy the castle's spires?"

"I'm not sure, but if the Kuroshi are as knowledgeable as the Iridians, they no doubt have the means to lay waste to your fortress."

"Damn Iridians. Kenshi foresaw the need for an alliance and they turned us away." He looks back in the direction of his fallen men. "Why don't these monks aid us, if they are so powerful?"

"I tried to convince them to join us, but failed as well. I will go to Mujong and try and stop the twelve."

"Is that a joke? You are Mujong's greatest enemy, second only to your father. None of you would make it past the border."

"Ha! That didn't stop us before," Jirai jibes.

Finn tries to temper their capriciousness: "You will be shot on sight if you are caught trying to enter my kingdom. We can help you gain entry." Makiko nods, determined.

Starov places a hand on Shotoku's shoulder and gives a not unthreatening look, "We're not letting you go, lad."

Shotoku's voice quiets as he speaks with his elder, "Starov, I'm sorry. For Devukai. For everything."

"I know you are. I can see it in you. That's why we're going with you. We ride together again." Chillson and Char-ton nod their heads in agreement. Behind them, Jirai smiles, pleased with himself.

Shotoku's eyes glisten as his emotions swell. "I may be young, but I doubt if I will ever share a spire with truer companions than the ones I see before me."

Finn speaks as if witnessing a moment in time from afar, "And you're the one. The one with the power to unite us and to defeat this terrible threat."

Shotoku nods, little left of the uncertain boy who began this journey. "I will see it done."

They exchange looks, each appreciating the others' rare abilities. Shotoku places his hand under Makiko's chin and moves her face gently toward his. "And don't try getting away from me again. I'm sorry we didn't meet you, but, when this is over, I want nothing more than a long holiday in your eyes." She smiles, eyes inviting, arms still around his waist.

Starov nods and steps forward, white knuckles on his sword hilt. "Then we go back in together and end this ... for our fallen brothers."

+++++

Mujong/Sterling Border

Hoards of loosely organized inazuma march across Mujong's borders. Horses, catapults and rava are driven by the Kuroshi monks. They fly through the air, spurning human and beast alike. Kurukov and Saiak stand on a bluff overlooking their forces. Kurukov smiles as he sees Maji drop less than gracefully from the sky some distance away.

"It appears he who fails not has finally done so." Then to the monk, "If you look like that, what does your prey look like, Maji?"

The monk stops before Saiak, slowly brushing dust from his battle garb.

"What happened?"

"It's as you'd feared: Shotoku's powers have matured."

"To what degree?"

"Not enough to seriously challenge me," he lies.

Saiak says, unconvinced. "And, yet, you could not defeat him?"

"He had help."

"So we can expect him tomorrow. Good. When Mujong is destroyed, he will have no choice but to join us." Saiak makes a show at jubilance, but a tremor sneaks into his tone.

Maji nods, "They are all headed to Mujong."

"Excellent. You are not to harm Shotoku. Leave him to me. I have a surprise for him. Feel free to kill the rest." He turns away from his generals, hands rubbing hard against one another.

Maji smiles, adjusting his silver rings.

Behind him, Kurukov's face betrays concern at the news concerning Shotoku.

Without turning, Saiak speaks loudly, composure slipping, "What's wrong with you, Kurukov? You look like someone took your spire. You will soon be the lord of your own kingdom. Is that suddenly a problem? Because I can reward someone else. Someone less …

skittish."

Kurukov recovers his grit. "No, Lord Saiak, tomorrow the gods and your plan place the advantage upon our forces. No one can stand against such might."

"Good," Saiak offers. "Now see to it. Force march all the way to Mujong." His nostrils flare and, in his imagination, the smell of earth and rain already swims with the miasma of corpses. Destiny washes over his body as his spirit passes the final fork in the road. No way but the one he has chosen now. The smell and the decision result in slight nausea and his mouth waters, but his jaw sets firmly. "Death to all who oppose me, now and forever."

FIFTEEN

Kingdom of Mujong

Upon news of the invasion, citizens and refugees crowd the streets of Mujong in an attempt to reach the safety of the castle's spires. In the confusion, hooded Kuroshi drive several carts into the throng.

A guard halts the cart and another moves around behind. "Stop right there! What's all this?"

The monk does not remove his hood. "Water for the possible siege, on orders of the king. And spires."

"Check it," says the guard as the other throws back the blanket, revealing large cylinders and hollow conical spires. He holds one high, showing his partner.

"And that? A spire?"

The monk affects a drawl: "Just what they gave me." The guard is unhappy, but, pressed by the masses, waves them on. Upon gaining the inner courtyard, the four wagons break off in opposite directions.

"Look! The sky!" yells a woman. The luminescence of the northern lights spreads, chasing nightfall. The Mujong people look up in wonder and fear.

"It's the zuma! They're coming!" someone yells. The panicking people crowd the gate. At the sound of hooves, they turn to look at who approaches. Finn reins in his mount forcefully and the horse rears. The people fall silent as their eyes fix upon their captain.

"People of Mujong!" His horse circles, but he is disciplined and pats his mount's sweaty neck. "War is upon us. Never before have we faced such a threat. But our Mujong defenses, ever like the resolve of her people, are unbreakable."

The eyes of the people find some calm; long has this man overseen the protection of their lands and families. "Find now in you again, the will and courage that have made our kingdom a bastion of hope upon these tortured plains. Restore order and make ready your swords. And let us send these foreign hordes back into the wastes from which they came. Fight! Fight and win!" The crowd and guards on the walls, inspired, hold their weapons high and bellow in agreement. Finn dismounts and calls the guards to him, allowing Shotoku and his disguised team to pass unnoticed in the crowd.

Finn confides in the men, "We have been infiltrated."

"But sire!"

"Just trust it is true. I do not blame any of you, but listen to what we must now do. The towers are being sabotaged. All our men must fly to those locations. There you will encounter the lightning monks. Use caution."

More Mujong soldiers approach Finn to learn his will: "But, sire, no munitions entered, much less zuma or monks. We'd have noticed …"

"Strange times make for strange allies. I have sent men ahead to aid you in this conflict. Princess Makiko is among them. Now go, quickly. You men come with me. We must protect the king."

+++++

Char-ton and Jirai walk down the hallway stealthily, stopping outside an open stairway entry. Two Kuroshi monks stand on the stairs, one placing a large cylinder of water into the wall. The other waves his arms and produces an orb of ball lightning, pressing it slowly into the wall. Molten rock drips down the wall from the newly formed hole. They place another cylinder in the new hole. Char-ton leans back against the wall, thinking. Jirai gives him a questioning look.

"Water?"

"You've seen a wall hit by lightning … or a tree, right? Didn't you listen when the Iridians explained this?"

"Yeah. Well, no."

"It's the water trapped inside that causes the explosion. The water heats rapidly, expanding with tremendous force. When the ion storm hits, this spire will be struck, the water will boil and the wall and spire will explode. Smart."

"Fiss me. Okay, I'm taking a shot."

"Wait 'til they're clear of the cylinders. Otherwise, they could still detonate them."

"Are you saying you think I'll miss, you bastard?

When have I *ever* missed? You are something." Jirai levels his crossbows, aiming carefully. Char-ton clasps his hands together, looking to the ceiling in prayer.

Suddenly, voices are heard behind them: "This way men! To the tower!"

The two monks jerk their heads toward Jirai just as he fires. "Fiss it!" Jirai turns to face the approaching soldiers. "Could you guys keep it down? Can a guy just get a moment?"

"Jirai, we've got to get them before—"

"Huh? Naw, they're coming down." The two monks' bodies slowly roll to the bottom of the stairs. One is shot through the throat and one through the eye.

"What in the hell were you so mad about then?"

"I was aiming for his neck. He ducked."

+++++

A mass of soldiers engage two of the Kuroshi monks at the second tower. The monks magnetically jerk the metal-wearing soldiers to the ground, while repulsing metal-tipped arrows and swords. Their lightning bolts burn swatches of men to the ground and they leap over the soldiers, attacking from behind and above. Some men haphazardly hurl mobile spires into where the fray appears to be, but only succeed in attracting the full fury of the monks.

For a moment, the two monks stand side by side, cool in the face of the terrified soldiers. Then Shotoku steps from the lines, challenging. The monks flex and stretch bolts of lightning between their hands, smiling and taunting Shotoku.

Shotoku speaks to the Mujong soldiers, feigning esteem: "Whoa. They are really good. I like that, ah, hand-stretchy thing you're doing. Chilling." The monks stop smiling and drop their hands to their sides. "Say, stop me if you guys have seen these." Shotoku pulls out two metal balls, as big as fists. "These are called damas." Magnetically, one monk jerks them from Shotoku's hands, examining them as they float in front of his chest. Shotoku looks at the other monk: "He must be the young one."

Motioning forward, Shotoku magnetically crashes the two balls against the monk, sending him into the stone wall. Quickly, he launches forward through the air, spinning, body glowing with gathered charge. The second monk takes a step back in surprise, but manages to fire off a charge. Shotoku deflects it easily and lands, spinning, a foot arching through the air and emitting a powerful bolt down across the stunned monk at the wall. As he falls dead, the other monk, realizing their mistake, flees over the wall, but Shotoku uses a magnetic push to launch himself and tackles the monk midair. They tumble to the ground, shock on the monk's face, but he rises, drawing his sword. Shotoku's sword is already out as he hammers the Kuroshi from all directions. As the monk loses his balance, Shotoku knocks the his sword aside and turns, stabbing backward. His black blade quickly and decisively penetrates the monk's chest. Withdrawing his sword, he walks away, sheathing his blade. The monk slowly sinks to the ground, still uncomprehending. Shotoku looks to the soldiers.

"Make sure the tower is safe."

+++++

Two Kuroshi monks place the last cylinder into the wall, dust off their hands and descend the staircase. After emerging into the inner courtyard of the keep, however, they halt. Portable lightning spires now wobble where none were before. Chillson places one last spire with some effort.

"Mobile, my arse. These are heavy."

Starov emerges from the stairway door. Startled, the monks split directions, positioning themselves with the walls at their backs so as to be able to see both attackers.

Starov eyes them eagerly, savoring the challenge. "You guys won't be able to use your lightning real well, *if* we can keep you where you are. This is what a warrior lives for." Chillson turns grim, drawing his sword. "Take your last sip of life, because we're going to kill you … and whatnot."

The monks recognize that the long, deep roof above them is more than just bad luck; it is a part of their enemy's plan. "No shadow monk has ever been bested, but by his equal," one of them utters.

"Well, that's a relief. I thought you were going to say by someone who's studied the old kata and learned the secrets of ancient lightning fighting … which the Iridians were kind enough to share with us."

"I sense no metal on you. Even your swords—"

Chillson looks at his blade. "Yeah, they depolarized our swords or something like that. You should know, too, that he and I are really good with our swords. Like, 'the best they've ever trained,' I think is what the Iridians said … ever."

One monk recognizes the insignia of the Bright Guard and speaks, "We've already killed one of you. He died like a pathetic coward. Not worthy of the Kuroshi."

Starov clenches his jaw and says, "You're right. He

was worth a thousand of you."

The monk on Chillson's right lunges back toward the stairwell, firing lightning at Starov, but it's sucked into the spire nearest them as Starov ducks out of sight.

The other monk rolls toward Chillson and comes up with a powerful bolt while springing for the open air of the plaza. Chillson hurls magnetic pebbles into the air at the first movement by the monks. The lightning refracts, splintering in all directions, and Chillson charges, drawing and attacking with his sword in the same motion. The monk barely gets his sword out in time to block Chillson, but he is driven back, deep beneath the roofing.

The other tries to enter the stairwell guardedly, but Starov emerges to meet him with a flurry of attacks, so fast and assorted that the monk can escape only by falling backward and rolling to regain his feet.

Both engage in close combat with the monks, who try short lightning bursts combined with sword attacks. Chillson and Starov use the spires and their newly learned techniques skillfully—jumping and hopping, separating themselves from the magnetic ground—and soon gain the upper hand. As the Kuroshi grow more fatigued and desperate for escape, Chillson and Starov manage to disarm them. Weaponless and uncertain, they back toward each other, seeking mutual protection. As they sheathe their own swords, the monks exchange looks of disbelief, then dread as the members of the Bright Guard produce the black magnetic spikes given to them by the Iridians. As they begin a series of dance-like movements, the Kuroshi attack with lightning blasts. The lightning, however, cannot seem to penetrate the strange shield they have created. Slowly, the monks begin to see a potent web of ions invisible to the men creating it. Suddenly, Chillson and Starov attack, punching the spikes one after another into the monks in a flurry of hand-to-hand legerdemain. Now they allow their foes free passage as they orient their backs to the castle wall. But the monks waver. Each spike is radiating a tornado of ions like the Kuroshi have seldom seen, but they understand well their lore. Exhausted and bleeding from the spikes, they teeter under the roofing's edge and feel the call of Aurora's skies, pining to discharge via their corporeal shells. Starov and Chillson draw close to their enemies and, with a final kick, send them tumbling out into the lightning storm. Frantically, they reach for the spikes and look woefully to the sky. When they are hit by powerful lightning bolts from the super-storm, they explode in every direction.

Chillson scowls at the miasma as Starov spits, "That's for Devukai, you sons-of-bitches."

+++++

In the gardens just outside the keep, a small group of Mujong soldiers attempts to slow down a disciplined cadre of 12 Kuroshi monks wearing amigasa. They fire and throw wooden weapons at their enemy, but these monks dodge skillfully and kill with lightning those in whom courage outweighs caution. The soldiers edge mobile spires closer for protection. The king is bound and held tightly by a monk in the center. The monks back up to the tower and two of them sink a canister into the wall while protected by the others. Soldiers begin to gather on the battlements around the tower above, firing down upon their foes.

Finn emboldens his men: "Save the king! Save the king!" Then he speaks to the monks: "Your masters have deceived you. We could live together in peace. I have heard that you can be just. Please, now, release the king and we shall give you free passage from this place."

A monk next to the king strides toward Finn, removing his amigasa and revealing himself to be Saiak. "As usual, you have no idea with whom you deal nor the extent of our powers!"

Wide, quick gesticulations lead to enormous emanations of lightning from Saiak's fingers. Mujong soldiers are cut down, screaming in the light and heat made more fierce by the storm. They attack bravely and with discipline, but Saiak bests them with sword and current until he is confronted by Finn himself. Saiak attacks with vehemence, but he cannot best Finn, who stays low, tosses metal into the air and uses his environment masterfully. Then suddenly he is stricken by a bolt from behind. Smoldering on the ground, Finn sees that Maji has approached unseen.

Maji curls his lips at Finn, "We were interrupted before. I owed you that."

Saiak approaches, glancing appreciatively at the darkening sky filled with northern lights. "It's a beautiful day. The consummation of my revenge, my victory and, yes, peace. My peace. The one I dictate." Slowly and smoldering, Finn rolls over and stares up at Saiak. Then his face changes, as if something has occurred to him, and he begins to laugh. Saiak, unaffected, smiles broadly. "Yes, futility. You see it now."

"He's better than you." Finn continues to laugh.

"Shotoku is better than you. You created a perfect opponent for yourself. Turned him against you. You're so *stupid*." Saiak's eyes burn as electricity courses visibly across his body. Finn sees death and his face sobers. His voice barely audible, he declares, "For justice …"

"He's a whelp! Where is he?" Saiak looks around quickly and sees a wisp of fear in Maji's eyes.

"… for vengeance, …" Finn looks to the sky above Saiak and bares his teeth. "… he comes for you!"

His enemies look up just as Finn covers himself. Shotoku falls from the sky into the center of the Kuroshi monks, doggedly pursued by a lightning bolt the size of a house that is visible for miles. He protects the king and himself at the center, as an invisible wave of heat and thunder rises from his landing, knocking friend and foe to the earth. The earth turns to glass and splashes through the air while some Kuroshi evaporate into the ether.

Saiak rises, dazed, to the vision of Shotoku releasing the king from his bonds. The storm peaks, striking a few of the tower spires, but to no effect. The skies glow behind Shotoku, illuminating his silhouette, eyes afire with inner confidence. Saiak looks at the towers in confusion.

"You are defeated, father." The rest of the Bright Guard arrives. "We have undone your sabotage upon the towers. The canisters will not explode. This castle will remain a refuge until the storm dissipates."

Desperation seizes Saiak's, and then resignation. "I raised you. Our blood runs thick. How could a son turn on his father?"

"Tell that to my brother. You're a father to nothing but strife and despair."

"Despair? Boy, you know not of what you speak." Saiak rises quickly up over the top of the battlements as the Mujong and remaining Kuroshi reengage in battle.

"Shotoku, no," Jirai yells, but too late.

Shotoku rises with Saiak, but midair Saiak conjures a tremendous bolt from the clouds and, with all his effort, channels it into the canister they just embedded in the castle wall. Deep within, the water in the canister superheats and expands fiercely. It explodes brilliantly, obliterating the wall for several yards and sending rock tumbling lethally in all directions. The tower and spire teeter and crumble in a great cloud of dust. Saiak is thrown by the blast through the air and into the trees surrounding the castle, while Shotoku plummets to the grass just outside the wall. The Mujong soldiers and Kuroshi monks in the area lay at random across the ground.

+++++

Thousands of inazuma coalesce in waves ready to crash upon the castle walls, red eyes glowing in the darkness. Lightning flashes and leaps from creature to creature, revitalizing them after their forced march. The Mujong soldiers look out at them in fear while the townspeople prostrate themselves on the grounds of the castle courtyard. Powerful bolts strike the protective spires, but they do not explode, protecting all within. The inazuma begin to move toward the castle while beasts move catapults into position.

+++++

Shotoku rises and sees Saiak by the tree line. As

Saiak sees the bolts strike the towers without exploding, he looks to Shotoku and sneers. Numbers in their favor, the Mujong soldiers press the weathered Kuroshi amongst the rubble of the destroyed tower.

He yells across the noise of the storm, "Can we find common ground?"

Shotoku frowns, "How many times I wished you'd uttered those words! How many times, for just a trace of understanding! Now you would hear me?" Saiak is silent. "You've made that impossible. I may have wanted to please you before, but look at what you've done …"

"So you would have joined me?"

"You're mad, Saiak."

"It's those friends of yours that drew you from me. I'd kill them all given the chance."

"No, you pushed me away and live or die, I'm on their side."

"Then you choose death."

"Yes, over a shameful life."

"Shotoku!" Jirai's voice makes it to Shotoku's ear and he turns his head. Jirai is fighting, but wants to make sure his friend is not hurt. Saiak scowls and launches into the air, fleeing, riding lightning in the same manner as the Iridians.

Shotoku looks back at Jirai. "It's our chance to end this. Destroying him may break their will."

"You can't go alone! Don't go!"

Although he wants to stay and help, Shotoku knows his father is the key to winning this battle. If he can show the enemy that Saiak is defeated, they may call off the attack. When Jirai is forced to fend off another foray by the enemy, Shotoku takes the chance to pursue his will without remonstration. He turns, running and leaping, ascending quickly in Saiak's wake.

Jirai sneaks a peeved glance at his friend, then grabs a spear from a Mujong soldier and breaks off the metal tip on his knee. "Like this," he says, showing a few soldiers next to him. He throws the splintered spear without the metallic head into the group of battling monks and one falls to the ground. The soldiers look to Jirai. "No metal!" They all begin to wrest the metal from their weapons and armor.

+++++

As the battle turns less one-sided, Maji pauses. His eyes find Jirai as he commands and pushes the monks out of his way. His ire conjures electricity from the air and it courses over his body. Jirai, he spits. Always this brat. Time for him to burn. He rises flipping over the battle and well behind his foe. Jirai seems to know he is there, but does not turn to face him.

"You seem to make a habit of interfering with your betters. The other day with Shotoku. Even when you were a boy. Getting his brother killed. Such a shame."

Jirai's back still faces him and his arms are busy doing something hidden. Current continues coursing across Maji as he savors the moment before Jirai's death.

"Yeah, that's me. I almost got you, too, didn't I? Wow, that would scorch, wouldn't it? All that training to be struck dead by an arrow. You'd be a fool to your friends." Jirai looks to the side. "Oh, yeah, well, if you had any. What, do you guys get together and charge each other?"

Maji just scowls, "Your precious friend is headed

into a trap. In the seclusion of Fulgurus Major, where the betrayal began, he'll meet his end."

Jirai's eyes betray concern, then anger.

+++++

Saiak leaps rapidly from bolt to bolt, while Shotoku struggles to keep up. His father seems to spring deftly off mountain and hillside, while he occasionally lands hard, falling painfully to his knees. He can now see clearly the talents his father had expertly masked for years. Recklessly quick, he jumps to the next mountaintop, clawing at the rocks, suffering cuts from the fulgurite, urging himself back into the sky. At one peak, his cuts bleeding, losing confidence, he wipes sweat and dirt from his face. His mind turns to Makiko, his friends, to Devukai and to his fallen brother. Rising again, driven, he clenches his teeth, finds a bolt and jerks back into the air.

+++++

Ruins of Fulgurus Major

Saiak stands amongst the dark ruins of an old monastery, wind blowing his cloak. Shotoku lands opposite him a good distance away, stumbling. He rises slowly as dark shapes spin, the shadows and light equally fickle in the storm.

"A good place to end things: at the beginning. This is where they betrayed me, sent me from the Order. But you know that already, don't you?"

Regaining his composure and readying himself, "It's just you and me now, Saiak. Finish it."

"No, you are mistaken. That is not how the strategist thinks. Perhaps, if circumstances had allowed you to gain years and wisdom, you'd have been a skilled leader. But, as it is—" Slowly, twenty Kuroshi monks materialize next to Saiak where there were none before. "—you have failed."

Shotoku closes his eyes as the air hums with the high frequency of this lethal enemy force.

+++++

Mujong Castle

"You underestimate him. Perhaps that is your flaw," jabs Jirai, still refusing to face Maji.

"This day belongs to a new order upon Aurora. Look at the skies. Who could doubt it is true?"

"No. No doubt. Faith." Jirai holds two hand-crossbows to his chest and takes a deep breath. Quickly spinning, he levels his bows, firing. Maji moves instantly, while Jirai rolls, even upside-down firing his arrows directly at Maji's moving form. When Maji urges the bolts away, his eyes widen as only half deviate. Changing polarity repulses the menacing arrows, but attracts the previously diverted bolts. In panic, he fires lightning, burning some, but not all, into dust. He is pierced by several arrows and writhes on the ground, enraged, like a snared beast.

"I saved those just for you, fisser. I—don't—miss."

Chillson and Starov mesh with Jirai's group and cut down the Kuroshi methodically, but there are too many and the small Mujong force is pushed back. Lightning strikes several Mujong as they battle for their lives, while thunder casts them to the ground.

Alone, confused, panicking in the storm, Junchi runs into the courtyard searching for consolation. He sees

Finn and runs toward him, but Maji's forces regroup. They press the Mujong and Maji finds footing again.

"Junchi, no, stay back," Finn yells, but too late. Maji manages to snatch up Junchi. Corralled and under threat of the boy's life, the Mujong hesitate.

Jirai sees history repeating itself. This is Lunabi, again. He knows that these men would die to save this boy's life, as Zarushi died for him. Jirai has a debt to repay and he would pay it. He knows it is his day to die. He walks toward Maji, accepting his fate.

+++++

Shotoku looks at the monks before him and slowly draws his sword.

"Fighting is futile, Shotoku. Surrender and I may still find a small province for you to run. After tonight, there will be no more Mujong, no more friends. Nothing for you, but me."

"The Iridians will see you receive justice."

"They did not help before, they will not help now and their apathy will be their undoing." Saiak's eyes narrow as he makes out a dark figure rising behind his son. The figure stops beside Shotoku. Lightning flashes and he frowns, recognizing Zensou's face. Shotoku turns, amazed.

Zensou speaks, wistfully, "I didn't believe that for so many years, but perhaps it is true. We should have continued to help the kingdoms, but we had lost so many. Lost my son. To this traitor." Saiak and the Kuroshi stand silently in the dark winds. "So we stand united, Saiak. A guilty conscience: our covenant." Zensou looks to Shotoku and back to Saiak.

Saiak smirks, "Well, the gods have sent me their

familiar himself. What fortune. Now you shall both come to an end here."

"Perhaps. Or perhaps there are others wishing to join us."

Slowly, the seven monks of the Iridian order materialize on either side of Shotoku and Zensou. The wind ruffles their cloaks. Spark Hand's and Silent Thunder's eyes shine as they nod at Shotoku. Midori places a hand on his shoulder, reassuring, consoling, emboldening. Several dozen blue-eyed inazuma rise from the hillside behind them.

Zensou amps up, sparks dancing in the very air around him, and his eyes shimmer: "You won't take another son from me, you bastard."

Saiak's confident façade crumbles.

+++++

Mujong Castle

Maji's silver-ringed fingers hold Junchi's neck tightly, as tears stream down the boy's face. Jirai squares off against Maji, drawing his sword. "You deserve a thousand deaths, you fissing scum. Get ready for number one."

"The boy dies. Nothing you do can save those you hold dearest."

Looking behind Maji, Jirai smirks, relaxing slightly, "Oh, I didn't say *I'd* kill you."

Suddenly, two of the monks arch in pain and lift off of the ground, lightning and blood erupting from their eyes and mouths. They fall limply to the earth, revealing Sprite, his blue eyes blazing. Behind him roll dozens of blue-eyed inazuma as they engage and slaughter the remaining monks.

Surprised to see the inazuma reinforcements, Maji allows Junchi to slip from his grasp. Panicking, he summons a bolt in an attempt to flee. As he rises up and away, however, Sprite steps into the bolt and sucks it from the sky. Maji gropes for another, but falls to the earth hard.

"Sprite! Sprrrrrite! You old lightning rod, you," yells Jirai in pure happiness.

Dubious, Finn joins Jirai. "Allies of yours?" Sprite places his thick fingers on Maji's head and picks him up. He is too exhausted to resist.

Jirai reassures Finn as he walks over to gloat at the monk. "Not allies. Friends."

+++++

The inazuma catapults launch their missiles at the Mujong fortress, drawing even more lightning from the skies. Within the walls, soldiers, women and children burn, the combination of the storm and attack too much for the fortifications. The red eyes of the creatures glow and flow like an evil, fluorescent scourge on the ebb of a dark sea. Reaching the walls, their skill at ascending the sheer rock of their mountain habitat is revealed. The Mujong know they must hold and attempt to repel them bravely and with discipline. A soldier looks out and is disheartened to see a second wave of inazuma rolling in from the west. When they reach the wall, however, the red-eyed inazuma scaling the walls are jerked back to the ground. The second wave has blue eyes and is engaging the others in intense combat. The tall blue-eyed inazuma shield the Mujong soldiers when they can, many dying to do so. Makiko arrives atop the battlements.

"Fire only at the red-eyes! Only into the red!" Hearing their princess, the soldiers focus their fire and begin to winnow the ranks of the red-eyed humanoids.

Several inazuma reach the top of the battlements and Makiko and her men struggle to repel them. Lightning arches from the invaders and her men fall. She stays low and near the smaller spires upon the wall, which save her many times from being scalded. "Use the spires," she yells, and her men take heed. Retreating a moment, she finds herself at the top of one of the main towers alone. A gigantic spire rises from its center ten feet thick, with ornate limbs adorned with glass trinkets, now mostly shattered by the storm. Several inazuma spy her and move in either direction around the spire. As they circle the tower, her heart sinks in dread. Then she hears the bravado of another soldier from the other side of the spire, but out of sight.

"Ha, ho, ho! Ouch, sparkie. Take that!"

Curious, but relieved, she waits at the ready. Three inazuma emerge, backs facing her as if something threatening approaches them.

"Haaaaaa!" Mesapato comes into view, rushing the remaining inazuma. He decapitates one with his long curved blade and the other two, frantic, back over the edge of the castle wall and fall to the earth far below. He looks after them, then turns to Makiko, wiping his long, curly black hair from his unshaven face. "Princess Makiko, may I be of assistance? Ha, ha!" His eyes and teeth flash white.

"Pato," she yells, allowing relief to overcome her; she runs to hug him.

+++++

From the killing fields in front of the Castle of Mujong, the sounds of suffering swirl through the air, inhuman and desperate. Sparks glint and fade, careening from the chitinous collision of inazuma exoskeletons. Smitten by their ancient brothers in a finale of fireworks, the attackers' lines fracture as their red eyes retreat, dim tracers in the darkness.

+++++

Ruins of Fulguris Major

From across the mountains, the screeches of retreat reach the ears of Saiak and his monks.

Shotoku smirks, "There is your force, Saiak, routed."

Saiak's face shows disbelief and panic. Then he looks to Shotoku. "You? You did this to me. This … world … is … mine!"

In an elongated moment and in the stretching silence, adrenaline surges and courses through veins, and slow jagged bands of lightning rip through the darkness, pulsing. The lethal flashes, the faces of fear, of hate, of despair make a mockery of the peaceful hopes of all good beings, great and small. From all sides, monks fly, dodge, crash, and scald and inazuma spring. Finally, the thunder from the exchange rocks the melee in a wave of pressure that disorients or flattens even the inazuma. All rise quickly and clash with great violence.

Saiak and Shotoku engage each other fiercely with swords. Saiak tries a flurry of lightning attacks, but his son only seems to absorb them. Then Shotoku lets the cumulative charge erupt at his father from the black blade of his sword. Saiak rolls away as the bolt burns down a Kuroshi behind him. Another Kuroshi attacks Shotoku from the side and he is forced to engage him. Suddenly, an inazuma grabs the monk, who purposefully channels enormous energy from the skies into its obsidian body. The inazuma crushes the monk's body in its arms and drops the corpse, but stumbles away, clearly wounded. Shotoku looks upon the creature in gratitude, when Saiak appears. Grabbing its neck from behind, his sword emerges from the wounded inazuma's chest, the lights in its intelligent eyes fading to black.

"Care for these creatures, do you?" asks Saiak, derisively.

"You bastard," says Shotoku, attacking. Swords clashing, Saiak is forced backwards. Seeing his father at a disadvantage, Shotoku rushes him, parrying his sword downward and striking Saiak hard in the face with an elbow strike. Saiak has not been idle, however; as Shotoku feels burning in his side, he sees a ball of lightning has eaten through his armor and scalded his skin. Both men roll away injured.

Like lightning, Silent Thunder descends from the sky, flinging bolt after bolt at Saiak as he closes on his old enemy. Saiak bats his lightning attacks aside without effort. "Don't bring that fissing spark at me, Thunder." They circle each other, a brief pause, assessing, searching for weaknesses. Saiak sneers, "Come on, Thunder. Let's see if you've learned how to die."

Just as Silent Thunder is about to engage, Shotoku grabs his shoulder, "No, why don't you teach us both." Silent Thunder and Shotoku attack in unison forcing Saiak to defend from two directions. He moves skillfully, using the rock and fulgurite of his environment to limit their angles of attack. Silent Thunder scales the rock face, climbing and hovering, striking with his legs at Saiak's head while Shotoku hammers with direct attacks to his torso and legs. The monk conjures a lightning bolt, but Saiak throws metallic pebbles into the air and rolls. The pebbles fragment the strike and Shotoku must roll away, as well. Saiak, having rolled through the razor-sharp fulgurite, faces the ground, injured. Silent Thunder drops from the rock face next to the king of Sterling. Two blue-eyed inazuma roll up next to Silent Thunder, who stands over Saiak, grabbing his cloak and pulling him to his feet. The monk cannot suppress the satisfaction of besting his old adversary as he meets Shotoku's eyes.

Shotoku breathes a sigh of relief. Then suddenly he sees Saiak spin, his sword slicing through one inazuma, then the next and across Silent Thunders chest, as face registers shock and pain. The inazuma sink where they stand as Saiak sends a bolt into the monk who is lifted off of the earth. "No," yells Shotoku, as he runs to defend the monk.

Sprite's father's eyes burn as he sees Saiak cut down two more of his inazuma. He plows through the melee making his way towards the corrupt king. Saiak considers fleeing by lightning, but eyes the inazuma and opts to bound quickly up the mountain slopes.

Shotoku looks down at Silent Thunder, blood oozing from a large gash in his armor. Spitting blood from his lips, he grabs the young warrior's leg. "Go. You can beat him. I *know* you can." He struggles to breathe. "You fight with your heart. Nothing can defeat that. Go."

Shotoku wants to help the monk, but with the

passing of his words pauses only a moment. A respectful nod and then he pursues his father upward, to the highest dome of the monastery.

Smiling, Saiak gathers speed, leaping large distances. Clutching his wound, sneering and in desperation, Shotoku follows Saiak, adopting the same gait. Sprite's father and other inazuma follow only a few steps behind.

+++++

Sheer cliffs descend into the clouds below. In the flashing light, two figures race across the mountain toward the drop. At full gait, Saiak leaps over the cliffs, falling as a bolt from Shotoku almost strikes him from behind. Saiak reaches for and finds lightning, raising him enough to reach the far side. Even though Shotoku is unable to see through the clouds above the chasm, he pursues his father over the cliffs without hesitation. His face shows only resolve.

The pursuing inazuma force halts at the cliffs, eyes dim and exchanging uncertain pulses. They know they cannot make the jump. A moment later, the sound of rapid footfalls draws near. The inazuma turn just as Sprite, with Jirai on his back, bursts through their ranks and over the cliff at full speed. Although unprepared, the inazuma manage to hastily give Sprite an extra magnetic push as he jets with all his strength from the cliff's edge. Sprite and Jirai disappear into the dark clouds.

Electricity strobes and snaps from Sprite's father's hands as his head twists in consternation. Sprite's friends approach the edge cautiously, eyes wide and sad, gazing after him and into the gaping, misty maw.

+++++

Aurora's Crown

The great wall of lightning, Aurora's Crown, ends Saiak's retreat. He stops, facing the immensity of its power. Razor-sharp fulgurite eagerly waits for a false move. Turning, father and son face each other, taking stock of their injuries. Both men labor to breathe.

"Now, Blind One, I will reveal what was in front of you all these years." Saiak closes his eyes as the rock and glass of the mountain shake. His arms rise slowly, struggling, as he grows an orb of magnetism that causes the lightning of Aurora's Crown itself to bow under his might. Metal plates are rent from the stone and swirl around him without pattern.

Shotoku steps back, gasping, eyes squinting, searching for a weakness in the whirlpool of plates. Lightning courses out of the orb, seeking ground. It seems to get smaller for a moment and Shotoku senses an attack. He opens his eyes and throws up his defenses only to have them negated by a magnetic blizzard of metal and glass shards. He is blown off of his feet and through the air. He turns in midair, eyeing the approaching fulgurite. Luckily, Saiak's discharge shatters most of the glass stalagmites as he skids across the gravel, still badly cut by the remaining shards.

Saiak floats inside the orb, closing the distance to Shotoku. He rises, trying to gather electricity to himself, but finds himself struggling to do so. Saiak is absorbing all of the latent energy, consuming it in order to keep his powerful orb in effect. Shotoku manages to conjure a bolt and then a ball of lightning and hurls them at Saiak, but they only disappear into the swirling orb.

As he feels the wind from the metal plates whisking by, Shotoku can only retreat. Suddenly, he feels static tug at his feet and realizes he is now forced to fight against tall crackleweed as well. As he wades backward through it, he senses his power returning. The crackleweed has become his new supply of power. But he must use it wisely. Now his mind turns and he reaches out again, searching for a chink in the orb's defenses. He sees the blue-white ion streams and senses an intermittent hole at the top of the orb. He drags his feet heavily through the weeds, sparks licking his legs and waist as his arms flex, drawing every amp of power he can manage. Clenching his teeth, knowing he has one shot, he plants his feet and thrusts both arms straight up, palms flat. An arch of lightning flashes, arching toward Saiak's magnetic pull.

Time seems to slow as father and son battle, Saiak pulling and Shotoku pushing the arch over the orb. Shotoku leans backward, as if pulling against a sail in the wind, hovering at an acute angle above the weeds, invisible magnetic forces holding him aloft. Shaking under the strain, he sees Saiak flexing, about to make a last great effort. As the arch of lightning reaches the top, Shotoku reverses direction and drives the bolt down through the center of the orb. Shotoku's push combined with Saiak's pull causes the arch to flow unimpeded into the orb and rip through Saiak's body and deep into the earth. The orb explodes outward, glass and metal ripping in all directions as the earth opens unto the sky, slowly raining red-hot splinters like fireflies, brilliant in the night air.

Shotoku finds his feet and painfully gets up. The

smoldering rim of a crater exists where his father once was. He limps over to the rim and looks down. Saiak's badly burned body lies at the bottom. Then it moves. Disoriented, it takes Saiak a moment to focus on his son. His weak voice stammers, "Perhaps you are a strategist after all. Mine seems to have been slightly flawed."

"So many trusted you—even loved you." Shotoku looks down upon his father in disappointment. "Two brothers did. And you tried to destroy us. You've destroyed so much. For what?"

Saiak only stares up at his son. "It could have been different. Should have been."

Shotoku turns to walks away, no longer willing to listen. "You will live with your failure and suffer the scorn of the good people of these lands. I hope your impudent, childish desire to rule everything was worth it," Shotoku spits, acerbically.

Suddenly, Saiak rises behind him, finding a huge vein of ions, and coalesces a charge. Voice still hoarse, he screams, "You will burn!"

"Shock," yells Jirai, emerging from the darkness firing crossbow bolts. The lightning leaps forth, striking Shotoku just before Saiak is forced to disintegrate two arrows. Shotoku falls to the ground motionless.

Saiak only glances at Jirai as he motions toward Shotoku's back and prepares to fire again. "Burn," he yells, his eyes maniacal in the gathering charge.

"No! Sprite!"

From the great curving curtain of lightning, a beam erupts to slap Saiak like paper across the terrain. He screams raggedly tumbling before melting into the unrivaled magnitude of the lightning sheets of Aurora's

Crown.

Sprite stops redirecting the wall, eyes aglow. He steps from the light, a dark figure emerging from an eternal flame. A once helpless child now his father's savior.

Jirai watches him approach, smoke in the wake of his cooling skin. Jirai watches in awe, "You are something else. Nice shootin', Sprite. Shock, you alright?" Shotoku's whole body continues to smoke as he lies. "Shock? Talk to me buddy." Jirai panics as his friend fails to move.

Then Shotoku inhales sharply, wincing. "Water. Do you have any water?"

Jirai smiles slowly, nodding, "Here." Shotoku reaches for the water skin and squirts it all over his waist; smoke billows forth from beneath his clothes. He closes his eyes, relieved.

"I think my underwear was on fire." Their laughter is slow, low and tired.

+++++

Mujong Castle

The sun shines on the Kingdom of Mujong as the castle hosts a gala affair, colorful pennants representing the five kingdoms flying from the spires high above down to the baroque tents and shops hawking exotic wares from the far corners of Aurora. A crowd surrounds a stage at the center of the courtyard as Kenshi addresses his people.

"… and so it is not without a great feeling of caution that we celebrate today. That our misunderstandings could lead to such a grievous outcome. We chose to cordon ourselves, to separate our interests from the welfare of all. We will not forget the bitter harvest of indifference. Will not forget the ones we loved and who we allowed to fall." Kenshi pauses, his face reflecting the guilt he feels so deeply. "Our spires have ever protected us against the lightning above, but they cannot protect us from the wounds and injustices that we do unto each other. In this, we must place our faith in ourselves and raise up those who prove themselves worthy. Let us rest our hopes for the future in beings such as these." The king motions toward the members of the Bright Guard, Makiko, Finn, Sprite, and the Iridians. "Today, we bestow upon them the highest award in our land. They are our shields. They are our protectors. I declare them: Spires of Aurora."

The crowd cheers.

THE END

ABOUT THE AUTHOR

Nate Covell is consummate geek whose heart has always been torn between comedy and a fascination with the pursuit of virtue. He is currently employed at Marine Corps Forces Central Command on MacDill Air Force Base in Tampa, Florida. Previously, he worked for the White House Military Office in DC, in cyber counterintelligence, in the Middle East, was a Japanese interpreter and lived in Japan and Italy. Nate has a B.A. in Creative Writing and has done graduate work at Harvard.

He currently resides with his wife and three kids in Valrico, Florida.

www.ingramcontent.com/pod-product-compliance
Lightning Source LLC
Chambersburg PA
CBHW071309170626
46809CB00001B/382